JOHN AND NANBAREE

JOHN AND NANBAREE

DORIS CHADWICK

COVER AND MAP BY
GLORIS SMITH YOUNG

The author wishes to acknowledge her obligation to the Trustees of the Mitchell Library, Sydney, and to the Trustees of the Museum of Applied Arts and Sciences, for permission to use original MSS and models in their possession.

This edition published 2021
By Living Book Press
147 Durren Rd, Jilliby, 2259

First published in 1962 by Thomas Nelson and Sons LTD

ISBN: 978-1-922619-38-9 (hardcover)
          978-1-922619-39-6 (softcover)

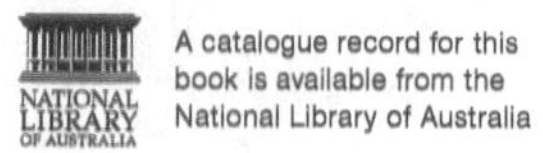

A catalogue record for this book is available from the National Library of Australia

To all who read
THE NEW SOUTH WALES SCHOOL MAGAZINE
1922-1960
To those who helped me edit
and produce it
and in particular to
V. C. N. Blight
New South Wales Government Printer

VENTURES in NEW SOUTH WALES
under Gov. Phillip
by Gloria Smithson, 2021
JOHN & MARTIN ON LORD HOWE ISLAND
birds of many kinds
RICHMOND HILL
where the Expedition ended.
corn & potatoes planted
Settlement at ROSE HILL where James Ruse had a farm.
Hawkesbury River
here the water is fresh
Natives attack!
Sydney Cove
Manley Cove
BOTANY BAY
PITTWATER
Lion Island
BROKEN BAY
THE WRECK OF THE SIRIUS
19 MARCH, 1790
Norfolk Island (8 Days)
Lord Howe Is. (4 Days)
Providence Petrel
S

CONTENTS

CHAPTER I

TO THE WOODS WITH NANBAREE

'WHATEVER you do this afternoon,' Mamma told John as he got up from the table to answer Martin's whistle, 'you must not be late home.'

'Because,' said Sue, 'it's the King's birthday, and we have to light the bonfire.'

'And then go to a play,' Mamma announced.

'A play!' This was the first John had heard of it. He almost disbelieved her. How could a play be acted in Sydney Cove, a mere straggle of huts in a place where white people had lived for only eighteen months!

'Yes, indeed,' Mamma's servant, Debby, explained, 'a real live play. The convicts are putting it on in one of their huts. You'll probably go to sleep, you and Sue, and your friends, Martin and Jenny, but your Mamma is determined that you should go because it is the first play to be acted in this new land of New South Wales.'

'And Nanbaree?' John asked, thinking of the black boy recently brought in ill to the settlement, who knew so little English.

'Yes, Nanbaree, too,' Mamma replied. 'We are all to have supper here before we light the bonfire and then go to the play.'

Martin was waiting outside when John emerged from the kitchen with the news, and with him was Nanbaree. The bonfire was stacked perfectly in readiness for the blaze to come. What, then, should they do on this short winter afternoon? Beyond the collection of huts that made up the town, the woods called, and before them gleamed the blue waters of the Cove upon which the *Sirius* and *Supply* lay snugly at anchor.

For weeks John and Martin had been waiting for Nanbaree to recover from the smallpox. 'We'll take him to the woods,' John said to Martin. 'He will be able to show us how to climb trees the native way and to get wild honey. Come on, Nanbaree. Honey! We want you to get honey,' and whistling to his dog, Gyp, he led the way.

'But we must not take him too far.' Martin was always the one to urge caution. 'If we do, he might go back to his own people, and the Governor does not want him to do that.'

John well knew of the Governor's wish. Ever since he and Martin had come with their parents to Sydney Cove, there had been clashes between the natives and the convicts. The Governor had tried to make peace by bringing in a native by force, named Arabanoo, in the hope that he would learn the white men's ways, and so persuade his own people that they meant no harm. But Arabanoo had died, had given his life for Nanbaree and a native girl, Abaroo, for when the black people had been found to be suffering from smallpox, these two had been brought into the hospital, and he had nursed them.

'The Governor wants Nanbaree and Abaroo to grow up here to learn to trust us, so that they can tell their own people that we wish to live at peace with them,' Martin reminded John. 'We'll have to be careful.'

But John was sure that Nanbaree would not try to escape. 'He is too interested in what is happening at the Cove,' he said to Martin, 'and in the new food he is getting—and in us.'

It was true. The boy had taken to John and Martin from the beginning, especially to John. On the very first day they had come with Governor Phillip to Port Jackson, they had landed in a little cove to boil the pot, and there John had seen the merry-eyed black boy and had given him a red ribbon. Often in their tramps through the woods in the months that followed, they had met him, and once he had saved them from hostile natives. John had become so attached to his 'black boy', as he called him, that he would have been very distressed had the boy died.

He did not die. He was there amongst them, and John was determined to find out many things about the natives that he had always wanted to know—how they climbed trees, and speared fish, and built canoes.

'To the woods, Nanbaree,' he said now, pointing to the green belt of trees around the Cove. 'We want you to show us how to climb trees and get wild honey.'

Nanbaree grinned. ''Oney! Nanbaree get 'oney!' He understood that. Time enough when they got there for him to understand what else they wished him to do.

These trees that the natives climbed in some unknown way intrigued the boys. How did the natives do it? Steps on the trunk so far apart that they could not be the steps of a man. Now they would find out.

John picked up a tomahawk from an out-house as he went through the back garden. Then, seeing a tinder-box that Pete, the gardener, had left there, he put it in his pocket. They might need it. They would have to hurry, or someone would call them back. Mamma did not look kindly on such excursions into the woods.

As they came to the trees, they glanced back on Sydney Cove. The tiny town looked so warm and comfortable in the bright June sunshine; the ordered rows of wattle-and-daub huts dipping down to the water's edge, creeping out along the western ridge above the hospital towards the observatory; the many-paned windows of the Governor's two-storied house on the east, dominating all, as they winked goldenly into the westering sun...

But the boys had no thought for the beauty of the Cove. Their eyes were on the marquee and the collection of huts that constituted John's home. Someone might see them—John's sister, Sue, or her friend, Jenny. They had purposely evaded the girls. A hint of colour in the garden made them hurry still more.

Nanbaree was now striding jauntily ahead. He had taken the lead, his three-cornered hat at a rakish angle on his head, his coat unbuttoned, his shirt tail flying, and his black feet stepping noiselessly but surely over stones and twigs and leaves.

John remembered the day when the black boy had been given white boy's clothes. Nanbaree had been so proud of his shoes, clip-clopping over the wooden floors of the hospital, intently listening to the noise he made. Then, within an hour, he had cast them aside, and no persuasion could get them back on his feet. Trousers, coat, shirt, and hat—particularly hat—he wore with style and pride, but shoes he kicked from him in disgust.

As John watched him striding along, he was secretly making up his mind to ask Mamma for permission to go without shoes. He had longed for some time to do that, but she had always refused. Perhaps she might relent now that shoes were growing so scarce, with no ships arriving from England, and stores becoming so low.

But what was Nanbaree up to? He had taken off his coat and was throwing it in the bushes.

John looked at Martin. Was he about to escape?

And now he was dispensing with his shirt.

'I think we had better take him back,' Martin said.

But there was no persuading Nanbaree—not with all the signs and pointing they could make. His face was set for the woods, and to the woods he was going, a quaint figure with only a hat on now, for just at that moment he was slipping his trousers from his waist.

The two boys followed more slowly. They had already come farther than they had intended. What if other natives came from the woods to join Nanbaree? Would they snatch him and take him away?

Suddenly he stopped. He had picked up a piece of pipeclay. And now he had caught a bee sipping quietly on the edge of a puddle. He was dusting its body with the pipeclay. He had let the bee go, and there it was sailing away, a speck of white against the green of the trees. So that was his way of finding a wild bees' nest! He was running in pursuit, and they were following. The flitter of white was moving straight in front of them. There was no mistaking the bee, for it veered not to right or to left. Then suddenly it was gone.

The boys slowed down. 'And that's the end of it,' Martin said.

But Nanbaree was running on, pointing in the direction the bee had taken. What was he trying to tell them? Was it that a bee flies from water to its hive by the most direct route? Dimly they realised that by training he knew more than they, and quickened pace. He had reached the tree, when they came upon it, a tall gum with a dead limb spreading like a finger above them, its trunk smooth and satiny and straight.

With a laugh Nanbaree grabbed the tomahawk. He was chopping at the trunk at the height of the left thigh. A slanting cut and a horizontal one, and there was a notch sufficient to hold the ball of his big toe. He was chopping another at the height of his right shoulder. And now he was up, his left toe in the bottom hole, his left arm around the tree. He was on the second notch; he was cutting a third, he was moving into it, the tomahawk held tightly between his teeth, his arms embracing the trunk to pull himself upwards. And so on to a fourth and fifth, the foot each time being raised nearly as high as the opposite thigh. So that was why the notches seemed so far apart!

'Perhaps we could do it,' John said.

But Martin was not so sure. 'It's harder than you think,' he replied.

Nanbaree had reached the curve of the limb. The bees were flying round in an angry cloud and settling on his dark skin.

'He'll be stung!' John gasped in admiration.

If he were, Nanbaree paid no heed. He was chopping at the limb; it was falling; he had begun to slide down, and John and Martin were stepping gingerly towards it. But the bees were about, taking revenge. John felt a red hot needle pierce the back of his hand. 'Did you get one, too?' he yelled to Martin. 'Take out the sting,' and they both ran to a safe distance.

Not Nanbaree! He was already at the limb, cutting out the hive, and offering them delicious pieces of comb. It was too tempting. They forgot their stings, forgot the bees, and taking the comb sank their teeth into the sticky sugary sweetness. All three expressed approval by soft murmurings and a loud sucking noise that Mamma would have called 'disgusting'.

They had finished the comb when John thought rather sadly that he should have kept some for Mamma and Sue and Jenny. There never were enough sweet things at the Cove. 'More,' he said to the black boy, holding out his hands. 'More honey for Mamma and Sue and Jenny, and Martin's mother.'

Taking the tomahawk, Nanbaree searched about again amongst the trees. ''Oney, no,' he said at length. '*Boo-roo-min*, yes,' and he pointed to scratchings on the trunk of a hollow tree.

Boo-roo-min, A possum! That would do. A possum meant fresh meat, and fresh meat was scarcer than sugar. Why, a lizard was acceptable, and snakes a dainty!

'*Gwee-un?*' Nanbaree asked.

Gwee-un, the native word for fire! So Nanbaree wanted fire to be made with the tinder-box. Eagerly John drew it from his pocket. He was thrilled. Now they were to watch the native way of setting a trap.

Already Martin was gathering dry leaves and sticks, and soon Nanbaree was placing them in the hollow, setting them alight with the spark John had struck from the flint, and dampening them with grass to make a long spiral of smoke ascending upwards in the column of the trunk. Then, seizing the tomahawk, he began again to cut a notch, and then another, and slowly to climb up and up, until he reached the top, where the smoke had now begun to emerge in a thin thread.

Would the possum come out? They waited expectantly, adding more leaves, more grass to the smoking fire at the bottom. Yes, there it was! It had come out at the bottom and not at the top. With a cry of surprise John grasped at its tail, and Martin fell over in his effort to seize the animal. But instead of catching it they found themselves gripping one another, watching the possum as it streaked across the grass and climbed another tree with a speed too quick for them, too quick even for Gyp, John's dog.

Nanbaree came down the tree and was convulsed with mirth. He looked at them as much as to say, 'Fancy having a possum within your grasp and not being able to hold it! These white boys!' and his merry eyes laughed, and his broad mouth grinned more widely than before.

But John was secretly pleased. Possums and flying squirrels were too beautiful and dainty to eat. He was glad the animal had escaped.

As he lay on the grass, resting and thinking about it, he looked at the tree, and again came the desire to climb. If Nanbaree could do it, surely he could. Impulsively he began to take off his shoes and stockings.

'You had better not,' Martin began to persuade him.

But John had made up his mind. 'I won't be cutting the notches, only climbing,' he said. 'Nanbaree thinks I can do it. What do you say, Nanbaree?' and he pointed upwards.

Nanbaree nodded pleasantly. After all, he thought it was easy.

With a skip John was at the bottom of the trunk, his left toe in the first notch. Now Martin and Nanbaree were helping him up, his right toe in the second, his left arm round the trunk. With a heave his left toe was in the third notch, and he was pulling himself up for the fourth. But what if he let go? He looked below and saw the two boys watching grimly. He looked up, and the top of the trunk seemed a long way off. But he had made up his mind that he would get there. Gripping the trunk firmly, he pulled himself up again. It was on the next step that his toe found difficulty in finding the notch, and for a wild moment he seemed to hang dangling by his arms as the other toe lost touch. No, he would not give in. Impulsive he might be, but he always carried out his purpose. Another heave, and he went on...

The top was close now. He reached it with a mighty pull, and sat on the first limb. With a feeling of exhilaration he waved to the others below. Well, he had got there. What would Cookie say when he told him—Cookie who had always laughed at his impulsiveness? Cookie, the cook on the *Supply*, with whom he had spent so many wild days at sea on the long trip to New South Wales! He wished Cookie could see him now.

He looked around among the tree-tops, idly enjoying all he could see, when suddenly a scratching behind made him turn quickly. The possum! It could not be. But it was its mate, sent up the hollow trunk by the smoke. Nanbaree would have grabbed it and hit its head viciously on the limb, but somehow John could not. The boys below shouted, calling him to catch it, but his attempt was only half-hearted. The furry body was too high now for him to reach. Let it stay there in peace.

This was the moment when he heard the voices of the natives. Guttural tones he knew so well! Friends of Nanbaree's! They were coming. He was sure of it. And they might try to take Nanbaree away. He must descend as quickly as possible. But how? For the first time he was afraid. How? Put his toe in each of the notches? Shinny down? The ground below him swam before his eyes, and with it the trees, the boys. Were there two faces down there or three? He shut his eyes, then opened them again. Surely there must be a third person!

They were shouting from below! Had he heard aright? Cookie's voice! There *was* a third person, and it was Cookie. Had he been with the natives whose voices he had heard? He could not hear them now.

'What be ye staying up there for, lad?' Cookie was yelling. 'Always did like getting into tight spots, didn't ye?'

John passed his hand over his eyes and dared not look.

'Come on, ye—we be a-waiting for ye. See, I ha' some birds for your Mamma. Maybe she'll cook 'em for ye for supper. 'Tis King's birthday, ye know, a day for a feast.'

John looked down again and recoiled. He couldn't, he just couldn't climb down those notches.

'Come on, lad. If ye stay up there all night, ye'll miss the bonfire and the play. What be the matter?'

John hated to say it, but he had to do so. 'I can't, Cookie! Every time I look down I'm giddy.'

'So that be it? Well, well, it's happened to better men than ye, lad. Wait a minute.'

There was scuffling and walking round below, the noise of voices, of sharp orders, and then for some moments quiet. John sat on the limb and did not dare look down again. But he was no longer hysterical. Cookie was there. Cookie would find a way.

'Ahoy there! Catch this!' He felt a vine slap his leg. So that was what they had been looking for in the woods. Another throw and he had it in his hands. 'And see that ye tie a proper knot, young land-lubber. None o' your grannies this time.'

John took the vine and tied it firmly to the limb, then sat back and closed his eyes again. Someone was testing the strength of the vine from below. It held—yes, it held strongly.

'Now come on. Shinny ye down,' Cookie was calling. 'Close your eyes and hold tight.'

It seemed easy enough explained like that. John clung to the limb and twined his legs round the vine. He was moving now, quicker, quicker; he almost seemed to be shooting through the air. With a thud he hit the earth, and they were helping him to his feet, laughing so at his discomfiture that he began to laugh, too. It had been nasty up there, but now, in safety on the ground, it did not seem so bad as it had appeared.

'*Boo-roo-min,*' Nanbaree cried, teasing John for the butter fingers that had lost the possum.

John shrugged his shoulders and pointed to Cookie's birds. 'It does not matter,' he said. 'Cookie has something for Mamma.' Nanbaree would not understand his compassion for the animal, why he could not bring himself to kill it horribly, as if he were murdering it.

Slowly John put on his stockings and shoes, remembering suddenly the voices he had heard. 'But the natives, Cookie? I heard them when I was up the tree,' and he got in a panic and looked around. 'They might have been coming for Nanbaree.'

'Aye, and so ye did, lad. They be a-gabbling to me. Saw ye, too, up yon tree. A-following me, they were, as I killed the birds. When I caught sight o' ye masted like that in the tree, I bade 'em begone. Saw young Nanbaree, too, I guess. Nothing 'ud miss their sharp eyes.'

Cookie picked up the birds and strode ahead to give them to Mamma, while John and Martin followed more slowly with Nanbaree, still wearing only the hat at a rakish angle on his head.

The sight of it made John remember the clothes that had been cast in the bushes. He knew now that Nanbaree had discarded them because they would only have been a hindrance. 'Trousers, shirt,' he called to the black boy, with expressive movements of his hands. But Nanbaree merely laughed and refused to search for them. Or was he in his own way searching all the time? Look where they would, this bush or that, John and Martin could not find the clothes. And yet when a giggling in front of them made them hurry forward, Nanbaree was there.

Sue and Jenny, of course, laughing at the rakish angle of the hat on the naked Nanbaree, and standing strangely with their hands behind their backs. And with them Abaroo, the native girl, who had been brought in with smallpox about the same time as Nanbaree. She stood there smirking, a gawkish girl of fifteen, only half understanding the reason for the merriment, Nanbaree's trousers held untidily behind her back.

So the girls were the culprits. They had seen Nanbaree discard his clothes and played this practical joke.

'Come on,' John demanded, 'give them up,' and as he spoke a gun boomed out from the Cove.

'The guns!' Sue shouted, and trousers, shirt, and coat fell in all directions as the girls made in the direction of the Cove, followed by the still naked Nanbaree.

John picked up the clothes and followed. He knew it would be useless to call Nanbaree. In any case he was just as anxious to get to the Cove. This was the final salute of the King's birthday. They must not miss it. Certainly Nanbaree must not miss it. He had been amazed at the burst of guns at dawn, by the joyous *feu-de-joie* at the parade of marines, by the second burst of guns at midday, and now by these. He had already outstripped the girls and would be the first to reach the Cove.

The guns were splendid, twenty-one from the *Sirius*, twenty-one from the *Supply*. Nanbaree was almost beside himself with joy.

'Not as good as last year,' Sue said regretfully. 'Then there were more ships and we had sixty-seven.'

Ships! Would they ever come again? That was the thought of everyone. For eighteen months the Governor and his little band of marines and convicts had been at Sydney Cove, and as yet no additional ships or supplies had arrived.

'Surely it won't be long now,' John heard Mamma say to Martin's mother, as they all gathered in the mud kitchen for supper. Nanbaree was in his clothes again, his black eyes alight in anticipation as he watched Debby grill the birds on the spit, the hat still at the same rakish angle.

It was a great night. When Papa came home, the bonfire went up in a flurry of smoke and flames and stars. The spectacle was worth all their effort—so John and Martin and the girls thought. All, especially Nanbaree, were inclined to linger as Papa hurried them on.

'Now come along,' he said, gathering his little band. 'You have something else to see—the very first play to be acted in this land.'

They looked about in amazement when they saw how the play-hut had been transformed. A stage had been prepared and around the walls stained paper had been hung in an effort to hide the wattle-and-daub. Candles fluttered and flickered in their sockets, and already the audience was being enveloped in a soft film of smoke. Soon the air would become heavy, but no one seemed to mind. The play was to begin—the first play to be acted in New South Wales—Farquhar's *Recruiting Officer*.

'Go to the front and sit on the floor,' Papa told the children. 'There won't be enough chairs for everyone.'

That suited them well. In the front they could see and hear; they would even be near the Governor.

'Hat, take off your hat,' John whispered to Nanbaree, as he removed his own, but Nanbaree was deaf to all persuasion—not even when the band struck up *God Save the King*, and the Governor took his seat. The hat still stayed at the same rakish angle on his head.

Then the play began, and all were carried off to the England of a hundred years before, where a recruiting officer was trying to raise troops for his regiment.

Once or twice John turned to watch Nanbaree. His bright eyes never left the stage. John wondered what he was thinking. The black boy could not understand the dialogue; for him it was only a mime, but as such it held his attention. Was he thinking of the wild dances and sing-songs that the natives sometimes held in the woods?

Nanbaree watched it all through, and so did John and Martin, but Jenny and Sue had fallen asleep before it came to an end to the ac-companiment of applause and praise for the fine acting of the convicts.

'Quite an occasion,' John heard the Governor say to Mamma, as he stopped to speak to her afterwards. 'The first play to be acted in this land.'

Perhaps some day, John thought, people would remember this day, when the little settlement of Sydney Cove would have grown to what the Governor believed it would be--a great city.

Nanbaree was moving off with Mr White, the surgeon, to the hospital where he lived, and Martin and his parents to the parade ground.

Slowly John followed Mamma and Papa and Jenny and Sue. The bonfires had burnt out and darkness had spread over the Cove. The second King's birthday in the new land of New South Wales had come to an end.

CHAPTER II

SPEARING FISH THE NATIVE WAY

MAMMA was distressed the next morning when John brought news that someone had run off with six cabbages from her garden.

'Oh dear!' she sighed. 'That's nine cabbages in two nights! And it takes so much effort to grow them. If the robbers would only ask me, I'd give them what I could spare.'

''Tis Caesar,' Debby declared. 'That black negro of a convict, 'tis he. I always said he would come to no good. Robbed his master, he did, and gone these ten days into the woods to live with the natives. How could they feed him, the great greedy glutton? 'Tis Caesar, ma'am.'

Mamma had kind remembrances of Caesar, who, when Sue had been ill, had brought her greens from the woods. 'Glutton he is, Debby, but how can he be anything else with that great big body? However hungry he was, I don't think he would steal from me.'

But Debby had made up her mind. ''Tis Caesar,' she muttered, as she went about serving the porridge for breakfast.

'Did you hear any noise last night?' Mamma asked John, sitting impatiently at the table.

'No, Mamma.' He was not interested in the cabbages, and was eager to be away. That day Nanbaree was to join Martin and him at lessons at the observatory.

'Nanbaree will at least learn something, just by looking on,' Surgeon White, his guardian, had said to Lieutenant Dawes, their schoolmaster, 'so I shall send him along.'

It was not far from the hospital to the observatory on the west point, where Lieutenant Dawes lived, and Nanbaree was already there when John and Martin arrived.

They knew at once that they would be set to do sums or grammar, for Lieutenant Dawes was already engaged, not in teaching but in learning from the black boy, and so adding to his vocabulary of native words.

'What name this?' he was saying, pointing to one thing after another. 'What name that?'

Earlier he had found out that Nanbaree had three names. 'Nanbaree, Bolderry, and Brockenbaw,' he proudly told them. 'And he seems to belong to a people called the *Cadigal*. That so, Nanbaree?'

'Nanbaree, *Cadigal*,' Nanbaree repeated.

The questioning went on for an hour or more. All three were glad when Captain Tench called in, and they were able to rush to the window and watch the life of the Cove, up and down the dusty roads, and over the blue waters of the great harbour stretched before them.

'I've come to say good-bye,' John heard Captain Tench say. 'I am to go to Rose Hill for a month to be captain of the guard.'

Rose Hill! That was where James Ruse was. Perhaps, thought John, Mamma would like to send him some presents--clothes, maybe, or even a pie that Debby would make. He had been such a great help to her in the days when she had first planted her seeds and shrubs and made her garden. Now he was at Rose Hill, the new settlement at the head of the harbour, of which the Governor had great hopes. The soil at Sydney Cove was disappointing, but up there, why, they grew cabbages as big as a man's head!

'Yes,' Captain Tench continued, 'while I'm there I'm going to do a little exploring. I think there might be a stream west from Rose Hill, and I intend to find it. I believe the Governor is setting out for Broken Bay tomorrow to search for the river he did not discover last time.'

So the Governor was going out again at last. More than twelve months before he had gone to Broken Bay and spent ten days there looking for a river. The boys had gone with him, and suffered all the hardships of an exploring trip undertaken in boisterous rainy weather. It was so bad that the Governor himself had developed a chill that had given him a pain in his side ever since.

'Did you hear that, Martin? The Governor is going to Broken Bay again looking for a river. He still thinks that there is one there. Perhaps he will take us.'

Mamma dashed his hopes.

Rushing in that afternoon from school, he told her about Captain Tench and his forthcoming visit to Rose Hill.

'Then Debby shall make a pie immediately and we'll send it to Jim Ruse,' she said. 'We must not forget Jim.'

'And the Governor is going to Broken Bay, Mamma. Do you think he might take us, too?'

'Not this time,' she replied. 'Papa is not going. You can't go without him.'

That seemed reasonable but, for all that, John was disappointed. He went outside to bring in some wood, and was disconsolately whittling away at a chip when Cookie came up the path.

'Now what be set upon ye, lad?' Cookie said, when he saw him. 'Something be a-troubling ye. Come on, out wi' it.'

'Just that I'd like to go with the Governor tomorrow exploring,' John replied. 'You understand, don't you?'

'O' course I do. I be a-going away myself tomorrow in the *Supply*, and mighty glad I'd be to take ye wi' me if I could. Now that would be a trip, wouldn't it?'

'To Norfolk Island?'

'Aye, to Norfolk, that wee speck o' an isle set in the seas wi' pine-trees enough for all the navies o' the world.'

'And birds?'

'Aye, birds enough to feed ye on fresh meat for months. Pick 'em up in your hands like, they be so tame. There and at Lord Howe's Island, too.'

For a while John forgot his disappointment.

'You don't really think I'll ever go there?' he asked.

'Maybe, lad, maybe. One never knows. Ye could be cabin-boy again like ye did from the Cape. D'ye remember?'

How could John forget? The long wild days from the Cape of Good Hope to Botany Bay after he had shipped from the *Sirius* to the *Supply* on the voyage out, the cramped little galley in the cramped little ship, with the water a-swilling always over the side.

'But I came to see your Mamma,' Cookie said, breaking the boy's reverie. 'See, I ha' brought her some fish.'

Mamma greeted Cookie in the manner he loved. ('A lady your Mamma be,' he had always told the children. ''Tis a pleasure to bring her gifts.')

'You'll stay and share them with us?' she asked him.

'Nay, ma'am. I must be away. I be a-sailing in the morning for Norfolk Island.'

'Then we'll have bananas,' Sue cried, for she was listening.

'And turtles,' said Jenny, who was also there.

Cookie scratched his head and wrinkled his forehead. 'I won't promise,' he said. 'Ye see, 'tis winter. But I'll bring ye back something from Norfolk. Just ye wait and see.'

The boats taking the Governor and his party were gone the next morning when John awoke.

'Will you be going with them next time, Papa?' John asked.

'Yes, and if I do, you and Martin can come. That's a promise.'

John went to school more light-heartedly.

'We'll be going, Martin,' he told his friend joyously, when he joined him on the other side of the bridge. 'We'll be going with the Governor next time.'

Not far from the hospital they met Midshipman Daniel Southwell.

'Ah,' he teased, 'two schoolboys "creeping like snails unwillingly to school".'

'Not unwillingly, Dan,' Martin protested. 'Lessons with Lieutenant Dawes are fun.'

'But all the same, I guess you'd rather spend the morning with that young Nanbaree. Cookie tells me that you tried to climb a tree and couldn't get down. Well, well, that's just what I'd expect of you.'

John grinned. His thoughts were on new adventures. 'Are you ever over at Garden Island, Dan?' he asked.

'Yes, sometimes, but I won't be for a while. We are moving the

Sirius to a cove on the north shore. Have to get her out of the water and careen her, to repair the damage she suffered when we took her to the Cape last year. You won't be seeing much of me for a few months. Why do you want to know about Garden Island?'

'Because Nanbaree is going to make us a canoe one day, and I thought we might be able to paddle over.'

From the moment he began John knew he should not have spoken of it. Dan's face gave evidence of this. Grown-ups were all the same; they always thought danger would come from some harmless adventure.

'Indeed! And the first thing you would do would be to scrabble a hole in the bark and let in the water. Don't you dare try to paddle across to Garden Island in one of those flimsy bits of paper. If you want to go, I'll come for you. Martin would have more sense than to do that.'

Martin was not so sure that it was good sense that kept him from doing the mad things that John attempted. It was just because he counted the cost, and so lacked the spirit. He wished sometimes that he could be as fearless and as impetuous as John.

'Perhaps,' he said now to Dan, 'you'll take us over to the ship at this cove while you are there.'

'I'll be glad to, Martin,' Dan answered. 'That is a promise.'

Two promises in one morning, and both before school time. They were sufficient to turn a dull morning into an exciting one.

Nanbaree's black head was not bent over a paper trying to write pot-hooks, when they arrived.

'He has not come,' Lieutenant Dawes told them with some concern. 'Perhaps you could look round the point and find him for me.'

It was pleasant in the bright June sunshine, its warmth like a woollen coat enveloping the body. They loitered, they dallied, they searched, they called, but no Nanbaree did they see.

'He may have gone over to the cast point looking for us,' they surmised, nodding to one another, and made off in that direction.

But neither Mamma nor Debby had seen him. They were both in a great state, for someone had robbed Mamma's garden and taken three more cabbages.

'Three more cabbages,' Debby wailed. 'D'ye hear, John? Here we are slaving like mad to grow vegetables—your Mamma and Pete and I—and those rascally convicts come at night and rob us.'

Mamma listening, smiled. John knew what she was thinking. Pete and Debby were convicts themselves, and here she was ranting at those rascally convicts for the theft. But no one thought of Debby as a convict, for she had been Mamma's devoted servant ever since the night of the storm, when they had first landed and had sheltered in the mud kitchen which the boys had helped Chips build for Mamma. As for Pete, well, one would expect anything of Pete. He was honest enough with Mamma, but with the rest of the convicts, he would be just as likely to cheat as any of them.

''Tis Caesar, ma'am,' Debby began again.

'Oh, Debby, how can you be so certain that it is Caesar?' Mamma reproved. 'I am not going to believe it of him until I am sure.'

Privately John was inclined to agree with Mamma. Caesar would not rob her, but he would not think twice of robbing anyone else.

'Have you seen Nanbaree?' they asked Sue and Jenny, playing in the Governor's garden.

'Yes,' the girls answered, as they disappeared into the house to get a titbit from Jenny's mother in the Governor's kitchen. 'He's down at the cast point near the cave making a fish-gig.'

So that was where he was. Making a fish-gig! Forgotten now were lessons. They were off at a gallop, in and out of bushes, up and over stones and rocks until they came to the cave at the water's edge.

Nanbaree had almost finished the fish-gig or pronged spear. It was not a new one. He had found the remnants from that store that once the boys discovered in the cave long months before. It had been left on a ledge unnoticed, when the natives had returned and taken away their weapons. Now he was busy repairing the barbed four-pronged head, and tying it with bark tightly to the shaft.

'*Moo-ting*,' he murmured, and they knew it was the native name for fish-gig.

It was long, some six feet, made up of two parts joined by gum, the head composed of four sticks inserted into the shaft with the same material, and tied together with strips of bark. At the end of each stick was a piece of sharp bone, also attached by gum. One had been detached and lost, and he had spent some time filing a piece of shell on the hard rock to make another. Rising, he searched the trees for another piece of gum, and now cemented it to the prong. The fish-gig was complete.

'Nanbaree catch fish,' he announced, and picking up a cockle or two, he made for a rock that protruded into deep water.

Taking off his precious hat, he laid it aside and peered over the edge of the rock. It was still fairly early in the morning, and the water was as yet unruffled by the slight breezes that rose as the day advanced. Besides, there was little depth, and even John and Martin could see the fish, big and small, swimming below.

Now he was opening the cockles and chewing the raw flesh.

'The bait,' John whispered to Martin.

For he was spitting out particles into the water. And the fish were swimming towards them, gobbling them up.

'Look, there's a big fellow!' Martin said softly.

It was a bream, darting from nowhere towards the smaller ones clustered round the bait. Nanbaree was moving the fish-gig gently towards it. And with a thrust the spear was going down, down, scattering the fish—all except the one impaled on its prong. He was drawing it to the surface and holding it up triumphantly.

'*Mau-gro*, fish,' he said, 'for Mamma.'

So it went on until a dozen silvery fish were spread upon the rocks. The boys were so fascinated that neither asked to have a try. The girls came down and joined them, obediently keeping quiet except for a squeal of joy when another fish was caught, and running hither and thither in search of more cockles when the bait gave out.

'Let's put the fish in the cave out of the sun,' Jenny said to Sue, and they carried them up and placed them on a ledge.

An hour had passed before Nanbaree drew in his fish-gig and made signs that he had had enough.

It was then that John picked up the gig and, chewing some cockles, tried to imitate the black boy. But no matter how many times he struck, he had no luck. The fish came, and were so close to the prong that it seemed as if he could not miss, but he always did. The same thing happened with Martin.

Strange to say it was Jenny who caught a fish, sturdy little Jenny who always acted with commonsense and determination. She struck once, twice, and there was a fish gleaming on the pronged barb as the spear came up.

With a squeal she rushed up the path to show it to her mother, followed by Sue, as Nanbaree looked round for the other fish.

'They're in the cave,' Sue shouted as she followed Jenny. But the fish had gone. There was no sign of them—not even one. They had completely disappeared.

Nanbaree gave a wry smile and shrugged his shoulders. 'Mamma, no fish,' he said, then bent to the floor to examine some tracks on the sand. 'White man,' he murmured, tracing the outline of a boot.

They watched as he followed the tracks out into the shrubs at the farther end of the cave.

'He'll lose them now on the grass,' Martin said, but he didn't. He seemed to know exactly which way the man had gone. A crushed blade of grass, a broken twig here or there on the bushes were sufficient to tell him that the thief had passed that way.

Slowly the boys followed him, skirting the back of the Government Farm and beyond it into the woods.

Martin was growing timid. 'Don't you think we've gone far enough?' he said to John. 'How do we know that we're on the right track?'

But John had complete faith in Nanbaree. He had been amazed at the boy's skill at tracking. The way Nanbaree had noticed small disturbances in the path was almost uncanny. Once he had picked up a thread from a leaf, and at another had found a fish-scale impaled on a thorn.

'We're on the right track. See, he's pointing to something. It's a wisp of smoke. Now we are going to find out the thief.'

Nanbaree crept forward, and was peeping through a screen of shrubs.

They followed as quietly as they could, but no matter how hard they tried they never seemed to be able to walk on twigs and dead leaves without making a noise.

'Black man,' Nanbaree whispered, and they drew back in surprise, then laughed silently when they saw it was Caesar.

Yes, Caesar! In spite of Mamma's belief in him! He sat at the fire, with two of the fish cooking on the hot coals, and the others at his side—a forlorn, dejected Caesar, his clothes torn, his boots bulging, as sloppy as any convict would be who had spent a week or more in the woods.

'Every inch a rogue,' Debby would say, and so he appeared.

His rogue's smile broke across his face as the boys burst from their hiding-place.

'Mas'r John!' he cried. 'Why be you heah?'

'Why be you here?' John repeated, eyeing the fish. 'Did you catch those fish?'

'Yes'm, I did,' and then with a twinkle in his eye,' I done ketch 'em in *my* way. Man mus' sure eat, y'know.'

'But they are ours, Caesar. Nanbaree caught them for Mamma.'

'Mamma?' Caesar rose slowly to his feet. 'Mamma?' he repeated. 'I's sorry, Mas'r John. I didn' know dey b'long t'you. I took 'em fum de cave, dat I did, 'kase I wuz hungry.'

John noticed that he made no attempt to tell any more lies.

The fish were for Mamma, That was sufficient. He was not surprised when Caesar began to drag the cooking fish from the coals to give them back. Nanbaree had already picked up the uncooked ones that lay on the grass, and was holding them possessively in his hands.

'No, Caesar,' John refused, 'Mamma would like you to have those. You are hungry and must eat. Will you promise me one thing and we'll say nothing about the fish?'

'Yes'm, Mas'r John. What's dat?'

'Come up and see Mamma tonight after dark. I'm sure she wants to talk to you. Besides, she will give you a good meal.'

Caesar nodded his head. 'I sure will,' he said. 'I promise.'

Mamma was interested in their meeting with Caesar. 'I'm glad you asked him,' she said to John. 'I'll try to persuade him to come back to the settlement.'

The fish she divided, giving some to Martin for his mother, and some for Lieutenant Dawes, then told them to go back to school.

'Why, I thought you had wagged it for the day!' Lieutenant Dawes said, after he had listened to their adventures. 'What name fish-gig?' he asked Nanbaree and got out his book. 'Two names, eh? *Moo-ting* and *cal-larr.*'

John and Martin looked at one another and sighed. Now they would have sums all the afternoon, while Lieutenant Dawes questioned Nanbaree about the fishing habits of the natives.

It became dark early in June, and supper was scarcely over, when John noticed a burly form near the marquee.

'He's come, Mamma,' he whispered, and gathered some bread and salt pork that Debby had laid aside as the meal of a hungry man.

'Don't forget to ask him about the cabbages,' she called as Mamma and John went out of the kitchen door.

Caesar fell upon the food ravenously. 'I's sorry, ma'am,' he said at length, when his hunger was satisfied. ''Tis days since I done eat much—'cept fer some fish,' and then paused, for John was frowning at him, and he knew that nothing must be said to destroy Mamma's faith in him.

'Why do you rob people and run away, Caesar?'

'I dunno, ma'am. I jes' can't help m'self. Den I reekon I'll live better wid the natives, bein' black, but dey woan' hav' me. Mebbe 'tis free I wants ter be.'

Mamma understood that. 'I suppose you realise that everyone has blamed you for the robberies from the gardens. Even my cabbages.'

'Yo' cabbages! No, ma'am, I wouldn' take yo' cabbages.'

As if to corroborate what he said, there was a stir from the brush fence at that moment, and they all saw a shadowy figure pause, then turn on his tracks and disappear down the slope.

'Dah, ma'am, you see it wuz not me.'

'I'm glad,' Mamma said, and John knew she was smiling confidently. 'I should not like you to deceive me, Caesar. I want you to allow yourself to be taken by the guard. The Governor is away at present, at Broken Bay. When he comes back, I'll say something to him about you. I'm sure he will treat you fairly.'

'You sartin?'

'Yes, Caesar, I am.'

Mamma was true to her word. 'Caesar,' the Governor said, when she spoke about him. 'The negro who was caught while I was away? He is one of the hardest workers. It's his appetite that gets him into trouble. I'll send him over to Garden Island. He can work in the garden there, and in addition to his rations can eat as many vegetables as he likes.'

'I still think he's a rogue,' Debby muttered, as she went about her work.

'Yes, a rogue,' Mamma agreed, 'but a merry one, Debby. I like him. How sensible of the Governor to treat him so humanely!'

The next morning three more cabbages were missing. Debby noticed Mamma smile and knew what she was thinking. At least Caesar could not be blamed.

CHAPTER III

THE RIVER AT LAST!

'DID you find the river?' That was what everyone wanted to know when the Governor and his party returned from Broken Bay.

'Aye, laddies,' Captain Hunter told the boys as they walked up from the boats with him, 'we think we ha'e foond the river. 'Twas just beyant Mullet Island, where we caught the fish last year. Dinna' ye ken?'

Of course they remembered.

'As grand a river as ye did ever see, winding aboot immense perpendicular hills and barren rocky lands. For twa days we rowed up it, an' then had tae come back.'

'Why?'

'Nae food, laddies. Oor provisions ran oot. But the Governor is going again when he has rested a day or twa. Maybe this time he'll tak' ye.'

The boys gathered their gear in the hope that Papa would go, and they would be allowed to accompany him.

'What about Nanbaree?' Martin asked John. 'Do you think he would be able to go too?'

They decided that there would be objections. 'Papa would say the trip would make Nanbaree want to go back to his own people,' John said. 'Don't let us say anything about him. Lieutenant Dawes will keep him from being lonely while we are away.

So when Papa mentioned that he was going with the Governor, and that John and Martin could go too, John remained silent about Nanbaree.

'You'll have to be in your best form,' Papa said. 'We are walking over from Manly Cove to Pittwater to meet the boats there.'

Neither of the boys minded how much walking they did. They were going, that's all they cared about. Gladly they packed their knapsacks and waited for the morning of departure.

'Could you spare Pete?' Papa asked Mamma almost at the last moment. 'I should like to take him to help with the baggage.'

Of course Mamma was willing. 'The garden is in very good order,' she replied. 'Debby and I and the girls will carry on, provided you give us someone to watch for robbers at night.'

John looked at Martin and winked. Both knew that Pete hated exertion, and wondered how he would fare on a trip that would be anything but easy.

'Tell me we have to walk ten miles, eh?' he grumbled when they spoke to him about it. 'Sounds hard to me,' but from the twinkle in his eyes they really thought he was pleased.

It was eerie sailing down the harbour in the darkness before dawn, picking out remembered landmarks as black masses against the night sky. The first thrusts of light were appearing in the east when the boats drew into Manly Cove.

'Now come on,' Papa said. 'Exercise your legs. You have a long walk in front of you.'

The boys tightened the straps of their knapsacks, and set off at a grand pace. But the way was long, across sandy beaches, through thick woods, up hills and down valleys, sometimes along paths beaten down by the feet of the natives as they had passed in the same direction. For five hours they went on, resting here and there, and coming at last to the shore of Pittwater, the southern branch of Broken Bay.

There it glimmered before them. 'The finest piece of water I have ever seen.' John remembered—the Governor's words for it when they had first found it the year before. It was everything that he had said it was: commodious, beautiful, inviting.

'This is where a boat was to meet us,' Papa explained. 'Two left Sydney Cove last night with our provisions. One was to pick us up here and take us to the entrance.'

No boat was there. They made a fire and cooked a meal, and still no boat came.

'We'll have to walk,' the Governor said at length.

Walk? Surely not. They had already come more than twelve miles, and now there were all those bays and hills between the southern end of Pittwater and the entrance to Broken Bay.

But it had to be done. Lifting their knapsacks, John and Martin set out again, languidly, wearily dragging one foot after another.

'What!' said Pete, as he passed them, chewing a twig as was his custom. 'Don't tell me ye're done. Thought ye were explorers, I did, hardy by this. See if ye can walk quicker than me.'

With that challenge there was nothing for it but to step out. Pete, true to form, had been until then one of the last, slouching along as lazily as he could, but now he became one of the first. He was certainly fresher than most, and strange to say seemed to be enjoying himself.

The boys were almost exhausted when they reached the narrow strip of sand and scrub within the bluff southern headland, where the boats had at last arrived.

Tired as they were, they were soon picking out landmarks remembered from their last visit—the island like a crouching lion right in the entrance of the bay; the west head, so steep, so high, its grey walls interspersed with shrubs and trees that grew outwards in their efforts to live.

'Do you remember the black boy whose father stole a spade?' John said to Martin. 'I wonder if we shall see them again,' but even as he spoke he knew they wouldn't. The natives moved about too much, seeking food where best it could be found.

The Governor was giving orders to set up camp. 'We'll start at daylight in the morning,' he told his men.

The party was quite large now, some forty in number; the Governor; Mr Collins, the Judge-Advocate; Mr White, the Surgeon-General; Captain Hunter, the commander of the *Sirius*, as well as others; Papa and his marines, the crew of the boats, and convicts like Pete.

'We must be well armed and protected,' the Governor had said, 'because we might meet opposition from the natives.'

Of the boats' crews, the one John greeted most enthusiastically was Chips, the carpenter.

'Ah, so you're here!' Chips teased the lads. 'Well, one never knows, you might be of some help. Governor's brought me 'cause boats are stove in by snags and rocks. You'll be useful to hand me the nails.'

They were away at daylight the next morning, rowing up the mighty waterway towards the island where they had the year before hauled in a fine catch of mullet, and so had called it Mullet Island. Beyond, they turned into the opening that the Governor believed was the 'river'.

It was certainly picturesque, grand too—a broad stream running between high craggy hills, rising steeply from mangrove swamps and reedy banks.

'No room for a camp,' John said to Martin. 'We'll have to sleep in the boats.'

But the Governor had in mind the parcel of rocks on which he had camped only a few weeks before. Here they raised their tents and spent the night as best they could.

Away again at daylight, they were soon past the point reached by the Governor and in new country.

On and on, rowing between immense hills of rock and scrub. Twice they came to a junction and chose to follow the stream that led to the north-west, only to find that it shoaled between high, steep, rocky mountains, and they had to return once more.

'We'll keep to the southern branch whatever happens,' the Governor said firmly, when they reached it a second time and went on.

Mile after mile. Day after day. It was hard on the boats' crews and the convicts. John and Martin, in the bow, often watched Pete, backwards and forwards, backwards and forwards. Only once in a while would he give them a wry smile and spit on his hands. They wondered if he now preferred gardening for Mamma, a much less arduous job.

At camps he was most joyful, sparing no effort to do a fair share of the work. 'Dunno, but I like this exploring,' he drawled one night with a wink. 'Makes a man think he's doing something worthwhile, eh?' then lazily closed his eyes and lay basking in the heat of the night fire.

The country was still unpromising, the high rocky shores or low marshy points giving no sign of the good soil for which the Governor was looking. Some felt that he would never find it. But he would not be deterred. He had determined to follow the river to the very end, and nothing would make him change his mind.

Natives were now seen at intervals, fleeing into the woods or gathered round their fires.

'Coo-ee,' John and Martin called to them, a word they had learnt from Nanbaree, which meant, 'Come here'.

Two eventually did come—with such confidence that the Governor thought they must have seen white men before. Cheerfully they exchanged a coil of fishing line for a hatchet and a wild duck that had just been shot.

'A good exchange for them,' Martin said, examining the line made of the hair of some animal and twisted like string.

The hills had moved back now, and the banks were covered with trees whose leaves were like those of the English pine. The ground between them seemed to have been ploughed up.

'Ye micht think a herd o' swine had been living there,' Captain Hunter said.

But when they investigated they found a great quantity of yams, and concluded that the natives had been that way, digging the ground with their sticks in search of food.

The Governor was happy. At last his river was showing signs of promise. 'A dark rich mould,' he called the soil when he examined a piece in his hand. 'It will be sure to run many miles away from the banks.'

As the stream became narrower, the boys were puzzled by the great masses of grass and reeds, and of huge logs, caught up in the trees thirty or forty feet above the river.

'But why?' they asked Papa.

'Because the floods have come down in torrents and left them there,' he explained.

It was hard to believe that the water could rise to such heights; hard, also, to believe that it could lay down the trees of the flats so that their tops pointed downstream.

'Like a field o' corn after a storm,' Captain Hunter said. 'The weight o' water must be tremendous tae cause that.'

At five o'clock on the evening of the seventh day, they came to a hill spread with lofty trees. Here they pitched their tents on its slopes.

In the stillness after supper, all heard distinctly the fall of water.

'A waterfall!' exclaimed John.

'And that means we cannot be far from the source of the river,' the Governor remarked.

They were up at daylight, climbing to the top of the hill.

John and Martin raced on ahead. 'Why!' they cried, when they looked north and south and saw the mountains stretching in both directions, and in between a gap, not five or six miles away. 'The Carmarthen and Lansdowne Hills!'

'Yes,' said the Governor, 'and the one we are standing on already has a name.'

'Richmond Hill,' they answered, and remembered how they had seen it from the coast—a stubby mountain on its own.

'The Blue Mountains,' most people had begun to call these hills, because from the distance they were so deeply blue almost purple.

'And in between the gap the river or a tributary might run,' the Governor said.

The soil was found to be very good.

'Let us plant some potatoes and Indian corn,' he suggested. It was always his custom to do this. 'Then when we come again,' he explained to the boys, 'we shall know if the soil is really rich. If it is, they will be thriving.'

John mused aloud to Martin. 'We've come farther than Nanbaree has ever been,' he said, pointing across the rich, flat country below to the east. 'And away over there, miles and miles, Debby is preparing breakfast for Mamma and Sue, and Nanbaree is getting ready to spend the day with Lieutenant Dawes.'

'Yes,' Martin reminded him, 'but what is happening in the west? What is beyond the mountains?'

It was a fascinating question.

'Perhaps some day we'll find out, Martin,' John said, 'some day when we are grown up and go over them.'

By mid-morning the tide was high, so they went on in the boats up the river, which was now shoally and very narrow, until it divided into two branches. From one the stream came down with a rush over a range of stones that lay across the entrance.

'The waterfall we heard last night,' John exclaimed.

'We'll examine the ground and then make ready to return,' the Governor decided.

All were glad to set out on their homeward way.

'Aye, that river's dangerous,' Captain Hunter remarked to the Governor. 'I wouldna' care tae think what micht happen if it rained in the nicht an' the water cam' doon in flood. Ha'e ye thocht o' a name for it?'

'Yes,' the Governor replied. 'I have decided to call it the Hawkesbury, after Lord Hawkesbury, the President of the Council of Trade.'

'The Hawkesbury!' thought John. So that was what its name was going to be. Lord Hawkesbury was certainly a lucky man to have such a fine river called after him.

With that they set off on the long row downstream. Seven days later they were back at Pittwater, and on the next day walked overland to Manly Cove.

CHAPTER IV

PETE IS THE HERO

IT was four in the afternoon when the Governor and his party reached the north shore of Port Jackson near Manly Cove. Although the way was clear now that they knew the path, the walking was arduous, for each man was carrying his own knapsack with two days' provisions.

Captain Hunter looked ruefully at his shoes, for only the soles were left, and they were tied to his feet with yarn.

'We can but hope the boats will meet us, or we micht see some fishermen in the harbour,' he said.

But there were no boats and no fishermen to be seen.

'We micht as well be fifty miles frae the Cove,' he sighed. 'I'm hoping we needna' ha'e to walk farther,' and he looked again at the remnants of his shoes.

The Governor ordered a fire to be lit, for the night promised to be cold. 'And tell the marines to fire muskets at intervals,' he instructed Papa, 'in case there may be fishing parties down the harbour.'

John and Martin rolled themselves in plaid and blanket and lay down beside the fire. 'What we always like to do most of all,' Martin whispered as they watched the logs crackling before they fell asleep.

The morning brought no sign of any boats.

'There is only one thing to do,' the Governor decided. 'We shall have to walk overland round the head of the Middle Harbour.'

Captain Hunter went unwillingly. 'But ma shoes,' he exclaimed. 'I'll be walking in ma bare feet yet.'

They were moving over a rocky hill towards a narrow stretch of the Middle Harbour, when the boom of a gun resounded across the waters.

'Ah!' said Captain Hunter. 'Someone awa' frae the *Sirius*. She's careened on the ither side of that point. Some puir laddie has lost his way in those wild hills.'

His fears were confirmed when a little farther on, the boys, walking ahead, discovered the print of a man's shoe on the ground. The party stood for a moment examining it, and almost immediately heard the boom of another gun.

'Ye ken I'm richt,' he emphasised. 'Some puir fellow in trouble.'

'Then we'll keep on firing a musket now and then,' the Governor said. 'If there is a man about, he will hear us.'

The first musket brought no reply, or the second, but to the third there seemed to be a faint answer.

'Did you hear it, John?' Martin asked.

'Yes, I thought I did. The crack of a musket.'

The Governor stopped to listen, and so had Papa and Captain Hunter and the others.

'Try again,' the Governor ordered the marines. 'Fire a volley.'

And again there was a faint reply.

They walked in the direction from which it came, firing, listening, and each time the reply became louder.

'Gi'e him a halloo,' Captain Hunter suggested, and so they did, the boys with all the power of their lungs.

And this time came a faint reply—a human voice.

So it went on until they were close enough to tell him to stay where he was, and at last saw him—a sorry figure, staggering like a drunken man, babbling like an idiot, his clothes torn and in fragments, his shoes ripped from his feet.

'Why!' cried John, who had sailed in the *Sirius*. 'It's White, the sailmaker!' And he rushed forward, as the man stumbled, tears of joy streaming from his eyes, then fell exhausted to the ground.

'He's starving,' the Governor said to Papa. 'Give him some food in small quantities and he'll come round. In the meantime, Captain Hunter and I will try to find a way of crossing the Middle Harbour.'

It lay before them, a narrow stretch certainly, with a long peninsula running into it from the other side, but still some four hundred yards in width.

'We micht as well be fifty miles awa',' Captain Hunter murmured gloomily again, thinking how close they were to Sydney Cove and yet how far distant.

John and Martin stayed with the lost sailmaker until Papa ordered them off. That is how they came to find the canoe. They had run down to the sandy beach and were exploring it, when, there before their eyes, sheltered by overhanging trees, was the answer to all their difficulties.

'The very thing!' the Governor said, as he examined it. 'I'll get two men to cross the stream in it. What about you, Chips? Think you could manage it?'

'I'll try, sir. Who'll go with me?'

'I'm willing, sir,' Pete said, stepping forward. 'I've been in one o' those canoes. Deserted, it was, down by the Government Farm, and I tried it out, I did.'

The boys looked at one another in amazement. It seemed strange for Pete to offer for some position of danger.

'Good, good,' the Governor commended. 'As you know, Chips, the *Sirius* is careened in a bay on the other side of the hill. Walk straight over and tell Lieutenant Bradley to send a boat round for us immediately.'

'Aye, aye, sir.'

The canoe was a poor sort of thing made of bark tied at both ends, with sticks across the thwarts to keep it open.

'Like the one Nanbaree is going to make for us,' John said.

Pete was the first to get into it. They watched him wade out in the water and gingerly lift his body into the canoe and settle on the keel.

'That's not the way,' cried Martin. 'The natives sit on their heels. It will turn turtle.'

And so it did. A slight movement of his body as he took a few strokes with the paddle he had fashioned, and over it went, and there was poor Pete squirming in the water and striking out for the shore.

'Sorry, sir,' he said to the Governor, as he dripped from head to toe. 'I should've known better. The natives squat on their haunches in those contraptions.'

'Never mind, my man. You did your best. I realise that they are tricky things to board.'

'Now if we only had Nanbaree,' Martin said, 'he would get us across.'

'They should have sent us,' John said impulsively. 'We would have been lighter,' but Martin was not so enthusiastic. He looked at the stretch of water and decided that a trip over it in a frail canoe would not be his idea of adventure.

The Governor was discussing the position with his officers. 'We'll try to make a catamaran,' he said.

'Yes, a raft,' Captain Hunter repeated, 'made o' the lighter logs aboot. Chips, ye are in charge. Everyone can help.'

John and Martin rushed off to find the right sort of log, and when enough had been brought, stood by as Chips directed the men to lash them together.

'Like the raft Robinson Crusoe made,' John said to Martin, and both felt a thrill to know that they were doing the same thing.

When the raft was ready, Chips himself prepared to try it out. Pushing it into deep water, he climbed upon it. A sigh, almost like a groan, came from those who watched when it went down like a stone.

'Wood's too heavy, sir,' he explained to the Governor.

'Sae that's that,' sighed Captain Hunter. 'What noo?'

'We'll have to walk round the head of the Middle Harbour,' the Governor replied. 'That's a journey of twa more days, and oor provisions are near spent,' Captain Hunter reminded him.

'I know that, but there is nothing else to do.'

Captain Hunter looked again at his shoes. 'I am sorry, Your Excellency, but I canna' gang wi' ye. Ma shoes wouldna' last. Rather than climb over rocky hills an' through those thick woods wi' bare feet, I'll gang back tae the boats at Pittwater an' come roond by sea. Ye can see what the exertion did tae the sailmaker.'

'But, my dear Hunter, you can't do that. You might meet some hostile natives.'

'Maybe some ithers will come tae,' he replied, and looked round at the officers assembled in a group.

Captain Collins was willing to accompany him. They were just about setting out, when Chips stepped forward again.

'What about swimming across, sir?' he said to the Governor. 'I'm prepared to try.'

'Good. But I think two should go. Is there any other volunteer?'

And for the second time that morning the boys were surprised, for it was Pete who offered.

'I'll go, sir,' he said simply, and then with a sheepish grin, 'Damp enough I be now. Won't matter if I get a second ducking.'

The Governor looked at them gravely. 'The water will be cold, and you might get cramps,' he warned.

'It's all right with me, sir,' said Chips.

'And me, too, sir,' said Pete. 'I have swum out to Garden Island even in winter.'

'Excellent!'

Soon both were stripping and wrapping their clothes in a bundle and tying it on their shoulders.

With a splash they entered the water and began to swim.

'It'd be freezing,' Martin stuttered, almost feeling, himself, the steel cold thrust of the water as it closed around their bodies. 'I'm glad it's not me.'

They were cutting the water, arms like knife-blades, heads down low, each with his bundle on his back. Every eye was upon them, every body taut, watching, watching... There was not a movement, not a word.

Closer... closer. They would get there. No, one had got cramps. It was Pete. He was in difficulties.

'He'll sink,' gasped John. 'He'll sink. Oh, Martin!'

But Pete had recovered. He was struggling on. Chips reached shallow water and was waiting. He held out his hand and drew Pete to the shore.

Immediately the tenseness was broken by a giggle from the boys. 'Pete's lost his bundle,' John said, and laughed again. 'He'll have no clothes.'

'Oh, John, how can you laugh?' Martin remonstrated. 'He'll be cold and get all scratched.'

But the others were smiling, too, and Pete took it in good part, for he waved his hand. Then sharing what clothes they had, he and Chips disappeared into the woods.

'Now let us hear what the sailmaker has to say,' the Governor said, and walked towards the spot where Papa and some of the marines were caring for him.

He had recovered sufficiently to sit up and was ready to tell his story.

'Four days, sir, I was lost in the woods. Went up the hill from the ship, an' all o' a sudden found I was lost, I did. Same sort o' look the trees have, an' one cove, why 'tis exactly the same as t' other. I kep' firing my gun, sir, that night an' the next day, an' the next, till the flint, it be worn to the stump. Didn't shoot a bird yesterday, 'cos I couldn't get fire out o' the gun. Come night, an' I expects to sit in the cold an' the black an' shiver, but marvel o' marvels, the flint, it worked again, so I lit some twigs an' be warm. An' this morning, too, naught a spark could I get from it, until I had to answer ye, an' then it worked again—yes, sir, it worked again, praise God. I be thinking Providence was looking after me.'

'And you didn't know where you were?'

'No, sir, all the time I did think I was a-walking back to the ship. An' instead I was a-walking round the head o' the Middle Harbour, an' along its north side, as ye know. 'Twas Providence that sent ye, sir, I am sure o' it. Another night an' I couldn't have gone farther, an' then one day someone'ud have found my bones in the woods.'

When the boat arrived from the *Sirius*, his fellow sailors were amazed to see their missing comrade.

'So that's where you got to,' John heard them say to the sailmaker. 'We've been looking for you night and day, sending boats into every cove, and firing guns every two hours.'

Midshipman Dan was in charge of the boat's crew.

'Been having a fine time, I guess,' he whispered to John and Martin. 'Did you find the river?'

'Oh, yes, Dan! The Governor is going to call it the Hawkesbury.'

'Is that so?' Dan turned to the Governor. 'Captain Tench found one, too, sir.'

'Indeed!'

'Yes, he went with a party from Rose Hill, and on the morning of the second day came to the banks of a river "as broad as the Thames at Putney", so he said.'

'Running north or south?'

'North, sir.'

The Governor looked at Captain Hunter and they nodded. 'Perhaps an extension of the river we discovered,' he said.

'And what will you call this one, sir?' John asked promptly. 'Perhaps the Nepean, after Mr Nepean, the Under-Secretary of the Home Department. I'll have to think about it.'

Mamma had supper waiting when John reached home.

'You'd never guess who was the hero, Mamma,' he said. 'It was Pete,' and he straightway poured out the events of the day.

Sue giggled, and so did Debby, when they heard of Pete's predicament. John guessed poor Pete would come in for some teasing from Debby.

'He came back late this afternoon, and told us you'd be here later,' Mamma said. 'So that explains the queer assortment of clothes he wore.'

She was horrified to hear about the lost sailmaker.

'There now,' she said, 'that ought to be a lesson to you, John. I always said that, if once you were lost in those woods, you'd never be able to find your way back.'

But John wasn't taking any notice. He was gobbling up a fine meal that Debby had prepared for the wanderers, and after sixteen days of salt pork and biscuits, it was so good that he didn't want to waste any time arguing with Mamma.

When at length he pushed away his plate, he said, 'Papa, do you really think that the river Captain Tench found is the same as ours?'

'It may be. We'll know in time.'

When the Governor gave some thought to the matter, he did name the other river the Nepean.

CHAPTER V
A NATIVE CANOE AND DANGER!

MAMMA was more cheerful than John had seen her for a long time. 'There's a load of bricks in the yard,' Sue told him. 'We are to have a real house.'

So that was why she was happy. John had realised long ago how much Mamma had desired that house. In the days that followed the fleet's arrival at Sydney Cove, he and Martin had helped Chips to build a mud kitchen for Mamma, the very one in which they were now having breakfast. At the same time Papa's men had pitched a marquee to serve as sleeping and living quarters for the family. John remembered the first night ashore, when a violent storm had sent them running to take refuge in the kitchen, and how Debby, an unknown convict, had come out of the dark to shelter with them, and so had become their servant. Other huts of cabbage-tree palm and mud had been added to the group, one for himself, and one for Debby. And when Sue had been ill, he and Martin had built a cubby for her that ever since had been her playground.

'Mamma, you won't let the men pull down my cubby?' he now heard her say.

'I hope not, dear. If it's in the way, we'll build you another.'

'And what about my hut?' John asked.

'Well, I don't think you'll need it,' she replied. 'There will be room in the house for us all to sleep. A real house, John, that won't leak, and will keep out the cold winds of winter. It is what I've dreamed of for months.'

'And I, too, ma'am,' added Debby. 'Now we'll be able to live as gentlefolk should live—even have a new kitchen maybe.'

John was thinking of the loss of his own hut, and the freedom that went with it. He did not want to sleep in a stuffy house any more. It had been so exciting to live alone—especially in a hut like Robinson Crusoe's. Debby's words gave him an idea. The kitchen! The kitchen he had built with his own hands. It was solid enough and quite watertight.

'But you won't pull down the kitchen?' he said to Mamma.

'No, dear, I shall never do that. Did you not build it for me, and have we not had many happy moments here?'

'Then perhaps I could have it instead of the hut. Please, Mamma.'

When she hesitated, John knew what the answer would be. Mamma was always so cautious. 'I don't know about that,' she said. 'I think I'd rather have you in the house with the rest of us.'

This was a time when Papa would understand. He looked at him pleadingly. 'Why, yes,' Papa said, 'let the boy have the hut! Teach him to be independent.' Papa was always one to lay stress on such a quality.

John finished his meal happily and got up to go to school, but before he went, Mamma, in her gracious way, made them all remember what they owed to the Governor.

'We are very obliged to him,' she said. 'It is he who has made this possible for us.'

'Yes, Mamma,' piped Sue, 'he promised you a house last Christmas when his own was finished.'

'Soon all will have houses,' Papa remarked, 'now we have a new kiln at the brickfields that will burn off thirty thousand bricks at the same time. If we only had more lime!'

Yes, it was the lime that was the trouble. The women convicts spent their time grinding oyster shells into lime, but there never was enough.

Martin was full of news when John met him at the wharf, for on this day Pete was to row them across to the observatory. 'I've seen Nanbaree,' he said. 'He's going to help us make one of those native canoes.'

'Yes, and mighty quick ye'll have to be to get into the tricky things,' said Pete. 'Before ye know where ye are ye'll be in the water like me,' and he laughed at himself.

The boys laughed with him.

'Was it cold, Pete? And did you get scratched when you lost your clothes?'

'Scratched? It be just as if I be rolled in the brambles. And cold? Well, no colder than for those natives! Don't know how they put up with it, I don't.'

Nanbaree was waiting for them at the door of the observatory.

'Been lost without you,' Lieutenant Dawes told them. 'Running to the window every five minutes, because I told him that you would come across the Cove. I guess he would have been at your home last night, John, if he had known you had returned. Your mother said he haunted the place.'

Nanbaree stood shyly and looked from one to the other, smiling all the while.

'Spent his time making a stone knife,' Lieutenant Dawes continued. 'Something to do with you. The three of you will have to look after yourselves this morning, for I'm to work on the plans for a new building for my observatory—a stone one.' He sounded almost as thrilled as Mamma.

That suited the boys admirably. It would give them time to get Nanbaree to make the canoe.

'Buildings everywhere,' thought John, as they walked back. 'Sydney Cove won't be the same place soon without its tents and marquees and wattle-and-daub huts.'

Mamma was so busy with the bricklayers when they told her that they were going to borrow the axe, that she did not appear to hear.

'Better take it,' Martin said. 'It might be sharper than Nanbaree's knife.'

They had looked at the knife rather critically when Nanbaree had proudly shown it to them. And why shouldn't he be proud? Had he not spent hours and hours of time grinding it at the smithy to some pretence of sharpness? Even so the boys did not trust it.

Turning into the path that led to the cave, they walked right out to the end of the east point before Nanbaree found the tree he wanted. Its bark was rough, but the trunk was straight and unblemished.

'Nanbaree make *nowee*,' he announced, and began by cutting the bark in a ring round the tree.

That was easy. But how was he to reach high enough to get even six feet off? Nanbaree knew. Looking round for a strong sapling, he borrowed the axe and chopped it down. The sharp point he leant against the bark so that it held tightly, then he walked up it as easily as a cat, and with the stone knife began to cut the bark right round the trunk. From the top ring he now cut down on the line of the sapling wedged in the bark, until he came to the bottom ring. This was the length he wished to make the canoe.

Now he had the bark, but how was he to get it off?

So far John and Martin had merely watched.

'You,' he called, beckoning them with a jerk of his hand, as he took the sapling wedged in the bark from the tree. 'John, Martin, you hold,' and with that they grasped the bark at the middle edge and helped him to loosen it with the axe, and then to lever it with the pole from the trunk.

It was a splendid piece of bark, and John in his impatient way saw it a canoe in a matter of minutes.

'Just tie the ends and there it is,' he said to Martin.

But that was not the way. Much more was to be done before it could be placed in the water. First Nanbaree chipped off the rough outer bark with his knife.

'Fire,' said Nanbaree.

John shook his head. He had brought the axe, but had forgotten the tinder-box.

So Nanbaree had to make fire in the native way, and the boys were happy to watch. He set about making his tools—a flat piece of wood in which he made a hollow, a rounded stick to move up and down within it, a third piece to balance both. Then he began to gather tinder—a tangle of dry grass, bark from under the logs, tiny sticks.

All was now ready. He was placing the third piece on the ground and balancing the flat one over it by means of his feet. He was inserting the rounded stick into the hollow of the flat one, he was twirling it between his palms, round and round and up and down. He was beginning to tire...

'Let me try, let me try,' cried John.

But John found that the art was not easily learnt. It was Nanbaree who set the powder in the hollow smouldering, and in an instant was tipping it on to the tangle of dry grass, picking up the tangle with his fingers and shaking it until it glowed into flame. With the help of the bark and the sticks, the fire was soon alight.

But why did he want the fire? Calling to them again, he made them pick up each end of the bark, one hand on each corner, and hold it over the fire, moving backwards and forwards to get it as much as possible into the heat.

'*Beial, beial*, good, good,' he said, as the bark responded and began to bend, and then ran off to look for something.

'Where has he gone now?' John complained. 'How are you getting on, Martin?'

'I'd like some dinner.'

'Yes, and so would I. We'll go as soon as he comes back. I'm tired of holding this thing.'

But Nanbaree would not let them go. He came running back with some vines with which he bound the ends while they held the bark together, then he placed sticks, one towards each end to keep the sides apart.

'Ah,' sighed John, 'now perhaps!'

It was not so. Nanbaree was off again, returning with long branches, and soon he had shown them how to bind these with vines round the inside edge of the canoe to make it stronger.

Rests to sit on, and now clay.

'For the fire to cook the fish,' said John proudly.

But Nanbaree corrected him. 'Cook, no,' he said. 'Fish, he come up fire.'

So that was it. The fire was carried round in the canoe to attract the fish, not to cook them.

Martin, who had been resting on the ground, got up to admire the canoe. Now that it was finished, it looked far more solid and seaworthy than that battered old thing they had found in the Middle Harbour. But he didn't relish the idea of a trip in it. John could have it on his own. What he wanted was his dinner.

'I'm hungry,' he said.

'Yes, so am I,' John replied. 'Dinner, Nanbaree,' he called, picking up the axe and moving off. Nanbaree obviously preferred his own stone knife.

Dinner was long over, when they reached the kitchen, and Debby was annoyed.

'Late, indeed!' she said. 'I should think you are. You'll have to be satisfied with a bit of pie, and cold at that. What I'll be cooking for you next I don't know, with the salt pork so dry and stringy. Nanbaree, you had better bring me some snakes.'

He smiled back, but did not understand until John said, '*Cahn*, snake for Debby.'

Thereupon they made short work of the pie.

'Where's Mamma, Debby?' John asked. When he was about to go on an escapade, he always wanted to know where his family was.

'Going over the ground with the head bricklayer. The house is to begin tomorrow, and she's as happy as a bird.'

That was good. She would be so interested in the house, she would not be thinking of him.

'And Sue and Jenny?'

'Gone with the parson and that native girl, Abaroo, to Garden Island. They took Gyp with them. I don't know why.'

Ah! So the coast was clear. Martin and he could go and fish in the canoe with Nanbaree.

Although she was fifteen and much older than they, the girls were becoming quite friendly with Abaroo, who now lived with the parson and his wife.

Back at the canoe Nanbaree found and shaped two paddles.

The time had come to launch it. John had brought the fishing lines from home, and was now busy gathering tinder and placing it on the clay, ready to light the fire that was to attract the fish. It floated smoothly, a neat little craft. Nanbaree was obviously proud of it, and so was John, but Martin looked upon it with misgivings.

'It'll sink,' he said to John. 'Like Pete in the Middle Harbour.'

'No, it won't,' John assured him. 'Nanbaree knows about canoes.'

'That's true,' thought Martin. 'Perhaps I'm being rather scared.'

How did one get into the thing? How did one balance? There seemed to be a knack of doing it successfully. Nanbaree was busy showing John.

Martin watched with interest. Nanbaree had, of course, dispensed with his clothes, and John had thrown off his shoes and stockings. So that was the way. One knelt in the canoe, buttocks pressed on one's heels, knees opened wide with their full weight against the sides to get one's poise. Like all things it was easy when one knew how.

And suddenly Martin felt the urge to try, himself. He would go with them. Quickly he threw off his own shoes and stockings, and going to the water's edge followed John into the canoe.

Nanbaree had the paddles, one in each hand, taking stroke alternately as the canoe moved out from the shore.

From the moment he saw how low it was in the water Martin's fears returned. An inch, two inches! A wave of any size, a lurch by one or the other, and the water would come in with a gulp. He didn't like it, and he didn't like the way he was sitting. He longed to move, to sit naturally on the keel, his legs stretched in front of him. The longing grew as the canoe moved farther and farther from the shore. He could see that John was enjoying himself, that Nanbaree was in his element; for once Nanbaree was in command, and the white boys had to obey.

And then the cramp came. He felt it in the arch of his right foot, aching, aching, making his instep taut, almost inflexible. He could not bear it. Lifting the weight of his body from the heel, he almost overbalanced. There was a sickening lurch, and it seemed as if all three would hit the water, deep, dark, and cold on that winter's day. But Nanbaree saved the canoe. With the skill of one trained from infancy to meet such an emergency, he threw his weight where it was needed, and the canoe glided on its way.

'Isn't it fun, Martin?' John called back. He was so excited that even if he had felt the lurch, he regarded it as part of a canoeing adventure.

'But John—oh, John—please—'

'Look, there's Garden Island. I can see Jenny and Sue. Hey! Hey!' he called to them, and in his excitement the canoe took another lurch, and once again they almost ended in the water.

'Oh, John! Please, John, put me on shore!'

Nanbaree was the one to pay heed. 'Martin, he *moo-la*, sick,' he cried. 'Canoe in there,' and he pointed to the headland to the east of the point on which they had built the canoe.

One glance at Martin, now slumped in the middle of the canoe, made John obey and right quickly.

'But, Martin, what is the matter?' he asked, as they brought the canoe to the rocks, and he and Nanbaree helped Martin out.

'A cramp, John,' and he sat down, holding his foot and trying to bring mobility to it by rubbing it with his hands.

Nanbaree soon lit a fire from the one in the canoe, and by relaxing in its warmth Martin recovered.

'Do we go out again?' John asked, eager to be gone, for the afternoon was rapidly passing.

'Not me, John. I'm staying right here.' Anything, thought Martin, would be better than that canoe.

John, although impatient, was not without some sympathy. 'But we can't leave you, Martin.'

'Of course you can. You and Nanbaree go on your own.'

Because he wanted to go so much John agreed. 'Just for a little while,' he said. 'When we have caught some fish, we'll come back and take you across to the east point.'

That suited Martin for the time being. 'All right,' he replied, but already he had made up his mind that he was going to walk home.

They had no sooner gone, then he drew his own line from his pocket and, breaking a cockle in two, began to fish, himself, looking up now and again to see what they were doing.

The fire in the canoe was burning brightly now, for they had built it up, and John was proudly hauling in a fish.

'He can have it on his own,' Martin thought, as he felt a rubble and also drew in a fish. 'Fancy sitting like that for hours!' and impaling the fish with a sharp stick he held it over the fire and began to cook it.

Voices came floating over the water. John? Nanbaree? No, girlish voices—Jenny and Sue and the girl, Abaroo. He looked up and saw them waving from Garden Island. Gyp was with them, and was leaping from rock to rock as far as he could go, barking in the direction of his master.

The canoe was drifting some twenty yards from the island, and John was holding up a half-cooked fish to show the girls, picking a piece and thrusting it in his mouth as if it were the choicest morsel there could be.

Martin never knew whether John called, or whether Gyp mistook his master's action for a signal. All he knew was that just as the girls turned to go back, Gyp struck out from the shore and made for the canoe.

What would happen when the dog reached it, and it so low in the water? If Nanbaree got the dog safely into the canoe, how would they restrain him?

Nanbaree was ready. He did get the dog into the canoe. With a clever movement he picked him from the water and swung him in. But Gyp wanted his master, not Nanbaree. He struggled, he barked, and leapt upon John. And John, remembering the fire in the middle of the canoe, turned suddenly to save the dog from hurt, the canoe lurched, the water lipped in, and over they went.

'No, no,' cried Martin from the shore. 'No, no,' as he watched them struggling and the canoe bobbing about on the surface.

Then with some relief he saw that Nanbaree had grasped it, and was bringing it within reach of John. Could they hold out? Could they?

Why hadn't the girls waited? They could have gone for help, he thought. He looked and saw their bright dresses a pattern amongst the green trees, but although he called, they went on. 'Jenny, Sue!' he yelled and yelled again, but there was no answering turn of the head, no looking back.

Gyp had already started to swim towards the point where he was. 'Then the canoe may come this way too,' Martin decided. Nanbaree had brought it to John, and both were clinging desperately to it. Even from that distance, Martin could see that John was beginning to be distressed. Nanbaree had thrown his arm around him and was helping to support him...

Where would the canoe drift? He watched it closely. The tide was coming in. It would float to the point. Yes, it was coming closer. But perhaps it would miss the point and sweep up the harbour?

Martin stared helplessly. What could he do? Go to the farm, and then be too late to help? Jump in, himself? All his being cried out to him to do just that, yet he held back. His reason was working, telling him that he could not swim that distance, would not be of any help. Then he saw the canoe break into pieces, and Nanbaree catch John as John slipped under the water. He couldn't stand by. He must help. Frantically he tore off his coat, his breeches.

He stood poised, ready to dive in, when he felt a hand on his shoulder, holding him back.

It was Caesar—Caesar with his face working with distress, as he watched the swimmers struggling right there in front of him.

'Oh, Caesar, can't you do anything?' and then he noticed that Caesar was shackled with a leg iron.

How could Caesar do anything?

He poised to dive again, but again Caesar was holding him back.

'Stay, young mas'r,' he said, and turned and went slowly and cumbersomely, but purposefully, with the iron held in his hand.

Was it a few minutes, or was it longer? It seemed half an hour to Martin standing there almost naked, waiting, waiting. What did Caesar intend to do? He had not dived into the water. And how could he with a weight like that? Some other means must be at hand. What? What? The dreadful uncertainty of it all!

And then he heard him, saw him. He was rowing a boat round the point from the farther side, he was rowing towards the boys, he would reach them in time. With a sigh of relief Martin picked up his breeches and put them on, for he was shivering with cold.

When Caesar brought John and Nanbaree—and Gyp—in to the rocks, Nanbaree was as fresh as he had been when he set out in the canoe, but John lay shivering and spent in the bottom of the boat, with Gyp quiet beside him.

'Git de fire goin', Martin,' Caesar bade the boy. 'We'll tak' him out an' mak' him warm.'

It was a real bonfire before they finished. 'Like a beacon,' Martin said. 'Someone will see it and come and rescue us.'

And so it happened. Parson Johnson with the girls, on the way back to the Cove, called in to find out the reason for the blaze.

'Thought you were in difficulties,' the parson said. 'So this is where Gyp is. We whistled and called and called and whistled, and then had to come away without him. How did he get here?'

It was a long story, and one that shocked the parson. 'Come, we must get the boy home,' and with that John was transferred to his boat, with Nanbaree and Martin and Gyp as well.

'Thank you, Caesar,' John whispered feebly.

'Dat sure be al' right, young mas'r. Tell yo' Mamma I done it fer her.'

'I will.'

Only afterwards, and when they were by themselves, did John and Martin wonder how Caesar had procured the boat. Had he stolen it from the island and hidden it on the point in order to run away again? They remembered that there were stores in the bottom, an iron pot and a gun. He should not have had those.

'Perhaps we interrupted his plans,' John surmised, for they heard nothing of his escape.

'Well, it's a good job he was there with the boat,' Martin concluded. 'It certainly saved your life.'

Mamma was worried about their escapade. 'Something always happens when my back is turned,' she complained.

'Yes, and so it always will, for boys will be boys,' Papa reminded her.

Within a month John was as skilful as Nanbaree with a canoe, for they soon made another. Mamma forgot to scold him when he came home day after day with fish, but she never failed to warn him to be careful.

'Are you sure it is safe, John?' she would say.

Of his small mishaps he told nothing. 'Of course it is, Mamma. Safe as being on the *Sirius*. Even Martin likes it now.'

Martin would nod and smile. Although he, too, had learnt to manage the canoe, he seldom went out in it, because he realised the risks and was not prepared to take them. While John and Nanbaree glided here and there, he fished from the rocks, for he had become the most skilful of all at striking a fish with a native spear.

So Mamma, reassured, would go back to her garden and watch with pride as the walls of her new home gradually rose.

CHAPTER VI

JOEY, OF THE COAT OF MANY COLOURS

OF the convicts who were building Mamma's house, the most ragged were those who drew the cart. And of them the most comical was a wizened little fellow with a limp, who seemed purposely to use his deformity to amuse the children.

Nanbaree, particularly, was entertained by the man's antics, and would mimic his gait amid roars of laughter from Sue and Jenny.

'Do it again, Nanbaree,' they would shout, 'do it again,' and they would go off into more fits of laughter.

Debby did not like any of the convicts and least of all the fellow with the limp. 'They're up to no good, ma'am,' she would say. 'Rob you in the twinkling of an eye, they would.'

Certainly the thefts from the garden were increasing. Mamma knew that there had always been robberies round the Cove. Convicts, too lazy to grow food, helped themselves each night to the vegetables grown by others. She had suffered less than most, but now, in the middle of winter, with green vegetables scarcer than ever, there was not a night when somebody did not steal some of her precious cabbages and cauliflowers.

'Too many convicts about,' Debby said to Mamma. 'They know the lay-out of the place too well, and just where to find anything. The cheek of them, too! The other day I saw a fellow pick up a couple of carrots and saunter off as if they belonged to him. That wizened little fellow with a limp, and as ragged as a scarecrow, ma'am.'

'Yes, I know. Did you let him go?'

'No, ma'am, I did not. I ran after him and pulled them from his pocket, and hit him over the head with them. Gave him a piece of my mind, too.'

Mamma knew the fellow well. His appearance and that of those with him distressed her. Their smocks and trousers had great tears in them, revealing their bare skin.

'Perhaps he's cold as well as hungry,' she now said to Debby. 'Do you think we could do something for him and those fellows with the cart?'

'How, ma'am?'

'Well, perhaps we could offer them some patches to mend their clothes.'

'They wouldn't thank you, ma'am. Just as likely to return your kindness by robbing you behind your back, as they are doing now.'

Mamma was determined to do something. Debby found her a few days later going through the boxes, casting out this and that in a colourful pile—plaids and checks, reds and yellows, greens and blues.

'But, ma'am,' Debby protested, 'we might need everything. What if the ships don't come?'

'Then we'll all be ragged. I can't watch these men going about as they do.'

Debby decided that her pleas would be in vain. Mamma could not bear the sight of the ragged lot day by day hauling bricks for the house, and was determined to clothe them as she thought fit.

Soon one or another began to appear with a patch—red or yellow, plaid or check, green or blue, and Debby concluded that Mamma had been handing out her patches.

Papa noticed it, too. 'Those fellows seem all to have donned coats of many colours,' he teased Mamma as he smiled at Debby. 'I hope you won't expect too much of them.'

'That is what I've been saying,' Debby said. She knew Papa realised how lazy and thieving and shiftless the convicts could be.

John and Sue also took notice when they saw the remnants of their clothes on the backs of the fellows in the cart.

'My tartan,' said Sue.

'And my check coat,' said John.

The patchwork of familiar colours amused them.

The wizened little fellow with the limp was so masked in patches that they began to call him Joseph. There were plaids and checks, greens and blues and reds, but the biggest of all was a yellow one on the seat of his trousers.

'Like a jackdaw, that fellow,' Debby observed, when she found him prying round the back of her kitchen. 'Always ready to snap up anything worth his while.'

But in spite of Mamma's kindness, the robberies continued.

'Just what I expected,' Debby told Pete.

He, too, was determined that Mamma should not be robbed. He had built a special yard near his hut, and into this, each night, he drove the livestock, and slept with an ear cocked for the slightest disturbance.

'With the stock so few, and them breeding more males than fe-males,' he told John, 'we can't afford to lose any.'

Of a litter of twelve that John's sow had had, only three had been females.

'Mighty funny,' Pete had remarked.

John thought of them only as roast dinners. 'Why worry, Pete? That will mean more pork for us.'

To the grown-ups, trying to build up their stock, it was a matter of concern. Of the livestock that had come in the ships, the cattle had been lost, the sheep eaten or dead; only the horses remained, and the pigs and goats and poultry of all kinds.

A few days later Mamma's goat gave birth to a kid.

'A female!' Pete announced triumphantly to Mamma.

'How wonderful!' she replied. 'Of seven kids born this month in this settlement, this is the only female. Now we'll have milk and butter even if the ships don't come soon.'

'Ma'am, they must come. Folks in England can't have forgotten us.'

'One would not think so, Pete. But we've been here eighteen months now, and there is no sign of them. Perhaps there has been an accident.'

'How, ma'am?'

'A shipwreck! If that were to happen, we wouldn't know, would we?'

Pete walked away scratching his beard. He would have to protect her garden. Mamma had a way with her. She always inspired loyalty in her servants. Pete had been inclined to shirk his work until he became Mamma's gardener. Now, although he took his own time to do things, and moved and walked slowly and leisurely, there was no question of his honesty, not where Mamma was concerned.

Sue's rabbits were so precious that she demanded that they should be placed each night in their hutch beside her bed in the marquee. They had had several families since they had arrived in New South Wales, but some mishap or another had kept their number at five.

Abaroo was particularly interested in the rabbits. Each time she came to see the girls, or on a message from Mrs Johnson to Mamma, she would gaze through the bars, and tickle their soft fur as Sue and Jenny did.

Sue became quite alarmed. 'She's not trying to take them from me, Mamma?' she complained.

'Of course not, dear. How could she if she wanted to do so?'

But Mamma decided to watch Abaroo. After all, but a few months before she had been wandering in the woods, catching possums and flying squirrels for her daily food. Perhaps she had some similar design on the rabbits.

Pete was alert from the time the convicts came till the time they went, and for long after, with the robberies occurring nightly.

'Probably tell their friends, they do, and are in league with them,' Pete said.

John took his share of watching with Pete, and Martin often stayed to help. Sometimes Nanbaree would come too, and they would squat round a blazing fire outside John's sleeping hut and wait for the robbers. But the robbers came at midnight and in the early hours before dawn, when the boys, thoroughly tired, had gone to bed; when Pete, exhausted after many hours of troubled sleep, failed to hear them.

Certainly the robberies increased through the month of July and into August.

'With the spring vegetables coming on, too!' Debby wailed. 'Oh, ma'am, what shall we do?'

Mamma and Debby were measuring the private stores of tea and sugar and flour and other special foods that Dan had brought when he went in the *Sirius* to the Cape of Good Hope some months before.

'They're going down, aren't they, Debby? Papa says it won't be long before all the butter in the public store has been used.'

'Oh, ma'am! I do wish the ships would come.'

'Yes, so do I. We can at least keep on making butter out of the goat's milk. The butter from the store hasn't been much good for a long time. And I'm told that they have served out the last shoes to the soldiers. Goodness knows what will happen when they are worn out. That reminds me, I must tell John to go without shoes except on special occasions.'

As if in answer to her call, he came barging into the kitchen at that moment, Martin and Nanbaree at his heels, and behind them Cookie—Cookie back from Norfolk Island with a mysterious bag.

'Now, now,' Debby scolded, as they crowded round the table while she hastily removed the foodstuffs to safety. 'If you knock over this flour and tea, Mamma will not be pleased. Besides, I must get Cookie a cup of tea.'

'Two cups of tea,' Mamma laughed gaily, 'and anything you have in the cupboard.'

It seemed as if the sides of the kitchen would burst when the girls squeezed in.

'What did you bring us? What did you bring us?' they cried.

'Tut, tut!' Mamma reproved. 'You must not ask for gifts like that. It's not mannerly.'

But Cookie, in spite of the bag, had brought them nothing. He sadly shook his head.

'Don't tell me there are no vegetables on Norfolk,' Mamma chided him gently. Cookie had always painted such a rosy picture of the island—birds a-flying, vegetables a-growing, fish a-baiting.

He had gone in the *Supply* with the first settlers soon after they had all come to Sydney Cove, and had been going backwards and forwards ever since.

'Nay, ma'am, 'tis sad. The black caterpillars, they ha' eaten the wheat and corn—aye, and the vegetables. Came in millions, they did, and folks a-picking 'em off the plants in handfuls, all for naught. But Lieutenant King, he kept some seed until the caterpillars went, so there'll still be a harvest.'

'And the birds, Cookie? Do they still come?' John asked.

'Birds? Why, there ha' been trillions and billions of 'em since April! Come at night, they do, back to their burrows at Mount Pitt, after feeding in the sea all day. Aye, and 'tis strange a-walking and a-slithering at that place, wi' the ground as full o' holes as a rabbit warren. Like a petrel this bird be, brown and ashy grey, that a-lays one egg in its burrow. At dusk the silly bird flies down, and be so tame it lets itself be taken.'

John and Martin were thinking of those roast dinners and the stringy salt meat that they ate each day.

'So you can catch as many as you like?' John mused, almost wetting his lips at the thought of such a plentiful supply of good food.

'Aye, lad, folks on Norfolk need never be wi'out fresh meat the months the birds they be there.'

'So this Norfolk is still a grand little place?' Mamma said, smiling at him.

'Just so, ma'am,' he agreed as he helped himself to one of Debby's pasties.

The children stood around, almost disconsolate. Cookie had never come back from Norfolk Island without something. More than once it had been turtles, at other times sugar-cane, bananas, and always vegetables.

'You have a bag,' said Sue pointedly.

At that he laughed. 'Thought I had forgotten, eh? Well, not quite like,' and he drew from his bag a pear-shaped ball.

'What is it?' they all cried together. 'What is it?' and begged him to open it there and then.

'Aye, I guessed ye wouldn't wait,' he said, and called for a sharp butcher's knife, which Debby readily produced.

A few skilful cuts, and the brown covering was off, and there, nestling snugly inside was another brown ball, but this time a hairy one.

'A coconut,' he explained, as he laid it on the table and they stood around. 'Came floating ashore over the ocean from some other island, and I did bring it back for you.'

'Why, it has a face like a monkey!' Sue said, pointing to the rounded end where there were three small holes.

'Aye, and one be soft, and I am going to open it.'

'Why?'

'To get the milk o' course. Can't ye hear it swirling about?' and he rattled the nut close to their ears.

Puncturing the hole, and another too, 'to let the air in and out,' so he said, he began to pour the liquid inside it into mugs.

'There ye be. Taste and see.' Each took a sip.

'Horrible!' Sue said, and put hers down.

Jenny persisted and began to like it before she was half-way through.

'Oh, Cookie, it's great!' cried John and Martin.

Nanbaree drank all in one gulp.

'Is there anything more to eat in a coconut?' the children were now clamouring.

'Aye, rich white coconut meat,' and he cut open the husk to reveal it adhering closely to the shell.

'Now, now, not too much at once,' said Debby, hovering close by.

Cookie cut a portion into pieces and handed it round. 'The rest will last for days,' he said.

Yes, it would last for days. Cookie always did bring the nicest presents.

Soon they were all out in the garden, examining the progress of the new house.

'Aye, 'tis time ye had a house,' Cookie said to Mamma, 'and proud I'll be, ma'am, to come and ha' a cup o' tea in it wi' ye. Maybe in my travels I'll find some trinket—something special for ye to put into it.'

'Like the ostrich egg,' John reminded him.

'Aye, I remember. Did I not promise to get ye an emu's egg and paint the *Sirius* on it?'

'Yes, Cookie, for the mantelpiece. Oh, do get it!' they cried.

'And now I must go. There be a storm a-coming. But I'll be back. 'Tis the Prince o' Wales's birthday next week on 12th August. What about a bonfire, eh? Will ye gather some logs?'

Right royally they agreed.

The light was fading fast, and great black clouds were riding up from the south.

'Come on, Martin,' he called, 'I'll race ye to the bridge. If ye don't hurry, ye'll get wet.'

They ran into the gloom, Jenny, too—all anxious to be home as quickly as possible.

Nanbaree lingered, grinning each time Mamma suggested that he go, until she gave in to John's entreaties, and suggested that they both sleep in the warmth of the kitchen fire.

For once Debby accepted the inconvenience without a grumble. 'At least the wet will keep those robbers in their huts,' she said triumphantly, 'and you won't have to watch tonight.'

Outside the storm had ushered in a night of heavy rain.

CHAPTER VII

NANBAREE SOLVES A MYSTERY

THE morning dawned clear and blue-shining, and the boys were early a-stir.

'Must have fined up at dawn,' John concluded, for the mud and slush were still sodden.

He was just about to make his morning visit to milk the goat, when Pete arrived.

'Ma'am, I'm sorry to tell ye, but the kid's gone.'

'Kid? Gone?'

'Yes, stolen, I think. 'Twould be easy for the rascals to come across in the rain and drive away the beast. Off my guard, I was. I should've known rain wouldn't keep those fellows in their huts.'

'There you are, ma'am,' said Debby. 'I told you they would take all they could get and rob you behind your back.'

'Yes, Mamma, and my rabbits are gone, too,' cried Sue, running across from the marquee.

'Oh dear, this is terrible!' and calling to Pete, Mamma hurried back with Sue to examine the hutch.

John ran instead to the goat's yard, followed by Nanbaree. The nanny was there, placidly nibbling at the short grass, but the kid was gone.

Nanbaree looked at John in astonishment. 'Leetle one?' he said, with a movement of his hands.

'Gone, Nanbaree, stolen right away,' John replied, and waved his arms about to make the black boy understand.

'Him taken?'

'Yes, taken away by someone; stolen.'

'Ah!' Nanbaree looked immediately at the ground. The soft mud had been marked in a criss-cross fashion by the hooves of the goat and the kid. Slowly he walked across the mud, noting this and that, for in amongst the marks were the imprints of boots and bare feet.

'Joey,' he said, pointing at one.

'How do you know?' John laughed at the idea.

But Nanbaree was quite serious. Pointing to his big toe, he said, 'Toe, it go this way,' and he pointed outwards.

John began to take interest. Perhaps the boy did know the imprint of feet. He was convinced when a few moments later Nanbaree pointed to a smaller one and said, 'That you.' And it really was the imprint of his foot. John placed his bare foot in the marked space, and it fitted exactly. Once again, as often before, he was forced to admire Nanbaree's cleverness.

Now they had come to a churned-up patch near the gate. Surely Nanbaree didn't expect to find a footprint there!

'Come on,' John urged. 'You won't see anything in that slush!'

But Nanbaree would not come. He had fallen on his haunches, and was dragging a hand through the soft mud. Whatever could he be looking for? And what could he find in the mud of all places?

'Oh, come on, Nanbaree!' John repeated again. 'I want to see what happened to Sue's rabbits.'

With a grunt Nanbaree rose, holding what seemed to be a handful of mud. But was it mud? He smoothed it out, and there on the palm of one hand was a triangular piece of cloth.

John watched fascinated as he wiped it on the wet grass. Its colour was yellow. The patch on Joey's pants! Now they knew. Joey was the robber. Joey! One would expect it of him.

But how had it got there?

John was about to ask, when Nanbaree explained in his own quaint way. 'Goat,' he began, and then mimicked a butting goat.

So that was what happened. The goat had butted the robber, and robbed him in turn of a portion of his pants, one of the precious patches that Mamma had gone to such great pains to provide. That was why the mud was so churned up, and Nanbaree had known the cause, while he, John, had merely looked on and scoffed.

'Come and let us tell them,' he called now, and opened the gate to go.

But still Nanbaree refused to budge. He was studying the imprints again, especially on the edge of the yard, where the grass grew more plentifully and the earth was firmer. Then, suddenly, with a leap he was over the brush fence and on the other side, calling to John, calling loudly and excitedly.

John joined him in haste. Had Nanbaree found the kid? No, not the kid, but footprints, many of them, leading away into the woods in the direction of the brickfields.

'Joey,' Nanbaree exclaimed, and again mimicked the gait of the convict. 'One foot so, other foot so,' and he matched the words to show that the good foot sank deeper into the mud than the lame one.

Now it was proved. Joey was the robber beyond doubt. They followed the footprints on the wet earth, on crushed grass, in and around the bushes and shrubs, until John thought they had gone far enough. He, for one, did not want to face the robbers alone with Nanbaree at that time in the morning.

'We must go back,' he urged Nanbaree. 'Mamma will not be pleased if we are late for breakfast.'

But again Nanbaree refused. He was patiently examining all marks on the earth, on the bushes around, then with a shout was going forward, for now the hoof marks of the kid ran beside the footprints of the robber.

The story was there for John to read: the robber had carried the kid, then putting it down had tied a rope round its neck. And the direction had changed: instead of going on to the brickfields, it went towards the Government Farm.

What next were they to find?

The two imprints went on side by side, sometimes clear, sometimes indistinct, until there was a definite tramping on one spot, and plain evidence that the kid had pattered hither and thither within a small area. Nanbaree walked around it, inspecting every mark, then pointed in different ways, first towards the brickfields, then towards the woods at the back of the farm.

Whatever was he trying to say?' Two,' and he held up his fingers. Two robberies? Two directions?

Then John saw what he meant. The path divided, and on each side were different sets of footprints. A meeting in the woods? And an accomplice—a friend to help him? Someone from the farm, waiting to take the kid, while Joey went on to his hut, for now the kid's imprints ran along with those of a bigger, burlier man.

And the purpose? To hide the kid, of course. No convict would take it openly to the brickfields or to the farm. He would very soon be seen with the animal and found out.

Nanbaree had realised all this. He was striding on, and John, no longer reluctant, was close behind him.

They had entered the woods, and gone a hundred yards or more, when Nanbaree pulled up with a start.

John looked round nervously, thinking that the black boy had seen someone, that there was danger in front and they would have to take precautions.

'What is it, Nanbaree?' he whispered, his heart beating quickly. 'Hadn't we better run home? We've found out enough.'

But Nanbaree was smiling, his eyes twinkling with the light of a great discovery, his finger to his ear. Without waiting to answer, he was off at a run, with John somewhat laggardly following.

It was just as he stopped to wonder whether they were being foolhardy that John heard the bleating of the kid, there in the woods in front into which Nanbaree was now disappearing. Nanbaree had heard, Nanbaree with ears sharpened by long training to every noise about him.

And there was the kid, tethered to a tree, in a small glade surrounded by thick undergrowth.

Triumphantly they burst through the bushes and untied the rope; triumphantly they led the kid back along the track to the kitchen.

'Now where have you been?' Mamma began when she came to the

door, then stood and stared at the kid, as if she were seeing something unbelievable. 'Where did you find it?'

'In the woods, Mamma,' and with Pete and Debby gathered as an audience, John told the story of the way they had solved the mystery. 'Nanbaree found it,' he ended. 'If it had not been for Nanbaree, we would not have recognised the footprints, and would never have known that Joey was the thief.'

'Going to kill it and eat it, I guess,' Pete said. 'Feast for the Prince's birthday. And those fellows down at the farm, they just stared at me and said nothing when I asked. Knew all the time, too, they did.' For Pete had already been to the farm believing that the kid might be there.

'Just what I'd expect of that Joey,' Debby sniffed. 'Always a jackdaw, that one.' Then she burst into laughter, for at that very moment, along came the same Joey, and in the backside of his trousers there was an unmistakable triangular tear.

As for Joey, he was so surprised to see the kid, that he almost dropped a load of bricks on his toe, then openly winked at the boys and began his strange lop-sided gait just to amuse them. Joey was certainly a good loser.

'You'll report him, ma'am?' Pete said.

'No, I couldn't,' Mamma replied. 'He would probably get a few hundred lashes, and I could not bear to think of that. I have the kid, and that is all that matters. Cookie promised me some fish today. If there are many, I shall give some to Joey in case he should be hungry.'

Pete and Debby gaped in astonishment. One could never persuade Mamma that a great many of the convicts were up to no good. To her they were human beings in poverty and distress, and as such needed her help even when they failed her.

'Come,' she said to the boys, 'you must be hungry,' and she ushered them into the kitchen, where Debby served them big platefuls of pease porridge and scrambled eggs. After all, they were the heroes; they had found the kid, and the kid meant butter and milk in the future, when few people round the Cove had such luxuries.

'Perhaps now you can solve the mystery of Sue's rabbits,' Mamma said, as she moved about doing her work. 'Sue and Jenny have gone looking for them in the Governor's garden.'

The rabbits! In their excitement John had forgotten the rabbits. 'Rabbits, Nanbaree, rabbits gone too!' But Nanbaree was enjoying his eggs. Slowly: he took his time. 'Rabbits, Nanbaree,' and pulling the black boy by the arm, John dragged him to the marquee. 'Rabbits gone,' and with his finger pointed to the empty hutch.

Straightaway Nanbaree lifted the canvas and slipped out of the marquee close to the hutch. On the earth were paw-prints of the rabbits themselves streaking across the soft earth, and beside these that of a human being.

'Abaroo.' he said instantly, and went back to the kitchen to finish his breakfast.

So it had been Abaroo. Mamma had feared it was, and now she knew for sure.

'I'll go round to the parson's hut,' she told Debby, 'and find out. Sue must never know.'

But before she set out, the parson, Mr Johnson, himself arrived with Abaroo, and with them in a basket, two of the precious rabbits.

'Abaroo is returning them, ma'am,' he said, while the black girl grinned beside him. 'She took them this morning, and brought them round to my place, but as soon as I saw them I told her that she would have to bring them back, because they belonged to Sue. That right, Abaroo?'

Abaroo nodded and grinned more broadly.

'You understand, ma'am, in Abaroo's tribe, no one owns anything; all things belong to the tribe. Maybe she thought she had a right to the rabbits. I have tried to point out to her that is not the white man's way.'

'Of course I understand,' Mamma assured him, and she placed her arm around Abaroo's slight shoulders to convey her meaning. 'But, Abaroo, there were five. What happened to the others?'

Patiently Mr Johnson explained to the girl in signs. 'Two,' she replied with conviction, 'two,' holding up two fingers. 'Abaroo, two.'

'Perhaps she left the latch undone, and the others escaped,' Mr

Johnson suggested. 'Let's show her the paw-prints.' Abaroo seized upon them immediately. 'Rab-bits,' she exclaimed, and waved her arms towards the direction they had taken.

'Yes, that's what happened,' Mamma said. 'Don't worry, Mr Johnson. 'I'll explain to Sue.'

No explanation was ever necessary, for at that moment, Sue and Jenny burst through the gate, with Sue carrying another rabbit.

'Mamma, Mamma, we found one—the gardener caught it in the Governor's garden—'

'Yes, dear, and Abaroo brought you two. Out of your five you now have three. Aren't you a lucky girl?'

Sue nodded doubtfully. 'But where are the others?' she asked, still puzzled about their fate.

'Gone into the woods, where you will never find them,' Mamma told her. 'But they'll be happy, dear. They'll have more rabbits and more rabbits, and now there'll be rabbits in the woods as well as emus and kangaroos. Wasn't Abaroo a good girl to find your rabbits?'

'Thank you, Abaroo,' said Sue gently, and then off they went, as the boys emerged from the kitchen and Martin came panting up the path to gather wood for the bonfire.

'Just like you, ma'am,' Debby said afterwards, 'that trusting little Sue. Never suspected that Abaroo might have taken the rabbits. And what for, I wonder?'

But Mamma would not let her entertain any other thought. 'I suppose Abaroo wanted them as pets, like Sue,' she said quite firmly, and then went to greet Cookie, who had arrived with the fish and to supervise the building of the bonfire.

That night Papa had to hear the story of the lost kid and the cleverness of Nanbaree in finding it.

'I made Pete tether it just outside his hut tonight,' Mamma said. 'I'm not taking another chance.'

'You need not worry any more,' Papa told her, and as she looked up in an inquiring way: 'Something is going to be done about these robberies. We are to have a night watch, and it starts tonight.'

John was interested. 'You mean those fellows who walk the streets with a lantern and a stave, Papa, and call out the time of the night?'

'Well, I don't know about calling out the time, but each will carry a lantern and a staff and go round looking for robbers. They'll have the right to go into the huts, too, if they think anything suspicious is going on after lights are out.'

'How many, Papa?'

'Twelve altogether. Sydney is to be divided into four districts, and there are to be three for each, one in charge and two to help. We are to be in the first division—the one on the east side of the Cove.'

'And who are to be these night watchmen?' Mamma inquired. 'Convicts or soldiers?'

'Need you ask,' Papa replied. 'You don't think Major Ross would let his men be night watchmen. That would be too much to ask of him. They will be convicts—honest men who wish to make good, led by a fellow called Herbert Keeling, and they will receive no reward.'

Papa spoke bitterly of Major Ross, who was in charge of the marines, for the Major had not allowed his men to do many things that might have helped Governor Phillip in his difficulties. He had claimed that the marines were there to guard the settlement, but there had been no threat from the natives, so the marines had spent their time in their own pursuits—building their huts, tilling their gardens, and hunting in the woods.

'What if one of the soldiers is caught stealing?' John remembered how, the previous year, six of them had robbed the public store.

'That's fixed, too, my boy. Any soldier or sailor found straggling in the convicts' huts, after taptoo has been beaten, is to be taken to the guard house.'

'By convict night watchmen?' Mamma asked incredulously.

'Yes, that's the arrangement.'

'Then there'll be trouble. Major Ross won't let his soldiers be treated like that.'

Four days later the bonfire went up with a crackle and spurt and a great show of flames, and right royally did justice to the occasion.

'God bless the Prince of Wales' the Governor called to the others, as it rose higher and higher.

'God bless the Prince of Wales!' the children echoed, and sadly watched as it began to collapse, then flicker and die down.

'Never mind,' said Cookie. 'We'll have plenty more.'

That was one lovely thing about Sydney Cove. There were always bonfires to celebrate important birthdays.

They went home to sleep peacefully while the night watchmen patrolled the Cove.

Mamma was right when she said that Major Ross would object. Before many weeks were past he was telling the Governor that it was an insult for a soldier to be stopped by a convict night watchman, and he was demanding that his men should come and go as they pleased.

'So the Governor had to give in?' Mamma asked Papa when he told her.

'Yes, but he was very bitter about it. If only Major Ross had tried to help rather than to oppose him, we would all be so much happier.'

'Never mind,' said Mamma, trying to be cheerful, 'the night watch has been a success. I haven't lost a cabbage or a carrot or a chicken since it started.'

'Yes.' Papa laughed. 'Captain Collins, who is in charge of it, boasts that many streets in London are not so well guarded and watched as the small but rising town of Sydney in New South Wales.'

'Ten o'clock and a windy night,' shouted the night watchman on his rounds, but Pete and John did not hear. The goat and the kid, the fowls and cabbages were in safe hands, and each in his cabbage-tree hut had no need to heed the suspicious sounds of the night.

CHAPTER VIII

WITH DAN TO CAREENING COVE

THE boys had not forgotten Dan's promise to take them to Careening Cove.

Chips, too, had promised them a trip to Rose Hill.

For weeks and months, as they roamed round the Cove in their leisure hours, they had stopped to watch him as he worked on a boat of local timber for the transport of provisions to Rose Hill.

'How much longer?' they teased him one day.

'Just you wait and see, my young fellows,' he replied, stung a little by their taunts. 'Before a month or two are out, I'll be taking you to Rose Hill. You mark my words.'

They hoped so. A trip to Rose Hill had been something to which they had been looking forward ever since James Ruse had gone to live there in the previous November. Occasionally Mamma had messages from him by word of mouth from other convicts, but that was not the same as seeing him. Besides, a trip even in a squat-looking boat such as the one building was something different, an outing to enjoy. They did indeed hope that Chips was right.

They were back at school again with Nanbaree in the observatory, studying hard while the masons cut and laid the stones in the new building that was to be Lieutenant Dawes's pride. Often he would leave them to supervise, often his friends would call to inspect what progress had been made.

Now it was Captain Hunter about to go back to Broken Bay to chart it while the *Sirius* was refitted, or to Botany Bay to do the same; now Midshipman Dan from Careening Cove to remind them that he had not forgotten his promise; or Captain Collins to talk with Lieutenant

Dawes about the differences he was having with Major Ross while the Governor was at Rose Hill.

Something was always happening at the observatory.

But the most surprising visit was from Mr White, the surgeon, who came for Nanbaree.

'I want to take him down the harbour,' he said, and Nanbaree jumped up readily, glad to be done with pot-hooks for a while.

The boys looked on jealously, but gave no hint of their desire to go too, until the surgeon and the black boy had left the room.

'I wonder why he did not take us?' John expressed aloud.

'Because it is the kind of excursion that he would not want you to share with him,' Lieutenant Dawes replied in a forthright manner. 'He has gone down the harbour with Nanbaree to try to interview the natives.'

'Why?' There must be a reason.

'Simply because the Governor would like to have one or two living with him again as Arabanoo did. He always intended to get some more, for he still wants to make friends with them.'

'But Nanbaree is living here, and Abaroo. Aren't they enough?' Martin asked. 'Can't they help the Governor to make friends with the natives?'

'I doubt it, Martin. We have found that they are too young to have any influence with the grown-ups.'

It seemed strange to John to hear Lieutenant Dawes talking so quietly about bringing other natives into the Cove. He had always in the past opposed the idea, so had Mamma, 'Because they are free people, and should be left to walk the woods freely,' she had said.

'But, Mr Dawes,' he could not help saying, 'I thought you did not like the natives to be brought here.'

'No, John, I don't—not if they are brought in by force. If they come in of their own wish and live freely amongst us, then I don't mind.'

'And that is what Mr White is going to try to do?'

'Yes. The other day the parson, Mr Johnson, went down the harbour with the native girl, Abaroo, for the same purpose. When they met some of her relatives, she told them how happy she was, how well she was treated, and tried to persuade one or more to come back with her, but they would not come. Now Mr White is going to try with Nanbaree, but I doubt if he will succeed.'

He did not succeed. The boys met him and Nanbaree on their way home from school, but there was no sign of another native with them.

'You did not get one to come back with you?' John blurted out.

'No, John, we could not persuade one to come,' Mr White said. 'In fact, I rather think our Nanbaree would have liked to stay with them. What do you say, Nanbaree?'

But the boy stood sadly digging his toes in the ground, obviously torn by different emotions.

'Oh, Nanbaree,' both John and Martin chided, 'surely you don't want to leave us!'

For answer he clung to Mr White, and his large mouth opened and grinned at all three. 'Nanbaree live here,' he said, and when the boys made off towards John's place, he went with them.

'I'm not surprised that he wanted to stay,' Mamma said. 'After all, the natives are his own people. And I agree with Lieutenant Dawes—I shall certainly object if any more natives are taken by force.'

Mamma in those days was very busy in her garden, and gathered the children to help her at every opportunity.

'We must work hard,' she told them. 'Otherwise there might not be enough to eat.'

They had often heard her speak thus, and were inclined to rebel. It was difficult for them to imagine a time when meals did not come at the exact moment, with sufficient to appease their hunger, even if the food remained unappetising.

Nanbaree did not understand at all this laborious pulling up of weeds, and Martin, too, would soon make an excuse to go home, so they would drift off together.

Jenny was always the most willing, and regarded the strawberries as her special care. Had not the Governor given them some runners, when, shortly after they came to Sydney Cove, Sue's had died?

'We'll have plenty of strawberries soon,' said Mamma gaily. 'They will taste good with the goat's cream, now that we have no butter.'

One of her fears had been proved correct. On 12th September the butter had run out in the public store, and Debby had come back with sugar instead.

'The children will like it,' Mamma had said. 'Did you ever know a child that didn't have a sweet tooth?' and she thereupon made them some toffee.

Nanbaree sucked and sucked and sucked, and did not understand when the sweet mixture locked his jaws together. 'M'm, m'm!' John laughed, and pulled the stickjaw from his mouth in long golden strands, only to be imitated by everyone else.

The children certainly did not mind if they had sugar instead of butter—not when there was always goat's milk in plenty. It was a lucky day for Mamma when she bought the goat, a lucky day when they saved the kid. But there were many round the Cove who had no goat, and they missed their butter.

With the spring there were fish—fish almost in abundance.

How then could anyone worry about the ships that did not come, when fish were plentiful, and the strawberries were ripe, and the vegetables just waiting to be cut?

And how could the boys worry, when the woods were gay with wild flowers calling them to roam among the shrubs in search of new plants and seeds to send home for Sir Joseph Banks?

'I do wish we could go somewhere,' John sighed to Martin, and then Dan returned to fulfil his promise.

'Well, here I am,' he said, 'and if your mothers will let you come, you can go back to the *Sirius* with me and stay for a few days.'

Once again the question rose, 'What about Nanbaree?'

And again the answer came, 'No, not this time. Some day when he is more used to us, and there is no fear of his leaving. I would not like him to sneak away into the bush when he was in my charge, and he might do that at any time, you know.'

So they went without Nanbaree. The girls promised to play with him, but they, too, were annoyed, because they were left behind.

'How can you go over to the ship without me?' Mamma explained to them. 'There are only men at Careening Cove. Wait until we all go to Rose Hill to see James Ruse. That will be the time.'

Yes, that would be the time. The boat was coming on well, and Chips's promise might come true very soon.

The boys thought it was grand to be slipping down the Cove into the main channel of 'the most beautiful harbour in the world' on a bright September day.

'Do you remember how the Governor called it that?' John reminded Martin, thinking of the day, almost two years before, when they had sailed down its great waterway soon after they had discovered Sydney Cove.

'Yes, and how we lay one night off Garden Island and slept in the boat.'

'And the day we went over to the island some months after, and had the skirmish with the natives,' Midshipman Dan reminded them. 'Mr Hill was there. Do you remember that?'

They certainly remembered it, and also Mr Hill, who like Dan was a midshipman on the *Sirius* and had often accompanied them on their outings.

'Why didn't you bring him with you today?' Martin asked.

'I did,' Dan replied. 'He is over at Garden Island getting a load of vegetables for the ship's crew. I have to pick him up on the way back, so you two can have ten minutes ashore.'

'Oh, good!' said John. 'We might see Caesar,' and he proceeded to tell Dan about the canoe and how Caesar had rescued him from drowning.

But although the boys searched every inch of the island for a glimpse of Caesar as they drew close to the shore, there was no sign of him.

'Caesar?' they asked the convicts, busily tilling the soil.

'Oh, him!' they replied. 'Find him nigh by the boat, ye will. Always a-pottering around there, a-caulking and painting,' and they winked at the boys to make their meaning clear.

John and Martin said nothing, but they understood. Why was Caesar always round the boat? They could only guess.

'H'm!' he said, when they came upon him unseen. 'Not gittin' drownd'd ag'in, eh? Reck'n I sure better patch up dis boat. Might need it y'know, nex' time John heah falls in der water,' and he, too, winked broadly at them.

It seemed to be all secrets, open secrets, with everyone in the know except the soldiers on the island. Well, they—John and Martin—would have to keep their own counsel, too. Caesar could have his little fun, though they guessed it would end, as it always did, in his recapture.

'Tell yo' Mamma I'll be a-seein' her soon,' Caesar whispered to them, as they answered Dan's call. 'So-on.'

The boat was loaded now with cabbages and cauliflowers and carrots and parsnips, and sitting in among them all was Mr Hill.

'Young John, eh?' he teased, as John came to sit near him. 'What will you be up to this time, eh?'

'Possibly get lost in the woods,' Dan chipped in, as he stepped into the boat, 'like the old sailmaker. Or have a scrap with the natives as we did that day at Garden Island.'

'The natives are not hostile now,' John began.

'For the time being, John. But just let something happen, and the beggars will throw their spears again.'

Dan steered towards a slim jutting point to the north-east of their Robinson Crusoe Island, and almost opposite them. The boys guessed at once that they were coming to Careening Cove, and were more sure than ever when he rounded the point and turned into another inlet.

'This is where the ship is careened,' he said.

They were already taking notice. The new bay was wide at first, but broke into two narrow prongs, like the root of a double tooth, and ran deep into high wooded hills.

'Careening Cove is the largest,' Mr Hill explained.

'There she is! Look, there's the *Sirius*!' cried Martin excitedly, as they turned a bend and the ship came into view, lying on her side in the shallow water at the head of the larger and deeper prong.

'Poor old ship!' sighed John, thinking of the happy days he had spent in her on the long voyage from England.

'She won't be poor old ship much longer,' Mr Hill reminded him. 'In another month we'll have her afloat, and she'll be ready to face the sea again, and go to the Cape of Good Hope, if necessary, for more food.'

That would certainly please Mamma, John thought.

The tents in which the crew slept and ate were clustered in a group at the water's edge, and around them lay the stores and guns that had been removed to lighten the ship.

'Can't have them spread out,' Midshipman Dan told the boys. 'The natives might sneak on those that were outlying and steal what they could find.'

So there were natives? The boys were not afraid. They had grown so accustomed to Nanbaree that they did not expect the natives to be hostile. Of course the fellows would steal, because they knew no better, but they would not throw their spears.

Mr Hill showed them round the camp. Here and there, as they walked about, they met one and another of the crew whom they knew, including the old sailmaker.

'Now don't ye two go a-trapesing into yon woods, as I did,' he warned them. 'Once ye are out o' sight o' the ship, ye'll never know one cove from t'other, an' the woods'll close in on ye, an' the trees'll all look alike, an' in a jiffy ye'll be lost.'

'So you must not go walking into them on your own,' Mr Hill impressed on them.

'We won't,' they promised, remembering how starved and weak the old sailmaker had been, the day they found him on their return from Pittwater with the Governor.

That night, as they sat eating supper round the camp-fire in the crisp cool air, the men promised them excitement. Among them were Mr Hacking, one of the quartermasters, and, of course, Midshipman Dan and Mr Hill.

'I'll take you shooting with me,' Mr Hacking promised.

'Yes,' said Midshipman Dan, 'he's such a good shot that the Governor has allowed him to shoot for us all, and mighty fine meals he provides. Like this kangaroo.'

It was a prospect they liked.

CHAPTER IX

THE NATIVES ATTACK!

THE boys waited impatiently for Mr Hacking the next morning.
'Keen, aren't you?' he said to them jocularly. 'Would you like to shoot, too?'

'Oh, good!' John replied impulsively. 'Papa has been teaching us, you know. He says we ought to be able to shoot, but Martin and I would rather fish with spears, as Nanbaree does.'

They set out about ten o'clock up the deep wooded hill and over the ridge towards the Middle Harbour.

'Do you remember it?' Mr Hacking asked them, when it lay before them.

Of course they did. On the other side they had come upon the lost sailmaker, and found the native canoe that sank, and built the catamaran, and across it Pete and Chips had swum for help.

'Do you ever get lost, Mr Hacking?' Martin asked.

'Me lost? Of course not.'

'But the sailmaker did. He said every cove was the same, and the trees were all alike,' John spoke up.

'Yes, and maybe they are if you have no eyes for the land, for the colour of the leaves and the shape of the rocks, for the rise and fall of the ground. Now we've come up a hill and down the other side, quite a long way down, haven't we?'

'Yes.'

'Well, if you had to go back, you'd go up and over, wouldn't you?'

'But what if we came out in another bay?' John asked.

'Then the best thing would be to walk to the point of the bay. You'd soon find out where you were because you'd see Garden Island and the one you have named after Robinson Crusoe, and there would be sure to be fishing boats handy.'

It seemed simple enough, but the boys were not so sure.

Just then a flock of parrakeets flew into the trees, a rainbow of brilliant colours, so lovely that John wished Mr Hacking had not to shoot. But he did, and brought down three with the first discharge of shot. Mechanically John helped Martin pick up the bodies and put them in the bag.

When it was almost full, Mr Hacking offered John the gun. 'Here you are. It's your turn now.'

John shook his head. 'I don't want to shoot,' he said almost abruptly.

Not all Mr Hacking's coaxing could bring out the real reason. But Martin knew why John had suddenly changed his mind. It was because he could not kill those beautiful birds, just as he had not been able to kill the possum when he climbed the tree. And Martin, being his friend, decided that he would not shoot either.

So they turned to go back to the ship. It was then, just as they had taken a few paces, that a stone crashed with a thud right in front of them.

The boys drew up with a start. A rock dislodged from above surely! What else could it be? But Mr Hacking had turned in an instant, musket held in readiness, ear and eye alert to every sound—the crunch of footsteps, the crackle of a twig—to the quiver of the leaves, to the fleck of black against the green.

'Nearly got me in the head,' he growled in an undertone.

'You don't mean it was thrown by the natives?' John asked hoarsely, and then remembered that he should have spoken in a whisper.

'Of course it was. You two go behind those trees, and if I tell you to run, then run for your lives. Remember, up and over, if I don't catch up.'

It did not seem possible. The natives had not been hostile of late. Thieves, they always were, but since the smallpox had killed so many, they had scarcely attacked anyone. Yet the natives had thrown the stone all right. From his position behind the large bole of a gum-tree, John saw them—three standing their ground, silent, menacing, spears and clubs gripped firmly in their hands.

Mr Hacking was moving back, presenting his musket before them, pretending to be about to fire.

'To trick them,' John said to Martin, 'so that he won't have to shoot.'

The natives ignored the gun. They were coming on, lessening the distance between themselves and the white man. And more and more of them were emerging from the woods, twenty, thirty, forty.

'He'll have to shoot,' Martin gasped. 'Oh, what shall we do. John?'

He had scarcely spoken when the crack of the musket split the silent air about them and resounded through the woods.

'It has only small shot in it,' John whispered. 'That won't hurt them. They'll go for all they're worth.'

But they did not. They came on, advancing with spears raised, clubs held high, making a great noise.

Mr Hacking was loading his musket again, getting ready to fire it a second time, but still they came on.

'Run,' he yelled to the boys, as he raised the butt to his shoulder, and they fled for their lives, fearfully, clumsily, twisting, turning, dodging, slithering and slipping on rocks, jumping over fallen trees. Up and over. Up and over. They must get up and over and down to the ship.

Behind them the musket rang out again. They paused a moment to ponder on what was happening. Mr Hacking had used buckshot this time and it would hurt. Had any of the natives been wounded? And what had happened to Mr Hacking? Was he coming behind?

'What do you think we ought to do?' Martin asked nervously.

'Wait a moment,' said John. 'He might catch up with us,' but even as he said it, he knew that he wanted to go on.

So they waited for a minute, fearfully, impatiently. Every moment they expected to see a black form—or even a score—emerge from the trees and corner them in an ambush.

'We'd better go,' Martin urged. Of the two he was the more afraid.

'All right. Up and over—that's what he said.'

Up and over. Up and over. They pounded on, panting, puffing, pulling themselves up the slope by shrubs and branches, pausing a second, and then going on, flagging a little now, until they came out on a small knoll, winded and exhausted.

'Do you think we are at the top?' Martin asked.

Yes, they were at the top at last. Dimly through the trees they could see the glint of blue that meant that the harbour was beneath them.

But where was Careening Cove? This was the test. And what of the natives? Had Mr Hacking stopped them? Or were they coming behind? Would a lance be hurled from the bushes as they stood to take their bearings?

'Come on, Martin,' said John, and breathing more freely they leapt down the slope, dodging tree-trunks, blundering through the bracken, down, down to the patches of blue so welcome through the trees.

But when they got down to the blue they could see no ship. Where— where was the *Sirius*?

They were in a cove, but what cove? There were so many coves in Port Jackson, and as the sailmakcr had said, they were mighty alike.

Which way were they to go now? East or west?

'Mr Hacking told us to get out on a point,' Martin said, 'then we would see Garden Island. Don't you think we ought to go out on the one that juts farthest out into the harbour? This one?' and he pointed to the east.

John agreed. There was sense in the suggestion, but it meant a long walk. Wearily they plodded on, jumping down, now and again, on to the rocks to slake their thirst and hunger with the juiciest and most succulent oysters they could find among the myriads to be found there.

'Mr Hacking will be worried,' John said, as the sun began its downward path. 'When he gets back, they'll send someone out for us.'

'*If* he gets back,' Martin reminded him, but that was a thought they did not dare to entertain.

They had almost reached the point when John formed his own conclusion. 'Martin, I know where we are,' he said suddenly.

'Where?'

'In the little cove next to Careening Cove—the second prong of the bay. The ship's over there,' and he pointed to the north-west, 'in the other prong. We'll have to walk back.'

Was John right? What if he were wrong? Then they would have to start all over again, and night would come, perhaps, before they realised where they were, and they would have to sleep in a cave. Now if only Nanbaree were with them! He would find the way.

Martin looked about. 'Hadn't we better go to the end of the point to make sure?' he said. He was always the practical one.

So they went on again, searching for landmarks—Garden Island and their own Robinson Crusoe Island. Yes, there they were, easily distinguishable as islands from the rest of the headlands.

'You were right, John, you were right,' Martin cried. 'We are on the east of Careening Cove, in the second prong. Come on, come on, we'll never get there before sundown.'

Joyfully they set out again, retracing their steps with spirit as if they were just starting out on their adventures. So keen were they to make the camp by dark, that they did not hear the splash of oars behind them.

'Hey, you two, what are you doing there?'

They stopped in their tracks. It was Dan's voice.

'Oh, Dan, Dan!' they cried, and raced down to the edge of the rocks to await his boat. 'My, we're glad to see you!'

Mr Hill was with him. 'We were fishing,' Dan said, 'and coming round this point there before us we saw you two. Couldn't believe our eyes. Went out with Mr Hacking, you did. Now get into the boat and explain yourselves.'

They did explain, and Dan's face became sterner and sterner as they went on.

'Nasty bit of work,' he said, 'and lucky you are to find your way back to the ship. There was the sailmaker now, and others—'

'Yes,' said Mr Hill, 'I think I'd get lost myself in those woods.'

If they hadn't been so worried about Mr Hacking, they would have sat up and taken the compliment proudly.

'He'll be there,' Dan said, when they expressed doubts about his safety. 'He's too clever a man to be ambushed by the natives.'

He was there all right. As they rowed up to the camp, it seemed as if every member of the ship's company was on the shore. And so they were, for they were just about to set out in groups to scour the woods until dusk—and even after calling, shouting, searching for the wanderers.

'Thank God!' Mr Hacking said and, laying his arms across their shoulders, ushered them up to the fires where the cook was already preparing supper. 'Have something to eat and then tell us all about it.'

He was proud of them when they told their tale.

'But what about you, sir?' John asked.

'I'm afraid a couple were wounded,' he replied rather regretfully, so John thought. 'But you know that I did not provoke them. The Governor will not be pleased.'

The Governor was very distressed, for he hated conflict with the natives. John and Martin noticed his concern when they returned to Sydney Cove a few days later and he questioned them about the attack.

'Thank you,' he said as he dismissed them. 'Someone must have provoked the natives, though I am sure it was not Mr Hacking.'

He looked tired and worried. 'Never got over that pain in his side,' John heard Mamma say to Debby. 'And there's been trouble with Major Ross again. All over the employing of a convict when the Governor was at Rose Hill. I believe the Major hinted that the Governor had gone to Rose Hill for pleasure. For pleasure, Debby, to sleep on bare boards with a pain in his side.'

Early in October there was one thing that brought satisfaction to His Excellency. Chips had, at last, finished the boat made of native timber, and it was put into the water.

All were there to watch, Nanbaree lost in wonder at the size of the *nowee*, as he called it.

'H'm!' commented Papa. 'A mere bed of timber! She'll never make speed.'

'What does it matter, Papa, as long as she gets us to Rose Hill?' John replied. 'We want to see James Ruse.'

But even John, in spite of his enthusiasm, had to admit that she was a sluggish-looking craft.

It was Debby who, a few days later, supplied the joke. 'Do you know what the convicts call the new boat?' she said to Mamma while John was in the kitchen.

'No. What?'

'The *Rose Hill Packet*.'

'And a packet is supposed to be a fast boat,' John murmured to himself. 'Chips will be amused.'

He joined in Mamma's laughter. 'That's just like their wit,' she said. 'One thing is certain—she'll never be speedy enough to be a packet.'

Pete a few days after produced another name. 'They call her the *Lump* now, ma'am,' he said.

And everyone smiled and agreed that was the more suitable, for a clumsier boat they had never seen. But she did what she was meant to do, transporting provisions to Rose Hill, and passing very well over the flats at the top of the harbour.

'Now, perhaps, we'll go and see James Ruse,' John said.

He did not know then that much was to happen before that long-awaited meeting was to take place.

CHAPTER X

WHERE IS MR HILL?

EARLY in November, Mr Hill came across from Careening Cove to stay the night.

'I have leave until the morning,' he told Mamma, 'and I was wondering if you would allow Pete to row me to the north shore before dawn, so that I can walk overland to the ship. Captain Hunter is bringing her back to Sydney Cove tomorrow.'

Mamma knew that the seamen of the *Sirius* often went that way. 'Of course,' she replied graciously. 'You must stay with us for the night.'

Mr Hill slept with John in the old kitchen.

'I shall have to be up early,' he said, as they went to bed, 'otherwise I'll miss the ship. She certainly won't wait for me.' John was thinking what a long walk it was from the north shore to Careening Cove. 'Then you'll have to see that you don't get lost,' he said half teasingly.

'So I shall, young John. I missed the path one day, you know, and the trees closed in on me and I didn't know where I was, just like the old sailmaker. But it's much clearer now.' John heard him rise long before daylight and disappear into the darkness with a cheery goodbye. 'See you soon, John. Don't forget to watch the good old ship come up the harbour today.'

There was no need to tell the boys to do that. Lessons were impossible when such a fine feat of seamanship was taking place. Lieutenant Dawes himself joined them as the *Sirius* appeared round the point and was cleverly towed up the main stream.

John had not thought of Mr Hill again until he saw Dan coming to visit Mamma that afternoon just as she was marshalling the children to water the garden.

'Hullo, Dan,' he cried immediately. 'I suppose Mr Hill got back.'

'No, indeed! Did he leave this morning? I have come to find out.'

'Why, yes!' said Mamma. 'Pete rowed him across to the north shore before daylight. Didn't you, Pete?'

'To be sure I did, sir,' Pete explained, leaving his buckets for a few moments. 'Told me he would probably lose himself as he did once afore. Maybe for a day or two this time. Jokingly, o' course.'

Midshipman Dan looked suddenly grave. 'Then I must go back to the ship,' he said. 'Someone will have to go over to the north shore to see if Mr Hill has returned.'

John gazed pensively after Dan as he walked through the gate. He was thinking how disappointed Mr Hill would be when he arrived at Careening Cove and found that the *Sirius* had gone.

'Fancy Mr Hill having to walk all the way back to the north shore!' he said to Martin, as Nanbaree burst out in a torrent of questions.

'Him lost?'

'We don't know yet. He is probably over at the north shore waiting to hail a boat.'

But Nanbaree had implanted a fear in John's mind. 'Mamma, you don't think Mr Hill is lost, do you?' he asked anxiously.

'Of course not, dear. He just missed the boat. That's all.'

Mamma spoke nervously as if she weren't quite sure. John knew that she was worried. Only that morning Papa had told her that the rats had eaten twelve thousand pounds of rice and flour in the store-houses. And a few days before, Pete had come home with the news that the ration for men had been cut to that of the women and children.

'Come on,' she now urged the children, as they carried water from the buckets that Pete had filled from the stream, 'we must grow things.'

'Yes, Master John,' Pete said, 'no more dilly-dallying. Five pounds five ounces of flour, three pounds five ounces of pork, and two pints of pease for each one of us. 'Tis not enough to put any fat on the likes o' you and me.'

The children did not mind this late afternoon chore. Watering a garden was much better fun than weeding. Sue had begun to go without shoes, and she found it a delight to run over the bare earth and grass, helping Mamma in her tasks, with Jenny always at hand to help.

But John's doubt about Mr Hill still pursued him.

'Did he come across from the north shore?' he asked Papa as soon as his father came home for supper.

'No, lad, not unless he came in at dusk.'

John went to bed thinking about Mr Hill, and woke up remembering, for at dawn the gun from the *Sirius* boomed, and he knew exactly what that meant. Mr Hill had not returned the night before. He was lost. He was roaming the woods somewhere on the north shore.

'He'll be found today, won't he, Papa?' he asked anxiously at breakfast, when a second gun boomed.

'I am sure he will be,' Papa assured him. 'Boats will go up and down all the coves on the north side.'

The day happened to be a Sunday. The children went to church under the great tree and came home again, and still the guns boomed at two-hourly intervals.

'Oh dear!' sighed Mamma. 'I do hope Mr Hill has not been in trouble with the natives.'

The natives! No, surely not! And yet they had tried to kill Mr Hacking. In the same area, too! Another fear began to creep into John's thinking.

Quickly he tried to thrust it aside. Of course Mr Hill would find his way back to one of the coves and be seen by a searching boat's crew. Had not he, John, and Martin done the very same thing?

But from now on this fear would not let John be sure. There was always the probability. Trouble with the natives! It was too terrible to think about.

'There it goes again,' Sue said at breakfast, when the gun was fired a second time on Monday morning, and Mamma and Papa looked at one another and sighed.

'I do hope they find Mr Hill today,' John said to Martin as they assembled for school.

'Him lost?' Nanbaree asked again, and they sadly said, 'Yes.'

All day at the observatory the boys waited in hope, but also with fear. As each two-hourly period drew to an end, they would go outside and watch for the signal that had come to mean a knell of despair.

On the third afternoon came disturbing news. One of the boats searching down the harbour had met with hostility.

It was Cookie who told John and Martin.

'Hullo, Cookie,' they cried, as they came upon him on their way home from school. 'We haven't seen you lately.'

'Aye, I been busy taking my turn a-looking for poor Mr Hill.'

'Is there any news?' John asked.

'Nay, lad. 'Tis getting bad now. Three days it be. He must be pretty hungry afore this. And there be those natives that attacked our boat today.'

'Today? What happened, Cookie?' they asked quickly.

'We be down the harbour a-looking—in the north arm, it be. They had come to meet us friendly like in a cove, then suddenly had gone like that into the skirt o' a wood,' and he flicked his hand. ''Twas then I saw the spears a-coming—two spears—and one was a-coming at me. Went through my hat. See!' He took it off and showed them where the spear had torn a hole in the canvas.

The boys looked on with something like awe. It had been very close. 'But, Cookie, how was it you weren't killed?'

''Cos I ducked, and the spear, it knocked the hat from my head. So ye can save your tears for another time. I be not dead yet.'

He grinned happily at them, and they grinned back in affection.

'And then what happened?' Martin asked.

'They came out from the bushes a-shouting and a-yelling. Ye never did hear such a row. But a musket ball sent them a-running. Aye, and gave us time to get back to the boat. I feel sorry for Mr Hill. I be o' a mind we shall see him no more.'

Silence fell on the boys, especially John. In spite of his fears, he had hoped that the news would not be quite as serious as this.

'I be a-going to Norfolk tomorrow,' Cookie said, a little more light-heartedly to cheer them up. 'Got to call in at Lord Howe's Island for some turtle, I believe. Maybe I'll be bringing ye some back?'

But the boys really had no thought for the turtle just then. Surely Mr Hill would be found the next day!

They watched the *Supply* sail, they listened for the guns to boom, they saw the search parties come and go, but still there was no trace of him.

'He must have been killed by the natives,' Lieutenant Dawes told them. 'There is nothing more we can do.'

Poor Mr Hill! And again John remembered how lucky they had been the day they had gone out shooting with Mr Hacking.

'The Governor must be worried,' he said.

'The Governor is very distressed,' Lieutenant Dawes answered. 'Now that the natives have shown themselves to be so hostile, he will try harder to get some more to live with him.'

'And you will think it right this time?'

'That will depend on the way he brings in the natives. I do not believe in forcing the men to come.'

Once again Mamma agreed with Lieutenant Dawes. 'I don't think anyone should be dragooned into coming into the settlement,' John heard her say when she discussed the matter with Papa.

'And what if the Governor can't get anyone in except in this way?' Papa asked. 'He has tried to bring them in peacefully. The parson took Abaroo down the harbour, and Mr White took Nanbaree, to do that, but they failed. The natives wouldn't come.'

This posed a question for Mamma. 'Can't he wait a little longer?' she said lamely.

'No, they're too hostile. They've found that they can kill the white men, and success has gone to their heads. Why, the boats can't pass any headland without spears being thrown!'

'Yes,' interrupted John, 'one went through Cookie's hat.'

'So you see, my dear, there is no other way. If the Governor wants to bring any natives to Sydney Cove in order to teach them to trust us, the men will have to be taken by force.'

'Well, I don't like it, Richard. I certainly won't be there to see them come in.'

CHAPTER XI

THE CAPTURE OF BENNELONG AND COLBEE

I T fell to the lot of Lieutenant Bradley, the first lieutenant of the *Sirius*, to capture the two natives.

'Bradley is to go down the harbour tomorrow,' Papa said at supper one night, 'to bring in two more black men.'

'I'm sorry.' Mamma sighed.

Lieutenant Dawes was quite outspoken in his sympathy for Mr Bradley when the boys arrived at school the next morning. 'He thinks it is the most unpleasant task he has ever been given,' he said, 'and very thankful I am that the Governor did not send me. Now, no running to the windows to watch for the boats!'

But how could he stop them? Nanbaree did not know what the commotion was about until they tried to tell him. From the instant he understood, he was more excited than they.

As soon as the boats appeared, Lieutenant Dawes gave up the attempt to restrain them. From all over the Cove people were assembling at the water's edge.

'All right,' he said, 'off you go.'

'Are you coming?'

'No, I am staying right here.'

Nanbaree was already out of the door and running down the road towards the bridge and so to the Governor's wharf. They followed, panting in their endeavour to keep up with him, dodging in and out among those convicts whose duties allowed them to take leave to watch the coming of the two natives. A little time off on such a day could easily be stolen.

The boat was almost in when the boys arrived. They saw at once that the two natives lashed to the thwarts were as terrified as Arabanoo had been, and that no one looked very happy, least of all Lieutenant Bradley.

Nanbaree had rushed on to the wharf and was now well out on the end. Surely he knew them, for immediately a great shouting came from him—a stream of unintelligible gabble, amongst which two words seemed to be repeated continually, 'Colbee! Bennelong!' Their names, perhaps?

For a few moments their eyes lit up with recognition, and they answered excitedly, then they lapsed again into terror, as the sailors motioned them to step out of the boat, and led them along the wharf, half dragging them, half pushing them, like puppies on a lead.

And beside them was Nanbaree. 'Colbee! Bennelong!' he repeated, and again went off into a torrent of gibberish.

The boys hurried after him, as the terrified natives were forcibly dragged up the slope to the Governor's house, running a little way ahead, and then stopping to watch the strange procession while it topped the rise.

For the first time John noted their bearing. One was younger than the other, about twenty-six years, tall and stoutly made, with a bold, open face, now sullenly defiant. The other was older, shorter, and not so robustly framed, but, for all that, seemed to carry an air of authority, and to be the leader of the two.

'Colbee,' Nanbaree whispered. 'Him big man, Cadigal.'

'And the other?'

'That Bennelong. Him fighter,' and he moved his arm in the action of throwing a spear.

The Governor was waiting at the door of his house.

'So you got them?' he said to Lieutenant Bradley, looking compassionately at the frightened creatures.

'Yes, sir. Lured them with two fish at the North Cove. When they dropped their spears to get the fish from our men on shore, I gave the signal from the boat, and they were seized.'

'Any bloodshed?'

'No, sir.'

'Good. Bring them in.'

John looked at the door-bell, thinking of the day when he had touched it to amuse Arabanoo. He was about to touch it again, as with a shout the girl, Abaroo, followed by Jenny and Sue, came running across the garden.

'GringerrykibbaColbee. WogultroweywolarawareeBennelongboin-babundebunda,' she screamed, and it seemed as if there were a whole tribe, so many names slipped from her tongue.

'Good, good,' said the Governor, pleased to see her. 'Abaroo and the boy, Nanbaree, will interpret for us.' Then turning to the smaller of the two men: 'What name this man?'

'Gringerrykibbacolbee.'

The Governor looked confused. 'Gringerrykibba—' he began. 'It's certainly a long name.'

'Him three names,' Nanbaree explained, and laughed loudly. 'Gringerry Kibba Colbee.'

'Oh, and which is the best one?'

'Colbee. Him big man, Cadigal, my people.'

'So Colbee it will be,' the Governor said, looking now at the taller man, still writhing in his bonds and muttering in protest. 'And what name this one?'

'Wogultrowey Wolarawaree Bennelong Boinba Bundebunda,' said Abaroo. 'Him five names.'

'And which name best?'

'Bennelong,' announced Nanbaree.

'Good, good!' The Governor praised the children, and then said to them, 'Tell your friends that we have treated you well, and that you are happy here.'

In another interlude of conversation with answer fired back at question, the two natives seemed to grow calmer, especially the taller one, who, a moment before, had so angrily protested against his bonds.

'Wish we knew what they were talking about,' John whispered to Martin.

'Clothes, of course. Look, Nanbaree is taking off his jacket!'

And the men were examining it, looking from it to the brightly uniformed soldiers and sailors around them.

'Tell them that each shall have a jacket, too,' the Governor said, 'and trousers, and a hat.'

It was the hat that amused them most. A sailor promptly complied by lending his, and the tall one, Bennelong, donning it, looked so coy in his new headgear that for a moment he seemed to be a pleasant fellow.

It was only for a moment.

'That's a rogue, if ever I saw one,' John heard Debby say, as she joined the outskirts of the group in search of Sue. 'He's just like Caesar. A scamp, he is!'

For immediately his pleasant mood passed, and he was ramping and raging again, stamping and swaying while his companion looked on in sullen silence.

Then John remembered the door-bell, and tinkled it as he had meant to do before the girls had appeared. The diversion was a success. The natives stood in wonderment, so John tinkled it again.

'Bell,' said the Governor, and invited them to try.

But Colbee would not be encouraged. He stood there, moving not an inch, yet ready at an instant to leap away to freedom should an opportunity be given.

'Bell,' said Nanbaree, rushing forward and ringing it with all his might.

'Bell,' Bennelong repeated, and tried to touch it, then felt the drag of the rope on his manacled hands and burst again into a stream of fiery abuse.

'Take them away and bathe and shave them,' the Governor ordered, 'and bring them back when they are clothed.'

The boys tailed after, while Debby gathered Sue and Jenny to take them home. 'Mamma said you were to come. It's not the place for girls,' she scolded. 'Why should you want to watch two dirty black men being bathed?'

They went reluctantly, but the native girl, Abaroo, stayed. She was

with the boys when they gathered in the hut that had been prepared
for Arabanoo, and where now the two men, who had been chosen as
the natives' keepers, were preparing a tub.

Nanbaree was highly excited. 'Bennelong, him fighter,' he told the
boys, and they readily agreed, for when he was forced into the tub—and
he submitted very unwillingly to be washed—they saw that there were
scars on his head, one on his arm and another on his leg, and that he
had lost half of one of his thumbs. 'He fight always,' Nanbaree ended.

It almost seemed as if there was to be a fight in the hut, for Bennelong was now lashing and thrashing his arms, and it took two men
to hold him down as his keeper continued to remove the dirt and filth
of days and weeks from his dark skin.

Then, strangely, as he stepped from the tub, the rage passed, and he
turned unconcernedly and gazed at the two girls, who had disobeyed
Debby and run back to join the group of onlookers. And again John
thought Bennelong almost grinned.

There was no smile on Colbee' s face. He sat sullen and morose in
the tub, enduring the torture in silence, anger and defiance mounting
until he seemed likely to spring up and make for the door.

'He been sick, too,' Nanbaree said, pointing to the pockmarks
on his own face, and then to those that deeply disfigured the face of
Colbee, and indeed of Bennelong, also.

The bathing was over now, and the time had come to shave them.
Once again it was Bennelong who protested most loudly; Bennelong
who made the most antics, pulling his face away from the blade, rolling his eyes, and moving from side to side. Was he terrified or having
a joke? John wondered.

But Colbee sat immovable, grim, silent, sullen.

'I like Bennelong the best,' John said to Martin. 'The other one's
too sulky.'

Bennelong was quite comic when he was paraded in his clothes.
He cut an almost elegant figure in his new trousers and jacket and hat,
and when shown his face in the mirror was first astonished and then
quite pleased with himself.

Colbee couldn't raise a smile. He grunted when his keepers drew on his trousers, he frowned when they put on his shirt, and refused to look in the mirror to admire his new hat. Then he turned to Bennelong, reprimanding him so harshly that the cheerful Bennelong suddenly lapsed into solemnness again.

'Because Colbee's the chief and Bennelong has to obey him,' Martin whispered to John.

Neither of the natives understood the purpose of the iron fetter now snapped on his leg, and for a moment or two each regarded it with curiosity, feeling the hardness of the metal, and listening to the clink as it fell on the ground.

Nanbaree was disturbed. He had seen many convicts in fetters, and knew exactly what the fetters meant. He had never been forced to wear one, so why should Bennelong and Colbee?

'Because they will run away,' John explained to him. 'The Governor wants to keep them here and make friends with them.'

A rope attached to each fetter was held by the native's keeper. Bennelong moved, and found that he could walk freely only the length of the rope. So did Colbee. Both began to protest, Bennelong with violence and loud language, pulling on the rope and dragging his keeper from the hut; Colbee with sullen defiance, sitting on the ground and refusing to budge an inch.

'Now, come on, come on,' Colbee's keeper urged, as an onlooker hauled Colbee up and forced him to walk through the door.

'Oh, the poor things! Oh, the poor things!' John heard Mamma say when he, too, emerged, and found her gazing compassionately after Bennelong and Colbee, now being pushed and dragged towards the Governor's house. 'Oh, why can't the Governor think of some other way!'

'Because, ma'am, there is no other way.' The Governor had appeared at his door and had heard her. 'How am I to teach the natives that we are their friends unless some of them come and live with us? And how can I keep them here without fetters? Come with me into my house and see the wonder in their faces when they see strange things.'

'But I came for my children, Your Excellency. They have already been called home, and have not come.'

'Then bring them with you, and they shall see how well we treat our visitors. Young Nanbaree and Abaroo as well. They must come to be our interpreters.'

The Governor's drawing-room was crowded when at last Bennelong and Colbee were persuaded and cajoled and finally forced through the door into the house.

Their terror was great. 'Perhaps it is because they think they will never get out again,' Martin said to John.

The Governor must have had the same thought, for he called to Nanbaree and Abaroo and bade them tell the men that this was where the white men ate and slept and lived.

'Tell them, too, that in a little while they can go back to the garden and to their own hut. I shall live here, they will live there.'

Bennelong seemed more satisfied. He looked appraisingly at the small man with the blue coat and gold braid, and for the first time appeared to understand that this was the person who was the chief of the white tribe. From the Governor he glanced at Mamma, and was immediately interested. Slowly he approached her, closer, almost too close, and studied her hair, her clothes.

She was becoming more and more embarrassed, when the Governor drew away Bennelong's attention by throwing some paper into the open fire-place and with the help of the tinder-box striking a light.

'Ah!'

This was indeed something to wonder at—fire from a box!

Both of them—Bennelong and the sullen Colbee—came jabbering to the fire-place, while Nanbaree told the Governor that they wanted to see it done a second time. They would have watched again and again, had not the Governor called for wine and biscuits.

Intently they stared as the red liquid was poured from the bottle. Bennelong even made bold to pick up an empty glass, feeling it with his fingers and looking through its transparent sides, until Colbee frowned, and snatching it from him, threw it on the floor to break into a dozen pieces. But the effect was almost electric. Terrified at the unexpected result, Colbee cowered towards the door, and would have none of the wine when it was offered to him.

Bennelong took his awkwardly, not knowing what to do with it.

'Drink,' said the Governor, sipping at his glass.

'Wi-dah,' said Nanbaree. 'Drink.'

Slowly Bennelong raised the glass as the Governor had done, matching every movement perfectly, then sipped, smacked his lips, and sipped again, then swallowed it all, his eyes growing rounded, his pleasant face all smiles with appreciation of this new drink.

'More,' said Nanbaree, as Bennelong held out his glass.

But the Governor would not give him any more. Nor would Colbee stay any longer. With a brusque command to Bennelong, he pushed his way to the door, and dragged on the rope until his keeper was forced to go, too.

And strange to say Bennelong obediently followed.

'See that they have a good meal,' the Governor told their keepers. Food might be scarce, especially fresh meat, but the natives had to be fed to satisfaction.

The children went with them. Remembering Arabanoo, they knew that Bennelong and Colbee would cook their own food. This always amused them, because the natives scarcely waited to singe the fur or feathers or skin before they ate the flesh raw.

As they walked away John heard the Governor say to Mamma, 'Well, ma'am, are you happier in your mind about our two natives?'

But Mamma shook her head. 'I know what you are doing is the only practical way to make friends with them, but oh, I do wish they had not to go about with fetters!'

'So do I, ma'am, and the fetters will be taken off as soon as possible. Don't you think it will be easier to make friends with the big one than the other?'

Mamma smiled as she remembered Bennelong and his cheeky approach to her. 'Rather a rascal, I'm afraid,' she said. 'Maybe one who likes the ladies—in his own tribe.'

'Yes, and a great boaster of his prowess as a warrior. We shall see.'

The children were watching the cooking of the fish when Mamma swept by and gathered up Sue and Martin and John for supper.

'Such a pile,' Sue told Debby, when she reached home, 'Twelve great big ones.'

'And mighty lucky they are not to have to catch them,' Debby said tartly. 'Now that big fellow I saw, I guess he'd take all he could get. They'll have plenty of waiting on, and not only by their keepers,' and she looked at the children with a twinkle in her eye.

'But, Debby, that won't make up for the loss of their freedom,' Mamma reminded her. 'How would you like plenty to eat if you had a shackle on your leg?'

Debby thought differently from Mamma. She had seen so many shackles among the convicts that the spectacle of fetters on the natives did not move her in the same way.

'It is no worse than shackles on the convicts, ma'am,' she replied, 'and the convicts get no waiting on and no pounds and pounds of fish.'

John was thinking over the matter as he ate his supper. The difference, of course, was that the natives were away from their own people.

Mamma was quick to remind Debby of this. 'How would you like to be kidnapped by the natives and led round among them with a shackle on your leg?'

'Yes, I suppose you're right,' Debby granted at last rather grudgingly. 'But the thought of all that fish when we are so short of food, ma'am, makes me rebellious.'

Bennelong and Colbee were sitting disconsolately with their keepers outside their hut when the boys returned for one last look before Martin went home to the parade ground. Nanbaree was there, and the girl, Abaroo, but neither was able to rouse the men from their melancholy. There they sat gloomily wrapped in their own thoughts, staring down the harbour where their own folk were.

John thought once that Bennelong's eyes twinkled when he tried to attract the native's attention with a broad grin, but almost immediately the fellow fell back into sullenness, for Colbee growled and seemed to call him to order.

Colbee himself had begun to examine the rope that was attached to his fetter, and was picking at it with his finger nail when the keepers dragged at it and motioned him to rise and go into the hut. He resisted with force, as did Bennelong also, in spite of the hurt caused by the pressure of the fetter on the leg.

'That fellow, Colbee, is the more cunning one,' Papa said to Mamma later. 'He'll have to be watched or he'll escape.'

Remembering the way Colbee had examined the rope, John rather agreed. Some ten days later it was known all over the Cove that the natives had tried to escape the previous night.

'Gnawed through the ropes tied to their fetters,' John told Mamma when he heard about it, 'and their keepers found them groping around in the hut, but they couldn't get out because they didn't know how to unfasten the windows or to unlock the door.'

'Oh dear, I wish they had got away!' Mamma sighed. For days they remained sulky, and took little interest in anything except their food, although their keepers walked them round the Cove—visiting the bake-house and the smithy and the farm-places which should have been a matter of wonder to them. Nanbaree and Abaroo followed them faithfully, talking, explaining, but the men would not be amused. Only the telescope at the observatory brought forth grunts of amazement.

Lieutenant Dawes sadly watched them as they walked away in their fetters and John told him how already they had tried to escape.

'They're not as amiable as Arabanoo,' the lieutenant remarked.

'Bennelong, the big one, is,' Martin said. 'He's a real lively fellow, but the other one keeps him sulky. Nanbaree says Colbee is a chief, so we think Bennelong is scared of him.'

Lieutenant Dawes was busy with preparations for an exploring trip to the mountains that the Governor called the Carmarthen Hills.

'It's my turn now,' he told them. 'You helped the Governor to explore the Hawkesbury, and Captain Tench discovered the Nepean

River. Now I am going out across the Nepean to see what is beyond the mountains that you have told me look so blue from a distance.'

For once the boys did not ask to go with him. They knew the trip would be strenuous and they would not be allowed. Besides, they were still fascinated by the two natives, and wanted to stay close to see what would happen to them.

Lieutenant Dawes had already gone two days, when one night at dusk the alarm was given:

'Colbee—he's escaped!'

John saw it happen, for he was on an errand to the Governor for Papa. As he passed the hut, Colbee was seated at the door, and Bennelong was inside with the keepers. All were eating their supper, Colbee grabbing his food, stuffing it into his mouth, smacking his lips and pulling faces, much to the amusement of the others. This was what one would have expected of Bennelong, not Colbee. Then John noticed that every time Colbee's hands were free, they returned to the rope attached to the fetter, and that the rope was out of sight of the door of the hut. Under the pretence of fooling his keeper, could Colbee be unsplicing it? Could he?

Indeed he was, for even as John watched in the gathering gloom, the native arose and, with the agility of a hunter, in spite of the fetter, was over the paling fence and immediately gone into the night.

'Colbee, he's escaped!' John screamed.

'Where? Where?' Soldiers, convicts, keepers verged upon John and asked the direction.

'Over there. Over the fence, that way.'

There was hurrying and scurrying, searching in and out of the bushes and behind trees.

'You're wasting your time,' the Governor told them all, when he emerged from his house. 'The man is gone, and you'll never find him in the night.'

'But, Your Excellency, he has a fetter.'

'Yes, I know, but that won't stop him. Poor fellow, I don't know how he will get it off.'

'And his clothes, too, sir,' John reminded the Governor. 'They may hinder him.'

'Not he,' the Governor replied. 'If he does not take them off and throw them away, they will at least surprise his friends. Where is the other native?'

Bennelong was cowering beside his keeper. John had never seen anyone so terrified.

'Maybe he thinks he will be put to death now that his friend has escaped,' Captain Collins explained.

'Perhaps he has been trying to unsplice his own rope,' said Papa.

The Governor bent to examine the rope and found it almost unravelled. 'H'm!' he grunted. 'We almost lost them both. A few more minutes and this fellow, too, would have gone.' He turned to Captain Collins. 'Give orders that the keeper be chained henceforth by the wrist to the fetter on Bennelong's leg. And see that the man who allowed Colbee to escape be punished.'

John hated to think of the punishment the keeper would get, but he deserved it, for had not the Governor entrusted Colbee to his care? And Bennelong? Would he be lonely now and sad, all alone among strangers? It seemed at first that he would be, for the next morning he took no notice of anyone, and sullenly resented the chain that joined his ankle fetter with the handcuff on his keeper's wrist.

Then suddenly on the second day, as if he had decided graciously to accept his captivity, or because his good humour could no longer be held in check—he became affable, inquisitive, even jovial.

He talked loudly and long with Nanbaree and Abaroo; he made his keeper take him round the garden again to see the ducks and the chickens, and across to Mamma's house, now nearing completion, where he frightened Debby by pulling the pin from her hair so that it fell like a swathe around her.

'P'ff p'ff,' she said in dismay. 'Just like his cheek!' while the boys smiled and winked at one another.

He also accepted the Governor's invitation to sit at table with him, and eat of the white man's food, and drink that strange red water that made his body glow within him.

'He's settled in at last,' Papa said. 'He must have been afraid of the other one.'

'Yes,' explained John. 'Nanbaree reckoned Colbee was a chief of the Cadigal.'

'A really lively, intelligent fellow,' Papa continued.

'And a rogue,' commented Debby, remembering her encounter with Bennelong that afternoon.

CHAPTER XII
JENNY FACES THE SNAKE ALONE

IT was now the middle of December, close to Christmas, and Mamma had plenty to do.

'Cookie ought to be back soon, and should bring some turtles from Lord Howe's Island,' she said to Debby. 'They might give us our Christmas dinner.'

'And the melons are ripening again,' Debby reminded her.

'Yes,' said Sue, 'and we'll be in our new house.'

Mamma and Debby seemed to go about their tasks more happily when they thought of that prospect.

'It's almost too good to be true. That house is the best Christmas present the Governor could have given me,' Mamma sighed thankfully. 'Just fancy, Debby: the week after next, and we'll be moving the beds and the chests and the tables into a real home.'

'And I shall have the kitchen all to myself,' John added. 'That's the best Christmas present you could give me, Mamma.'

'And goodness knows what you'll get up to in it!' exclaimed Debby.

In the circumstances John thought Mamma would refuse when Papa suggested that they should all go for a day or two to Rose Hill.

'The children can take Jenny and Martin,' he explained. 'We'll go in the *Lump*. Chips always promised them a trip to the head of the harbour, and he can take us now.'

'But, Richard, there is so much to do—' Mamma began.

'Tut, tut! Debby can do that, and when we come back, I'll get help to move the furniture and set you up as a lady should live.'

John noticed that Debby smiled broadly at Papa, and thought that there was some secret between them. Now what could it be? Something concerning Mamma.

'Well, it would be very nice to see James Ruse again,' Mamma said. 'I did promise him that we would visit him someday.'

'Yes,' said John, 'on the farm he is going to own.'

Papa looked round at them all as if to prepare them for a surprise. 'He has the farm,' he said quietly.

'You mean it?' Mamma was so overjoyed that she was really excited. 'Oh dear, I am glad! Of course I'll go.'

And again John noticed the look that passed between Papa and Debby.

There was no need this time to worry about Nanbaree. He was too absorbed in Bennelong to leave the Cove. They had seen very little of him since Colbee had escaped, he was so busy being an interpreter whenever the Governor wanted him.

They were away the next morning on the slow-sailing *Rose Hill Packet*, otherwise named the *Lump*. The girls were particularly interested because they had never been up the harbour before. The boys had gone that way with the Governor in search of a river, not long after they came to Sydney Cove.

Now they were full of reminiscences.

'Do you remember the crescent-shaped hill?' John asked Martin. 'That one the Governor afterwards called Rose Hill?'

'Yes, and the creek that ran round it. I wonder how much it has changed, since people went to live there.'

They would soon know. The settlement of Rose Hill was begun in November 1788, some months after their exploring trip with the Governor, so it had been there almost a year.

'And the fine meal we had when Cookie stuffed a duck with salt pork.' John stiffened as he spoke, and his voice hushed to a whisper. 'Martin, there's someone hidden by the trees over there—a convict in a boat,' and he pointed towards the northern shore, where another branch led to the west.

Two pairs of eyes were now glued to the spot, two pairs of eyes watching for movement, while the others, blissfully unaware of what was causing their interest, gazed idly from one side to the other.

Slowly the *Lump* made its way, closer and closer as it tacked towards the northern shore.

The convict was there all right, the boat was there; the boys recognised it as the small boat from Garden Island.

'Caesar!' they whispered to one another. 'Caesar escaping again.' Had not the Governor ordered the irons to be taken from his leg? This was what he would do.

The man was lying behind the boat, which was drawn up and half hidden behind the rocks. They saw him as the *Lump* turned to make again for the southern shore. Yes, they were sure it was Caesar, his skin was so dark.

'Don't tell,' John whispered again, thankful that the grown-ups had not seen or suspected.

But innocently Jenny babbled as they drew out again, 'There's a man over there.'

'Where? Where?' Sue and the boys, as well as Mamma, turned to look.

'Aw,' said John, 'that's only a native!'

The *Lump* was so far away now that no one disputed him. As for the boat, it had been so cleverly camouflaged that it could not be detected at that distance.

For another two hours the *Lump* sailed on while Chips pointed out the landmarks to Mamma—creeks and inlets, islands and peninsulas, the high sloping shores of the north side, the flat swampy land as the stream narrowed.

It was past midday when the boat at length came to the landing place at Rose Hill, and Mamma stepped ashore. The country had improved now, and the stream ran like a limpid pathway between the green trees.

'I like this place,' she said to Papa. 'It would be a pleasant place to live.'

The children had landed before her, and had begun to run along the wide track that Chips said led to the settlement.

'Maybe it'll be a road some day, ma'am,' he told Mamma, as he pointed towards it, 'but at the moment you'll find some fields astraddle it. The Governor has not got round to laying out this town as he did Sydney Cove, but he will, you mark my words. And this'll be the main street, a mile long, leading right up to the Governor's house on Rose Hill. I'll wait here for you tomorrow to take you back.'

Rose Hill was certainly a primitive place as Mamma saw it after a half a mile walk in the heat of the December day.

'Well, this is a surprise,' Mr Dodd greeted her, after Papa had gone to acquaint him of their visit.

Mr Dodd was well known to them all. He was the Governor's servant, and had sailed with them in the *Sirius*. Because he knew more about farming than anyone else, the Governor had put him in charge of the agriculture at Rose Hill.

'The young ones, too,' he exclaimed, as he turned to the children. 'John and Martin always avoiding the garden, I guess, and Sue—have you those rabbits still?'

That was a story to tell—of the rabbits born, and of the rabbits lost.

'But how are you getting on?' Mamma asked when Sue had finished. 'That's what we've come to find out.'

'Fine, ma'am. The harvest has just come in—two hundred bushels of wheat, sixty of barley, and a small quantity of Indian corn, flax and oats. Now what do you think of that?'

'Splendid! At the Government Farm at Sydney Cove they grew only twenty-five bushels of barley.'

'Yes, so I heard. But this is the place, ma'am, richer soil and drier climate. Next year we aim to plant our harvest as seed.'

Too dull for the children to listen to, especially Jenny and Sue. They were kicking up the dust on the edge of a cornfield while they watched the convicts break the cobs from the stalk.

'Maize, ma'am, or Indian corn, some call it. Seems to do better than wheat, and grows like magic. But I am sure you need some refreshment, and if you will do me the honour of visiting my home, I shall be only too glad to share with you all I have.'

He led the way up the cleared track, skirting a wheatfield here and there, towards a collection of huts that huddled round the redoubt, nestling snugly at the foot of a crescent-shaped hill.

John and Martin recognised it as soon as they reached it.

'This is the place the Governor called The Crescent, Mamma,' John said, 'and then renamed Rose Hill.'

'Yes,' said Papa,' after Mr George Rose of the Treasury.'

'Never had occasion to use the redoubt,' Mr Dodd told them. 'The natives do not worry us. The barracks and stores are built within it.' He waved his hand towards an enticing footbridge across the river. 'The Government Farm is over there. That is where I live.'

The house was comfortable enough, though built of twigs and plaster. Its coolness was certainly a relief from the heat outside, as they sat and ate a meal of pork pie and cabbage and potatoes, with a water-melon to follow.

Mr Dodd was full of enthusiasm for his little settlement. 'I shall show you round my garden later,' he said to Mamma. 'I have grown the biggest cabbage you ever saw. Now that you are here, I'll cut it and send it back to the Governor when you go. We have vegetables in plenty just at present, but our rations, of course, are the same as yours. I wonder why the ships haven't come.'

'Something has happened to them,' Papa suggested.

'A shipwreck, eh? Then the food position is serious?'

'Yes, and will be more so if the ships don't come in the New Year.'

Mamma looked up from her melon. 'I have a house now, Mr Dodd, a real brick house. If only the ships would come I'd be truly happy, for I like this place.'

'You mean you'd like to stay here always?' Mr Dodd seemed surprised. 'And not go back to England?'

'Why not? It's a beautiful climate, and when we really begin to farm, there'll be plenty of food. The longer we are here, the more comforts we'll get. And there's adventure, too, for John, when he grows up. The mountains, for instance.'

Papa laughed loud and long. 'She's telling you what I have been telling her for two years, Dodd. That's why I brought her to visit Rose

Hill. Some day, perhaps, I'll be able to get a land grant, and why not one at Rose Hill?'

John sat and listened. To stay in New South Wales would be just what he wanted. But the mountains would be conquered before he grew up. Hadn't Lieutenant Dawes gone out to try to climb them?

'Dawes hasn't come back?' Papa asked.

'No, but he should be here any day. He went out with two others, as you know. They seemed to think it would be easy to climb the mountains, but they'll have to do it quickly or their food will run out.'

The meal was finished now, and it was cooler outside. Mr Dodd suggested a walk in the garden, but Mamma, much to John's delight, said she would like to visit James Ruse.

'James Ruse? Ah, yes! He was a convict gardener to you, wasn't he? And you begged me to bring him here?' Mr Dodd said. 'Well, I'm happy to say that he has been everything you said he was. Honest and industrious.'

'Oh, I am so glad! I knew he would be. My husband says he is to have a farm of his own?'

'Yes, ma'am, we have cleared an acre of ground and turned it over, and built him a hut. Now he is in possession. If he makes good, the Governor will give him the land. It's an experiment, if you understand.'

He led the way out of the gate, as the children followed, then ran on as they always did, while the grown-ups came behind.

'How do you mean, an experiment?' she asked.

'Well, the Governor wants to see if a convict can support himself as a settler. Ruse's time has expired, and he is really a free man. Many think he won't be able to keep himself off his land, but I believe he will.'

'Surely he's not to keep himself straightway?' Papa asked.

'No, he's to continue to get rations from the store, and he has been given tools, grain for sowing, and two sows and six hens. He also has a convict to assist him.'

Mamma was smiling proudly as she listened. She had believed in James Ruse, and he had proved himself worthy of her faith.

They had partly retraced their steps of the morning and crossed a creek, when they came upon a clearing with a lone figure wielding a hoe. Down, down, down, came the hoe in rhythmic strokes, deep into the dry clods of earth, smashing, breaking them into a hundred fragments. Never a moment to look round at the pleasant prospect, never a moment to stop to watch something ungainly bobbing up and down at the far end of the clearing.

But the children saw them. 'emus!' and with a yell of delight they were after them, twisting and turning among the trees as the strange birds stopped and eyed them, ran on, stopped again, then taking fright dashed off into the wood.

'Come back,' Papa ordered. 'John, do you hear? Do you want to get lost?'

So they swerved and made for James Ruse, standing at last with his hoe poised, astonished to see his visitors.

'Oh, ma'am, ma'am,' he cried, dropping his hoe and doffing his hat, 'ye have really come at last!'

'Yes, Jim, I've come to see your farm. My husband told me about it, and although we are just about to move into our new brick house, I just had to come and see it.'

'Yes, ma'am, it came right, just as ye said it would. The Governor, he says if I do well, he'll give me thirty acres. Thirty acres, ma'am! 'tis hard to believe.'

They were all gathered in a little group around James Ruse, the children gaping and listening but still watchful for the emus.

'But well deserved, Jim,' Mamma assured him. 'I'm so glad.'

Mr Dodd looked around at the evidence of fires in the stumps and trunks of trees. 'You've been burning a bit,' he said.

'Aye, sir, that I be. Burn the timber, I say, and dig the ashes into the ground, then hoe it up like I be doing now. And excuse me, sir, for saying it, but I never do more than eight or nine rods a day. The convicts, sir, do sixteen, and only scratch over the soil.'

Mr Dodd smiled at the hint. 'And then what will you do?'

'I'll clod-mould it, sir, then dig in the grass and weeds, and let it lie as long as I can open to the sun and air. Last of all, I'll turn it up again, and sow my crop broadcast. Now if we only had a plough and some oxen—'

'Yes,' said Mamma, 'it would be grand, but how could you use the plough with all the stumps in the ground?'

'Dig 'em out, ma'am. They'd come out in time. But I'll grow my crops, stumps or no stumps, if it be only to please ye. Told the Governor, too, I have, I'll be able to keep m'self in eighteen months, so I got to do it.'

The girls had run over to the hut, where they had found some kittens that were just meant to be petted. The boys followed them, as the grown-ups continued to discuss the boundaries of the farm, and the possibility of crops in the next harvest.

It was then that they saw the emus again, queer heads bobbing up and down above the smaller trees and shrubs.

'Just like sea serpents,' Martin said afterwards.

How could they remember Papa's command not to follow?

Never before had they been so close to the big birds. There they were, and they simply had to go. Not a thought of the danger that lay in the woods, not a thought of what might happen to the girls if they followed. Off they went at a gallop, the strange heads luring them on, the girls in hot pursuit.

But they soon lost the heads of the strange birds in the mass of foliage, soon lost the girls. They stood within a few hundred yards of Ruse's farm, and did not know where they were.

'The girls followed us,' said Martin guiltily.

Both were penitent, knowing well that they should not have been so impetuous. *They* could find their way back. Had not they returned to Careening Cove in a moment of greater danger? But what of the girls?

'Let us follow our footprints and try to track the girls, as Nanbaree would do,' Martin suggested.

That was an idea. Slowly they retraced their steps, marking them on the flattened grass, and by the twigs broken from the prickly shrubs.

'This is where they ran a different way,' Martin said, when they came to the spot where the footprints divided from their own. 'Here is the way they went.'

That is how they came upon the girls, and were amazed at what they saw. For they were bending over a hollow in the ground, and in it were a dozen or more of dark green eggs.

Emus' eggs! Of course they were emus' eggs. What other birds could have eggs as large as those! What John had longed for, what Cookie had promised him—an emu's egg with the *Sirius* painted on it, to be a companion to the ostrich egg that Mynheer Jan had given Mamma at Capetown.

He could see them closer now, a whole nest of them laid out in a pattern, small ends inwards, large ends outwards. He must have one. With a spurt he ran on, outstripping Martin, then stopped, stiffened with horror. For Jenny had picked up a stick and was raking in among the eggs, and out of the nest a snake had wriggled—a brown one with a yellow front, head upraised, fangs extended—and was about to strike at Sue.

Now he saw one of the bravest actions that he had ever seen, or ever would see, so he told himself afterwards. Thrusting Sue behind her, Jenny faced the snake alone, backing away, deliberately enticing it on. Then suddenly she swerved as it struck into nothingness. She had done it on purpose to allow Sue to escape, for Sue was now stumbling back towards the farm. What courage, what coolness of mind!

But the snake was coming again.

What should he do? Oh, what should he do? He must do something, and something quickly. If Jenny could be so brave, so cool-headed, then so should he. A stick! A stick! Where could he find a stick?

He picked one from the ground to wield it as he had seen Pete do and Jim Ruse many a time. Would that Jim Ruse were there now!

But there was no one—only he and Martin to protect Jenny. For Martin had a stick too, and was coming to help.

The snake was about to strike again, when with all the force of his strong young arms he came down on the back close to the head.

Whack, whack, whack!

Then it was Martin who had raised his stick, and was coming down again and again.

They were beating out its life together.

And there it lay at their feet, as Jenny, unnerved at last, burst into tears and sobbed convulsively.

It seemed natural to find Caesar watching them, when they looked up.

'Caesar!' John said.

'Aye, never seen a snake deader, dat I hav' not. Dah's no need fer Caesar ter come an' git you outer a mighty bad fix any mo.'

No one thought to ask him his business, why he was there, whence he had come. Caesar himself offered no explanation.

'I jes' watchin' 'tween der trees,' he said, and placing his finger on his lips, slipped away into the foliage, carrying the snake on a stick. 'Good fer supper,' he told them with a wink.

'That means we mustn't tell,' John warned the others. 'Jenny, do you hear? You must say nothing about Caesar. If you do, you'll get him into trouble.'

Jenny nodded solemnly. She was still too unnerved to speak. But John knew that he could trust her. There was no one more loyal to them in all their schemes.

John picked up an egg, and Martin did likewise. 'Take one, Jenny,' he said, as he felt the weight of the egg and passed his hand over the granulated surface. 'You deserve one.' Then in single file they retraced their steps in the direction they had come.

They found Sue in tears and being comforted by Mamma and James Ruse with the gift of a tabby kitty.

'Whatever happened to the child?' Mamma asked.

'Oh, nothing much, Mamma! We found an emu's nest, and a snake ran out,' and John displayed his egg.

'Where?'

'In among the trees,' he explained vaguely, for he didn't want his mother to know that they had gone so far.

Jim Ruse looked at him queerly from the corners of his eyes, but merely said with a grin, 'So that's why those birds have been running about this farm.'

'How about watching the nest, Ruse,' Mr Dodd suggested, 'and when the young hatch, we'll send some down to His Excellency. Maybe he'll be able to rear them.'

'That I'll do gladly, sir. No one'll get those eggs. P'rhaps there'll be a little emu for the children.'

'And how are we going to divide these eggs?' Mamma asked. 'You have three—and there are four of you.'

'I should like Jenny to have one,' John spoke up, remembering how stolidly she had stood up to the snake. 'Sue can have mine.'

But Sue preferred the kitten, so all was well.

The sun was setting as they said good-bye.

'We'll be back next year when you reap your harvest,' Mamma called gaily to Jim Ruse, as he stood at attention and watched them go. 'Be of good cheer, Jim. You'll get your thirty acres, and maybe the Governor will call it Experiment Farm.'

At night as the boys lay side by side in the barracks—for that is where they slept with Papa, while Mamma and the girls stayed in Mr Dodd's house—they talked about Jenny and the snake and about Caesar.

'He must have come up and landed,' John said, 'and now he's gone off with the natives again. Silly fellow!'

'And before the month's out, he'll be back, and the Governor will have to punish him again.'

By the next afternoon Chips had brought them safely to Sydney Cove, with the wonderful cabbage, and the emus' eggs, and a kitten, and melons and pumpkins from Mr Dodd's garden.

'We've brought you a cabbage that weighs twenty-six pounds, sir,' Martin informed the Governor when they saw him as they passed through his grounds on their way from the wharf.

'Yes, sir,' said Jenny, 'and emus' eggs. Look!' and she held out hers for him to see. 'My mother will use it to make something nice for you.'

He was very interested in the large green egg, and weighed it in his hand, as he examined its rough surface.

'Jim Ruse is going to watch the nest, and when the young ones hatch will send you some, Your Excellency,' John added.

'Good,' said the Governor. 'I'm glad you've had an interesting time.'

'We have,' they cried, and went to their respective homes.

But when Mamma and her children came to their gate, they looked about in astonishment. The marquee had gone! And so had John's wattle-and-daub sleeping hut. Before them was the new house, its shuttered windows held open with sticks, for there was little glass except what went into the Governor's house. But for all that, a comfortable, substantial house, with verandahs beside which to grow creeping plants to give shade on hot days—a house to withstand storm and wind and heat—a real home.

'But—' said Mamma.

Debby was there laughing at her. 'The master, he said I was to move the furniture into the new house while you were away,' she explained, 'and his men were to come and take down the marquee. Just as a surprise, ma'am.'

'Yes, yes,' said Papa, coming in behind. 'To surprise you,' and picking up Mamma he carried her over the threshold of her new home, just as if she had been a bride.

And Mamma, because she was so happy, was just like a young girl, rushing here and there to the rooms and noting the furniture in the places where she and Debby had planned it would be. Although she had been taken aback at first, she was glad now it was all fixed.

'I left the curtains, ma'am, and the ornaments, and all those small things that you would like to place yourself,' Debby said. 'We'll have it all finished before Christmas.'

John sneaked out of the house into the old kitchen. His bed had been brought in, and his chest with his clothes, and all the things that he treasured so much—Robinson Crusoe, the ship in the bottle, and the crooked stick. Even the spears had been leant against the wall.

Carefully placing the egg on the bed until he could get something to stand it on, he washed his hands in a basin that had been left for him, then took up his comb and passed it through his hair. He would have to look his best. For this was an occasion. Supper in the new house, with the best linen, no doubt, and the silver, brought from the chests where they had lain so long.

Yes, it was an occasion indeed. Whistling because he was happy, he crossed from the old kitchen, now his very own hut, into the new house for the first meal.

And what a meal it was!—one to remember in the years to come, a meal that marked the beginning of a life that Mamma had dreamed about ever since they had left England.

A real house! She had got it at last.

CHAPTER XIII

CHRISTMAS IN MAMMA'S NEW HOUSE

MAMMA kept open house in her new home, and for the intervening days before Christmas she had a constant stream of visitors—Lieutenant Dawes fresh from his journey to the mountains, Cookie back from Norfolk Island, and the Governor, most honoured of guests.

'Did you find a way across the mountains?' John and Martin inquired excitedly when Lieutenant Dawes appeared up the path with Nanbaree.

'Yes, did you?' asked Mamma. 'Tell us first, and then you can inspect my house.'

'No, I am sorry I did not,' he replied. 'His Excellency asked me to reach the summit of the Round Hill, a clear landmark in the Carmarthen Hills. From Rose Hill we went across country to the Nepean River, which you will remember was discovered by Captain Tench. Above us were the mountains. They did not appear to be particularly high, so the next day we commenced to climb them, expecting the journey to be easy.'

'And you met trouble?'

'Yes, ma'am, for when we reached the top, we found that our way lay over one ridge after another, with deep valleys between. For three days we pushed on, but covered only fifteen miles.'

'So you did not get to the Round Hill?'

'No, we did not. On the fourth day on the mountains we came to a ridge on which was a small outcrop. This we named Mount Twiss. Below us lay a waving valley of hills and more hills, covered with trees and blotched with purple cloud shadows, and beyond it the Round Hill. To reach this hill would have meant great effort and more provisions, so we turned back.'

'What a pity!' Mamma sighed.

'You never saw such magnificent scenery, ma'am. Great precipices of yellow sandstone form the walls of the valleys, and over all is a filmy haze of purplish blue. That is why we have begun to call those hills the Blue Mountains.'

Debby had entered with the tea-tray, and laid out the best linen and silver on the table. Mamma began to pour the tea into the cups.

'Some day a way will be found over those mountains, I suppose, but it won't be easy,' he ended.

Four days before Christmas, Cookie came jauntily up the path with a wide grin.

'Turtles?' Sue cried.

'Aye, I brought your Christmas dinner. There be only three, but enough for the Governor and ye and some others.'

'Then that solves our problem,' Mamma said graciously to Cookie. 'I did not want to kill any of the pigs or the fowls, for I am sure there is a bad time ahead.'

'Aye, ma'am, I be so surprised to see no ships when we came in. 'Tis strange. They should ha' been here by this.'

John was at hand with his emu's egg.

'My, and ye got that, eh? Now how?' And when he was told, 'I'll blow it this very day, and your Mamma, she can make ye an omelette.'

'No, Cookie,' Mamma interrupted, 'I'll use it to make a pudding for Christmas. Debby found some raisins yesterday among our stores that I thought I had used. The pudding will not be rich, but it will be a pudding, and you must come and help us to eat it. Papa will light some brandy round it, and we can think we are back in England, with the snow outside and the holly laden with berries.'

'And instead it will be so hot that we won't want to eat the pudding and will eat some melon instead,' Debby said gloomily.

The same afternoon, the Governor came with Bennelong, dressed in a jacket of red kersey and a pair of trousers, his keeper trailing behind.

'I have brought him, ma'am, to show you that he is happy, and so to ease your mind. Bennelong, what do you call me?'

'*Be-anga.*'

'*Be-anga*?' repeated Mamma.

'It means, *father*, in his language,' the Governor explained. 'And I call him '*Dooroow*', which means *son*, So you see we are getting along quite well. Why, we are such good friends that he carries my sword, don't you, Bennelong?' and the Governor pointed to the scabbard hanging at the native's waist.

Bennelong strutted with pride before Mamma, moving his hips, and dragging so much on his fetter that his keeper had to hurry. The children could not help smiling.

'Debby was right,' Mamma said. 'He is a rogue—a likeable rogue, but I'm still not happy about his fetter.'

'It's a necessity, ma'am, a necessity. It'll be removed as soon as possible. Bennelong, tell the lady how you were caught.'

Then followed a pantomime with gestures and signs as Bennelong described how the boat came into the shore, and how he and Colbee were decoyed with a fish. '*Beial, beial,*' he cried, and went on to show how he was seized and dragged into the boat. And again he led his keeper a pretty dance, as he moved here and there, lifting his arms and throwing his body about.

'*Beial*, I must tell you, means *very good*,' the Governor explained. 'He likes fish, and now he gets plenty without the trouble of spearing them. I am told that he can manage the share of six men with ease.'

'That may be all right for him, but what of his wife and children? Haven't they been left with no-one to provide for them?'

'He has none,' said the Governor. 'His wife died a short time ago. That's right, isn't it, Bennelong? *Mau-gohn*, your wife, she *bo-ee*, dead?'

The mention of the native word for wife seemed to send Bennelong into a state of gloom. He immediately sat on the ground, and began to sing in a sad monotonous way, moving his body from side to side.

'Poor fellow!' sighed Mamma. 'He's mourning her. Oh dear!'

'It won't last,' the Governor whispered. 'Just you wait and see,' and almost at once Bennelong rose, grinning in his most friendly manner, and with his hands making motions of drinking to Mamma.

'That means he wants wine,' the Governor explained again. 'He has taken a great fancy to it.'

'Then he shall have some,' Mamma replied.

'No, ma'am, not yet. Let us see you dance, Bennelong. If you do, the lady will give you wine,' and the Governor made the same motions of drinking.

Bennelong needed no further inducement. He began very slowly chanting in the same sad monotonous way, but gradually quickening the tempo of song and movement, until he was throwing himself into the most violent postures, shaking his arms and striking his feet on the ground with great force, so that he seemed to be in a fit of madness.

'Oh dear!' cried Mamma. 'What energy—and on this hot day!'

'Yes, and exercise for his keeper!' The Governor smiled, for the poor man was looking very exhausted.

'Wine—' began Bennelong, and Mamma called to Debby to oblige.

She came carrying the glass on a tray, her eyes expressing disapproval, but stayed to smile when she saw Bennelong throw back his head and drink almost at one gulp.

'*Beial, beial*,' he said, bowing before her, as he placed the glass on the tray.

'You've taught him manners,' Mamma remarked approvingly.

'We are trying to, ma'am,' the Governor replied,' but it is not quite as easy as it was with Arabanoo.'

Bennelong had unbuttoned his red kersey jacket on account of the heat, and Mamma could not stop staring at the scars on his body. 'How dreadful!' she said.

'Yes, his chief pastimes seem to have been love and war. And sometimes the ladies gave him the scars. Bennelong, that wound on the back of your hand there, *tam-mir-a*, How did you get it?'

With a great laugh Bennelong went into a long conversation in his own tongue.

'Nanbaree interpreted it for us,' the Governor said. 'He got the wound when he was carrying off a lady from another tribe. She stuck her teeth into his hand.'

'Oh dear!'

'So he knocked her down and beat her.'

'The terrible fellow!' Mamma was evidently not so sorry now for Bennelong.

'Tea is served, ma'am,' Debby announced, coming out of the house again.

'You will do me the honour of joining me?' Mamma began, and His Excellency bowed, and motioned the keeper to take Bennelong back to Government House.

But Bennelong was not ready to go. He was eyeing Debby, and then, so quickly that she was completely taken by surprise, he took a step or two, and roughly putting his arm round her waist, kissed her soundly on the cheek.

'*Beial, beial*!' He laughed, and turned to go, but not before Debby had struck him a stinging blow across the face. '*Beial, beial*!' was his teasing reply, as he swaggered down the path after his keeper.

'The great big cheeky brute,' Debby began, flushed to the roots of her hair. 'The rogue! The ruffian!'

The Governor began to apologise. 'I'm sorry, Debby,' he said. 'I'm sure he was only copying someone he had seen kissing in my household. He meant no harm. Now come, you must forget it.'

But Mamma doubted if Debby would ever forget what she considered an insult. 'Oh, sir,' she said, 'but he kissed me! A black man!' and then went inside and with a clatter laid out the cups for Mamma.

When she had disappeared into the kitchen, Mamma asked the Governor, 'What do you think of that?'

'Just that he copies whatever he sees. Poor Debby! I must see that he doesn't do it again.' He smiled as he drank his tea. 'Are you satisfied now about his captivity?'

'Not exactly. I still hate to see him shackled, just as I hate to see the convicts in the stocks and in leg irons, but I think he is quite capable of looking after himself, and I think he could and would escape if he wanted to, in spite of all your precautions.'

'Excellently said, ma'am. I agree with you. Bennelong is no fool.'

Meanwhile, the children had followed Bennelong and his keeper.

'Get the spears,' Martin suggested, 'and let's see how far he can throw them.'

There never was such a spear-thrower. The spears whirred through the air to a distance of ninety feet. And with them followed such violent exclamations of rage and vengeance, that the children looked at Nanbaree for an explanation.

'He great fighter,' Nanbaree said. 'He throwing them at *Cammeraygal*,' and they smiled, for they knew that the *Cammeraygal*, the most powerful tribe on the north shore, were his bitterest foes.

Bennelong had become a never-ending interest to the girls always, and to the boys when they were free from their lessons.

As Christmas approached, Lieutenant Dawes told again in the classroom the story of the Child of Bethlehem, hoping the black girl and boy would understand. For Abaroo had come, and Sue and Jenny, because this was a special occasion. If they did understand, there was no sign. The story was just a story, for as yet the native children did not know enough to appreciate its meaning.

But they had already realised that Christmas was a time for feasting. Had not they heard mention of turtle and pudding and water-melon?

'Catch possum, bird?' Nanbaree suggested when Lieutenant Dawes let them go, and off they went towards the brickfields and the head of the stream.

'Yes,' said Sue, 'and get some of those red and yellow flowers like bells for Mamma,' knowing that Mamma had prized them the year before.

But they did not go together, for the girls knew that the boys would explore farther afield than they dared to go. Beyond the fringe of the settlement there were still the natives and the wild strange woods.

Nanbaree had never been so quick to track the tiny animals as he was that afternoon. They took the spears with them, and he used them to advantage. Their bag included a small rat-like kangaroo, a strange animal with quills like a porcupine, a fair-sized lizard, and what seemed to be a common rat.

'Poof!—we can't take that,' John protested, looking with revulsion at the rat, but Nanbaree laughed.

'*Beial, beial*,' he said, 'good, good,' and stopped to pick some white grubs from holes in a nearby gum-tree, which John had already discovered that he regarded as a great delicacy.

'And not those,' he protested again. 'Mamma would not eat those.'

'Good, good,' Nanbaree replied, and placing the grubs in his pocket and handing the other animals to the two boys, he bore the rat home in triumph.

Trekking across towards the head of the stream, they came upon the girls at a fairly deep basin where wild ducks and other water-fowl sometimes came to rest.

Nanbaree pulled up with a start, and made a gesture for the others to stop.

What was happening? Sue and Jenny were sitting quietly on the bank, flowers beside them, watching the water-birds as they flew down and floated on the surface of the water.

'Where's Abaroo?' asked John, but Nanbaree quickly silenced him. 'But why?' he began again, and was silenced this time by a loud squawking from the stream.

For out of it, seemingly from the depths, her head camouflaged by a lily leaf, Abaroo appeared, and in her hands she triumphantly held a wild duck.

'But how?' he asked mystified, yet full of admiration for her cleverness.

'Abaroo, under water,' explained Nanbaree. 'Bird on water. Abaroo catch feet.'

So that was it. What a clever way to catch birds! Mask one's face, then hide under a lily leaf in a water-hole or swamp, and wait for the birds to alight so as to grab one by the legs. Clever, yes, but when John remembered that she would have to hold her breath and remain still, he wondered if it were as easy as it appeared.

'Can you do it?' he asked Nanbaree.

But Nanbaree shrugged his shoulders. 'Abaroo,' he said, and by that John knew that as long as she caught birds like that, he would not exert himself.

Mamma was overcome when they all appeared at her door with the flowers and the duck and the lizard, the animals and the grubs.

'Chris'mas,' said Nanbaree simply.

'Well, that was nice of you,' she replied. 'But don't you think Abaroo should take the duck to Mrs Johnson with whom she lives? And perhaps you and Abaroo should keep the grubs for yourselves.'

John watched her smile as she spoke, guessing that she did not like the look of the 'disgusting' things, as Debby would call them. He was surprised when she accepted the lizard.

'I'll have that,' she said. 'It might taste like iguana. And of course the tiny kangaroo. I'll get Pete to skin it, and then perhaps Debby will make a pie.'

He could see that she was repulsed by the rat and the porcupine and came to the rescue. 'Could we keep the rat and the porcupine, Mamma, and roast them in the old kitchen?' he asked.

'If you like, dear, provided you take care not to burn yourselves.'

Here was a new pastime—roasting animals caught by Nanbaree in the fire-place of the old kitchen, now his bedroom! A fascinating pastime—eating without knives or forks or plates, tearing at the flesh with good strong teeth like Bennelong and Colbee.

They did not hear Debby say, when Mamma presented her with the tiny kangaroo and the lizard, and told her about the rat and the porcupine, 'Might as well get them used to eating anything, ma'am, now that food is becoming so short.'

They lit the fire, but were horrified when Nanbaree wanted to put the animals on the embers and roast them as they were.

'No, no,' John cried, and ran off for a butcher's knife.

'Of course not,' said Martin. 'White boys don't eat fur and quills and the insides.'

As for Jenny and Sue, they were beginning to wonder if they wanted any at all. But their appetites were whetted when John had skinned the animals, and the delicious smell of roasting flesh began to fill the hut.

Nanbaree picked up the entrails and placed them on the fire. 'Nanbaree and Abaroo eat,' he said, and the others were quite willing to let them have the offal.

The porcupine was so delicious that they devoured it with relish, smacking their lips; the rat—well, a rat was always a rat, so Martin observed, and they left most of it to Abaroo and Nanbaree, as well as, of course, the entrails.

'Maybe if one were hungry,' John said, as Nanbaree remembered the grubs and, producing them from his pocket, placed them on the ashes.

'Eat,' he said, offering each a grub when they were roasted, but Sue turned up her nose in disgust, and John and Martin and Jenny declined.

'What, a-eating grubs?' sounded a deep voice from the door, and they looked up and saw Cookie. 'Well, maybe ye'll be eating worse afore long.'

'Eat,' cried Nanbaree, offering him one.

'Can't turn a good thing down.' He winked at them, and popped it in his mouth. 'H'm, like marrow!' he declared. 'Now what d'ye think o' that? Ha' ye got another?' And when he had eaten, 'Tastier than weevils, young John. Ye had better learn to eat 'em.'

After that, the boys had a try, eating with their eyes closed, and decided that Cookie had been right. But the girls could not be coaxed. It was the ugliness of the grubs that made them so repulsive.

'Well, what d'ye think I ha' brought this time? It be sitting on your Mamma's mantelpiece.'

'The egg!' cried John, and he was up and away, followed by the others.

'The egg!' they cried, and gathered round to admire the fine painting that Cookie had placed on it of the *Sirius* in full sail.

'Be ye pleased?' he asked John, and the boy nodded.

'It's fine, Cookie. Isn't it, Mamma?'

'Yes, indeed,' she said. 'Now we'll always have the *Sirius* with us, even when she is not here.'

John placed his hand in Cookie's gnarled one. 'Thank you, Cookie,' he said. 'I'll keep it always in remembrance of you.'

The next day was Christmas Day, hot and humid, which made them think of England far away, and the snow that possibly blanketed the earth, and the tall straight forms of the leafless trees, and the robin redbreast pecking at the window for crumbs.

Mamma took them to church under the great tree, and then, gathering Nanbaree and Jenny and Martin's family, ushered them all back to have the first Christmas dinner in the new house.

There Cookie joined them, and they manfully ate of the hot fare that Debby had so laboriously prepared--pie, turtle steak, and raisin pudding, over which Papa poured some brandy and set it alight. Then what fun they had, especially Nanbaree, as they plunged their hands into the flames to grab the very last of Mamma's raisins. They were soon so hot that it was almost a relief to turn to the water-melon.

Over at the Governor's house, Bennelong sampled the turtle steak and asked for more and more and more.

For amusement afterwards, when all had gathered to pay their respects to the Governor, Bennelong danced and capered as he had never done before, while Abaroo beat her hands to keep time, and Nanbaree clicked two sticks.

'The ships haven't come,' Mr Johnson, the parson, afterwards reminded Mamma, as they walked homewards. He had remembered that Mamma had said, the year before, that their coming would be her best Christmas present.

'No, but I have my house, and you will soon have one, too,' she replied.

But the thought of the ships cast a gloom over the festivities. When would they come? Two years now, and no ships from England to bring more food!

'If they're not here by next Christmas, ma'am,' Debby said, 'we'll be living like the black men—wearing no clothes and eating rats and porcupines like the children.'

'They must come, Debby. The Governor expects them any day. He's putting up a lookout at the South Head to watch for them.'

John knew that men went over to Botany Bay each week to see if the ships had gone there—and now in addition there was to be this lookout.

'At the South Head,' he repeated. That would be another place to go with Martin. Someone would be sure to be stationed there—Dan, perhaps?

He looked at the mantelpiece where Cookie's emu egg stood beside the ostrich egg that they had brought from Capetown, and he rejoiced in its possession. Any Christmas that gave him such a gift was a day to remember.

And when, next day, Papa told him that Caesar had returned and stolen a musket from Garden Island, and gone off again, he felt that even this was like a greeting from a friend.

It wasn't such a bad Christmas, in spite of the ships that did not come.

CHAPTER XIV

AS STOWAWAYS TO NORFOLK ISLAND

WITH Christmas over, there was no thought in anyone's mind except the ships that did not come.

It was now 1790. Early in January, Captain Hunter went down to the South Head with some of his men to erect a flagstaff and build a hut for those who were to watch there. From the observatory the boys looked each day for the pole, and when they saw it for the first time, they rushed to tell Lieutenant Dawes.

'It's up,' they cried. 'We can see it. Look down there to the ridge. We'll see the flag run up when the ships arrive,' and even then they lived in imagination what a great day that would be.

They were on the tiptoe of expectation. If a rumble of thunder was heard in the sky, or a gun resounded in the woods, 'The ships!' they would cry and rush to the window to look for the flag.

But the days went by and no ships came. Captain Hunter returned, and Lieutenant Bradley went down to take charge of the Lookout. The *Supply* set sail for Norfolk Island. But still the ships did not come.

Towards the end of the month Caesar returned. The boys saw him being led into the hospital in a sorry condition.

'Yes, indeed, the rascal,' Mr White told them, when they asked after him. 'He has been brought down from Rose Hill, and a tale he will have to tell, I'm sure.'

Bit by bit they heard that tale, for Mamma sent them over with some broth, and they were allowed to see him.

'Want ter know what happen'd, eh?' he said, answering their questions with a wink. 'Foun' a way dis time ter git food, I did. Stole a musket fum de islan', den rusht 'ponder natives as dey wuz roun' der camp-fires eatin', an' dey lef' me de meal. I sure got wits y'know. But I lost de musket in a gar'n at Rose Hill when der guards chas'd me. Arter dat der natives, dey drew der spears, an' now I be in a mighty bad fix, see,' and he pointed to the bandages that enveloped his arms and legs and body, and gave him the appearance of a wounded soldier home from the wars.

'And you did live in the woods for a month, Caesar,' John said.

'I did, m'lad, an' I foun' out sumf'n. Come close, an' I'll tell you. D'you r'member de cattle dat wuz lost at Sydney Cove? I seen 'em.'

'You saw them?'

'Yes. Dah wuz two calves wid 'em.'

'But how? And where?'

'Out o' Rose Hill, lad. Natives hav' 'em. Mus' hav' been natives dat drove 'em 'way. I done try to bring der cattle back, an' dat's when I got de spears. I's a hero, y'know,' and he winked at them again.

John blurted out Caesar's story at supper that night, expecting it to be hailed joyfully.

He was rather surprised when Papa laughed it to scorn. 'So Caesar has been telling you that tale, too,' he said. 'Well, you can take it from me, John, that Caesar never saw a sign of those cattle. He's just telling lies to see if he can save himself from the punishment he expects. Always going off into the woods and robbing the gardens and doing everything he shouldn't. He deserves what he got from the natives.'

'Oh, Richard, aren't you being hard on him? He might have seen the cattle.'

'Yes, Papa, truly!'

But Papa was quite convinced. 'Lies, lies, that's what the Governor thinks, and so do we all.' Mamma and John exchanged glances. Both knew that they each had a sneaking hope that Caesar had seen those cattle, and that some day the cattle would be found.

'Poor fellow,' Mamma sighed. 'He escapes only because he wants to be free.'

Mamma grew more worried each day. In addition to food, she now had to think of clothes. Sue and John had but one pair of shoes left, and one outfit that was really presentable. She had patched and turned the rest, and remade her own and Papa's clothes for them.

'Real ragamuffins,' she called them, as she watched them go around in worn and faded garments. 'But they are at least tidy.'

'Well, if you had not given those clothes to the convicts, ma'am, if I may say so—' Debby began.

'Now, now, Debby,' Mamma reproved. 'You know I could not help doing that, and it did win their loyalty.'

'Yes I know, ma'am. 'Tis one of the lovely things about you—your thought for others. For me especially, when you took me out of the rain and the night. God bless you, ma'am. You'll have your reward when the ships come.'

But they did not come. On 12th February the *Supply* returned with no turtle but continued reports of an abundance of vegetables on Norfolk Island.

'And the birds, ye never did see such crowds and crowds,' Cookie told the children as he distributed plantains which he had brought. 'There be millions and trillions, and 'tis nothing to catch a thousand in a night. Just pick 'em from their burrows when they a-come in at dusk from a-feeding in the sea.'

'Do you think we'll ever go there?' John asked wistfully.

'Maybe, maybe. I'll think o' it. Want to be cabin-boy, again, eh?'

'Any way, Cookie, as long as Martin and I can see those birds in their thousands and millions and trillions...'

And then came startling news, news that the boys believed could definitely fulfil their dearest wish. They heard the story in half a dozen places round the Cove. Instead of going to China for food, the *Sirius* was to sail immediately with the *Supply* for Norfolk Island. And she was to take hundreds of people from Sydney Cove to live there.

'Perhaps we'll go,' John said to Martin, and made for home.

Cookie had just brought some fish, and Mamma and Sue were standing with him in the garden when John rushed through the front gate.

'Mamma, Mamma, some of us are going to Norfolk Island.'

'Norfolk Island?' Mamma repeated. 'Do you know anything of this, Cookie?'

'Aye, ma'am, Gov'nor thinks more food can be grown on Norfolk, and there be more birds and fish, and he be a-sending some folks from here in the *Sirius*. Heard it acoming up from the wharf, I did.'

'Then maybe we'll really go to Norfolk Island and see those birds,' John cried joyfully.

'Yes,' said Sue, 'and have plantains every day.'

'And what o' your Mamma? I be sure she would rather stay wi' her house and garden. Eh, ma'am?'

Mamma smiled rather sadly, so John thought. 'I would, Cookie—of course I would, but my husband's a soldier, and if he is sent, then I must go too.' And for the first time John realised that it would be a great wrench to part Mamma from her house and garden.

As soon as Papa came home, the children plied him with questions. Was it true that some of the people at Sydney Cove were going to Norfolk Island? Why? When? Were they to go, too?

'Yes, what is it to be?' Mamma asked, quietly standing by.

'We are to stay here,' he answered simply. So there were to be no birds, no plantains, but Mamma would be happy.

'Then who is to go?' she inquired.

'Two companies of marines and about two hundred convicts. Lieutenant King is to come back on the *Sirius* and to go to England to make the Government realise that we need food regularly. Major Ross is to take his place as Lieutenant-Governor at Norfolk Island.'

'Well, that's one good thing,' Mamma remarked rather coldly. 'He'll certainly be no loss.' She did not like the carping, critical Major, for he had never tried to co-operate with the Governor.

John was impatient to meet Martin the next morning. He was relieved when Martin told him that his father wasn't going to Norfolk Island either. John could not bear to be parted from Martin. They had been through so much, and if they were to meet those birds, it would have to be together.

'Oh, Cookie, we're not going!' they moaned, when next they met him.

'Aye, and 'tis a good thing. Norfolk be a grand place, but your Mammas, they both ha' their roots here now.'

'And we won't see the birds in their millions.'

'No, that ye will not. I'll tell ye what,' and he lowered his voice: 'I'll take ye down the harbour in the *Supply* the day we sail. Some o' the gentlemen be sure to come a-down and go back by cutter when we get to the Heads. Ye can come home with them. Understand?' and they knew that he wanted them to make a secret of this adventure. 'I'll ask your Mammas, but no one else must know.'

Midshipman Dan, too, was very disappointed that he was not going on the *Sirius*. 'The Governor says I must take charge of the Lookout while the ship's away,' he told Mamma when he came to see her. 'I suppose he means to honour me, but I'd much rather go with her to Norfolk Island. Perhaps the boys will be able to come and stay a few days...'

Well, that would be something. If they couldn't go on the *Sirius*, they could at least visit the Lookout.

The Cove was very busy in the days that followed. Three hundred all told were about to embark. The convicts had few belongings to gather together and pack, but some had poultry and vegetables which they were willing to barter for clothes and money. The marines had livestock, too, and Mamma, always wise in these matters, took care to add to her collection by the purchase of another goat as well as some more fowls and pigs.

'A real farm,' Debby called the place now. 'We just want a horse, ma'am, and a plough, and some haystacks, and we'll be right.'

Mamma smiled at her joke, and remembered that there was not a plough in Sydney Cove.

'I don't know what the men in the Government were thinking about when they sent us out without a plough,' she sighed.

'Yes, ma'am, and not enough beds for the women, and bowls too small, and tools so bad that they broke into pieces at first using. And there be those convict women with not a strand of thread to mend their clothes falling to pieces on their bodies. Now if a woman had been ordering these things, she'd have ordered plenty, don't you think so, ma'am? And good things, too!' Debby was always so impatient of blundering.

'Never mind, there'll be some soon on the ships,' Mamma reminded her.

'When they come,' Debby sniffed, and then made a remark that both remembered the next day. 'You know, ma'am, I have a feeling those convicts are eating hearty tonight. When I came up from the Cove a little while ago, there seemed to be a smell of roast fowl and duck everywhere. Just like Christmas, it was.'

'But, Debby, how could it be?'

'Well, it was, ma'am, and I couldn't help thinking those convicts were all killing their birds and eating them. The Governor said that the ones going on the ships could kill, but you take it from me, there's more than those killing.'

'It would be dreadful if they were.' Mamma was horrified at the thought. 'That would mean no more eggs or chickens or ducklings. They wouldn't be so foolish.'

But that was just what the convicts were doing. All round the Cove they were eating heartily. Roast duck, roast turkey, roast fowl—there never was such a feast since they first arrived at Sydney Cove. In the morning the greater part of their livestock had been gobbled up and was no more.

'Thought the Governor was going to take their birds from them, I suppose,' Debby muttered grimly, 'and they made sure they were going to keep them, even in their own stomachs.'

'And is he?' Mamma asked Papa.

'No, but he is determined that in future they must get his permission to kill.'

'And them about to get the gardens of those who leave,' Debby went on bitterly. 'There'll be many a lazy one who has never planted a turnip or a potato will now have whole beds full of them grown by someone else. The worthless rascals!'

On 3rd March, with colours flying, the two companies of marines marched to the water's edge, and were rowed out to the ships.

'Convicts' turn tomorrow,' Cookie told the boys, 'and yours, too, for a short trip down the harbour. We sail the day after. Ye'll ha' to be aboard the night afore, for it'll be early in the morning,' and he winked at them broadly.

'Good-bye, Mamma,' John called, when Cookie came for him and Martin. 'I'll be back tomorrow.'

Mamma was glad they were to have this enjoyment. Sydney Cove, once so busy, was desolate and lonely now that so many had gone.

'Let them be happy,' she told Debby. 'We don't know what is in front of us.'

Debby was amusing Sue and Jenny by cutting out some dolls' dresses from bits of old clothes, because they were feeling once more that they had been left out of an adventure.

As for Nanbaree, he knew nothing about it, for it was now dusk, and he was well at home with Mr White, his guardian.

The ship's great light at the stern was winking at them as the small boat drew alongside, and they leapt into the *Supply*, and down into the galley.

It was fine to be back, John thought, among the pots and pans, remembering the long days he had spent in it when he was a cabin-boy on the way from Capetown to Botany Bay.

'See, I ha' a hammock for each o' ye,' Cookie told them, 'and mind the rats, they don't tickle your toes.'

John grinned. That was an old joke with Cookie.

Before six in the morning they were away—a gusty squally day.

'If I be a-thinking right, we won't get out o' the Heads—' Cookie winked at them again—' and ye two boys, ye'll be wi' me another night.'

'But, Cookie, haven't we to go back?'

'Aye, I ha' forgot. Some o' the gentlemen be on the *Sirius*, saying good-bye. They'll take ye back,' and much to their surprise he winked again.

Cookie was right. When the Heads came in sight, there was so much sea that the ships were forced to anchor off a little island low down in the harbour.

'Till tomorrow, I guess. I said ye' d be wi' me for another night,' he told the boys, and they did not mind.

But with the coming of the new day they asked once more, 'When are we to go back, Cookie?'

He looked at them and winked again. 'Too late now,' he said. 'The gentlemen, they did go back yesterday. Ye see, they forgot. Now wasn't that strange?'

'You mean we can't go back?' they cried together.

'Aye, that I do. Ye'll ha' to come on now, but ye'll ha' to work your way, see. Cap'n o' this ship, John, ye know, be Lieutenant Ball. He says he can't spare a boat to take ye back to Sydney Cove, and that ye'll ha' to help me in this galley.'

It was too good to believe! They would go to Norfolk Island, they would see the birds, they would gather plantains for Sue and Jenny...

'But, Cookie,' John hesitated, when he thought of it,' what about Mamma? And Martin's mother? They won't know.'

'Aye, they will. We'll send a signal to the Lookout, and your friend, Dan, will tell them. But I don't know what ye'll do wi'out clothes!'

Clothes! They would wear anything—canvas petticoats and smocks—anything to be able to go to Norfolk Island and the millions and trillions of birds. They might even see Lord Howe's Island.

They asked no questions, but they believed Cookie had something to do with it. Wasn't that why he had winked so broadly at them?

CHAPTER XV

LORD HOWE'S ISLAND

FOUR days out from Port Jackson, the *Sirius* and *Supply* did approach Lord Howe's Island.

'Where is it? Where is it?' the boys asked Cookie when he called them to look from the port of the galley. They had heard so much about it, they were impatient to see the famous island from which the turtles came.

It was a fine sight and a fine island, with two mountains, one cone-shaped and the other square-topped, and a low shore to the north-west sweeping round like a crescent and breaking away into a jumble of rocky islets.

'Aye, a pretty little island, like a piece o' jade in a blue setting,' Cookie called it. 'The cap'n, he did call those mountains Gower and Lidgbird the first time we did pass on the way to Norfolk Island.'

'Will anyone go ashore?' they asked eagerly.

'Aye, Lieutenant Ball, he be a-going to visit Cap'n Hunter on the *Sirius* to ask for permission to go and turn turtle.'

'Then we'll be going in?'

'Aye, I guess so, and maybe ye'll get a chance to turn one; and if ye don't, there'll be birds by the millions just a-waiting to ha' a look at ye.'

'Oh, Cookie!' Norfolk Island they had expected, and now it was to be Lord Howe too! They were certainly being lucky.

The morning was well advanced when the *Supply* stood into the bay at the north-west, to allow the boats to make their way through the reef to the low shore, whose white sands showed up so clearly against the deep green background of palms and more palms.

'I ha' only been on this island but once,' he told the boys, 'and cap'n, he has given me permission to go again. 'Take your boys, too," he said, and here we be a-waiting for the boats.'

John and Martin looked at Cookie gratefully. He had a way of getting them their dearest wish, and it had happened again. To go with the sailors would have been exciting enough; to go with Cookie was all that they desired.

They looked at the great mountains rising straight and naked from the sea, only their sloping saddles rich with the thickness of trees and vines and palms and ferns.

Those mountains were certainly lovely; rugged and massive, but gentle in the morning sunlight; mountains to remember always, to picture in their minds when they were far away.

This Lord Howe's Island fascinated them—it and the tiny islands threaded like a curving necklace before them.

And now they were going ashore. They clambered down into the pinnace and waited for more adventure.

They had it, too, when the pinnace nosed its way through the reef, where the seas broke endlessly in a white swirl.

'Got to be sure o' the right opening,' Cookie told them, 'or the cruel rocks, they'll rip the bottom. That be what happened to Cap'n Cook.'

There were a couple of close shaves before the coxen found the way in and brought his boat through the fast flowing channel into the quiet of the lagoon.

'Ha!' exclaimed Cookie. 'Now if ye look into the water as we come a-closer in, ye may see a thing or two.'

'What, Cookie, what?' they cried, but he would not tell.

John saw it first, a glimpse of colours—red, blue, green—under the water.

'What is it, Cookie? What is it?'

'Coral, o' course! Ha' ye not heard o' coral? Think ye it be white? Nay, it be vermilion and jade and sapphire and lilac, and all the colours there be. Sprigs like flowers, pillars like organ pipes, leaves like lettuce—aye, and crawly bits like sheep's brains. Ye shall see. Ye shall see.'

They were close to the silvery beach now, and they could see that it was whiter than any beach they had known.

'Made o' coral sand,' Cookie said. Bits flung off the rocks and a-broken by the pounding o' the waves.'

As soon as they could, they jumped from the bow on to the beach, and almost immediately stopped to pick up something that took their fancy.

'See, John,' cried Martin, 'a piece of sponge.'

'Yes, and a piece of that coral that Cookie said was like brains.'

So many things lay strewn on the beach-shells in their myriads, sea-eggs, seaweed of many shapes and colours.

'Come on, come on,' called Cookie. 'I did not bring ye here to a-pick up baubles. Look ahead! Look ahead!'

They drew themselves up and could scarcely believe their eyes. So absorbed had they been in the wonders on the beach that they had forgotten for the moment the birds. And there they were before them at the head of the bay—seeming millions of birds walking about without fear like geese in a farmyard, millions of birds winging up into the sky to darken the sun.

'No, it couldn't be. There couldn't be so many as that,' John murmured, and yet there were.

'Gannets,' Cookie called them. 'It's their rookery. They be a-bringing up their young. Black and white the big ones, and white mottled with brown the young fellows. We'll ha' gannet soup for supper. Eh, what?'

He followed the sailors up the beach and, bending, picked up a young bird. The boys did the same. The larger birds made no protest; they merely walked around as tamely as if they had been pets. John grabbed one by the neck, and was surprised when he held it.

'Goodness,' he said to Martin, 'we could catch enough of these birds to feed everyone in Sydney Cove. I wish Mamma and Sue could have some.'

Only when they made a commotion, cried aloud, or waved their arms, would the birds scatter to some ledge of rock that provided a runway, and take wing, but they soon came back to attend to their young.

'Oh, Cookie!' was all the boys could say.

'Aye, I told ye so. And now we'll go a little way into the woods, and I'll show ye some more.'

It was rough walking, for they had to squeeze between the thick vegetation, but they did not mind scratches in the wonder of that great natural aviary.

For there were birds of many kinds—pigeons that sat in the trees and allowed the boys to take them off with their hands; coots and wood-hens that ran a few steps, then stopped, almost waiting for someone to come up and seize them; parrots and parrakeets that eyed them in friendly fashion from above; tiny grey-capped black birds that remained on the tips of their fingers or their shoulders or heads, entirely without fear.

'But why are they so tame?' John asked Cookie, in wonder.

''Cos there be nothing to kill them, I be a-thinking—not animals o' any kind. They know not man—nor rat, nor dog, nor cat.'

Now the boys were having a game to see which could entice the greatest number of birds to himself. It was so easy, with birds all around them, at their feet, winging above.

Such lovely creatures they were, too—pigeons with head and breast of purple mauve, the throat white, the mantle or back of the neck green, the rest of the body brown; the coot or fowl, some bluish-grey and white, some blue with red bills; the wood-hen, dusky brown; parrakeets of green and red and blue.

'Aren't you going to kill any?' Cookie asked them, smiling.

'Kill them? Oh, Cookie, how could we? We'd like to take them away in a cage and keep them.'

'And that would be crueller than a-killing them,' Cookie reminded them. 'Ye came ashore to get food, ye know,' he told them with a sly smile. 'We ha' got to ha' fresh meat.'

But no coaxing would make the boys wring the necks of such lovely creatures.

'The sailors can do that,' they said, and from the noise of whacking sticks and triumphant shouts, they were sure that there would be plenty of birds for them to pluck.

The vegetation had changed as they went farther into the woods. As well as palms in plenty there was a strange tree with many roots like the guy ropes of a tent meeting to form one hardy trunk.

It was Cookie who decided that they had gone far enough.

'Got to do something to earn our passage ashore,' he said. 'If ye won't kill these birds, I'll show ye something else,' and he turned and led them back towards the beach.

Soon they were floundering in sand—loose, greyish-black sand, and could not understand why their feet did not get a firm footing. First one leg up to the shin, and when they extricated that, they found that the other had plunged into an equally unruly morass.

Cookie waded his way across, and then stood and laughed at them.

'Come on, ye boobies. Slow-coaches ye be. There still be the turtles.'

Yes, turtles—but how could they get towards him?

'You're having a joke with us,' they complained.

'Nay, nay, 'tis birds' burrows ye be a-falling into; the birds, they be at sea-ye look there, black lines of 'em a-fishing. When we come a-back we might be able to catch one—come a-flying in at dusk they do, and land at your feet, just like that.'

As if to explain what he meant, one did come flying in right at his feet, and Cookie picked it up in his hands like any old tame duck that ever waddled in a farmyard.

'Come on,' he cried, letting the bird walk away. 'We were ordered to turn turtle.'

But there were no turtles. He trudged them along the beach, teaching them to look for marks in the sand, high up near the line of palms.

'Ye see, the turtle, it comes up to lay its eggs, so they say, and puffs and sighs and crawls, and puffs and sighs and crawls, until it gets beyond the tide-mark, then digs a hole and lays its eggs. So, ye see, it leaves a mark upon the sand, and if ye be lucky, ye will find the turtle up there a-laying eggs, or a-flurrying back to the water.'

'And then what do you do?' they asked.

'Turn it,' said Cookie triumphantly.

'Turn it?' they repeated.

'Aye, and then the turtle, it can't get away like. Leave it a-floundering and a-flurrying and a-sighing in the sand, ye do, and then come along with the boat and a-heave it on board.'

Marks were there, high beyond the tide-mark, but no turtles, only a few dead ones smaller than the palms of their hands.

'Young ones come from the egg,' he told them. ''Tis too late for turtle now. Ye'll ha' to wring the necks o' some of those duck-like birds.'

But not until they had waded into the lagoon and looked into a coral pool—with its myriad colours of lilac and green and yellow and blue and red, the tiny striped rainbow-like fish that darted from side to side, the brilliant lips of the clams waiting to clamp down on the body of any luckless creature that passed into their shells...

'Now watch, now watch, ye little ninny,' Cookie warned, when John pointed his toe at one, and suddenly saw the brilliant lip disappear. 'It could a-grab your foot and break your bones, and there'd be no getting ye back to your Mamma safe and sound. Sometimes I do think ye ha' no sense. Martin, here, he doesn't do such silly things.'

John lowered his head, and walked slowly up the beach. For a few moments he felt abashed, because Martin was always being held up as an example to him. But he was too interested in his surroundings to dwell on Cookie's reproof, and if he had he would have remembered that he was the old man's favourite, and would have immediately forgotten.

A few of the black birds were returning early from fishing, and landed with a squawk and a clatter close to his feet.

'Petrel or shearwater,' Cookie called them. 'We'll wring the neck o' one or two and have a good feed.'

The boys were ready. Within minutes they had a fire going, and Cookie provided the fare.

'Let's cook them as the black men do,' John suggested, and so they did, singeing the feathers, and laying the birds on the hot coals.

It was a delicious meal, out there in the bright sunshine, with the mountains rising forbiddingly behind them, and the white sand and blue bay stretching out before them.

'Now a few more, and we'll join the sailors,' Cookie said, and, taunted by him, the boys tried their hand at killing a few, and, so loaded, they returned to the boat.

Seated in the bow, they did not look at the mass of slaughtered birds the seamen had brought. They knew that they would have more than their share of plucking them; they knew, too, that when cooked they would enjoy the tasty morsels as well as any. But for the moment they could not forget the beauty and trustfulness of the birds they had handled and petted.

'I do wish we could have taken some back to Mamma and Sue,' John whispered, 'just to keep in cages,' and then he wondered if Mamma would not have regarded them as a good dinner. He knew Debby would.

That was the strange thing about Lord Howe's Island. When one heard of it, and of the birds in their millions, one wanted, in hunger and longing for fresh meat, to knock them down in hundreds and gorge and gorge and gorge, but when one was there it seemed so different. One wanted to kill just a few for oneself, just a few, and leave the rest to live their lives in freedom.

By nightfall they were back on the *Supply*—plucking, plucking, plucking! John got up for a moment and, going to the port, thought of those millions and millions of birds settling down to sleep. In the fading light he could still see the two mountains like dark blobs against the horizon.

'Now come on,' Cookie called. 'Ye had a holiday today. There be no time to waste a-thinking o' those birds—only these dead ones.'

Walking back, John stood and looked at the pile.

'Are the birds on Norfolk Island like these, Cookie?' he asked.

'Ye mean the' ones that a-come in millions? Aye, they be like the petrel we caught and ate, but they be not the same. Different colour, they be, although they burrow in the ground just like those other birds. Maybe ye shall see.'

John began his plucking again. Birds, birds, birds! Would they never end? And it was for the birds that he and Martin had wanted to come with Cookie on this voyage. To see so many birds. Well, they had seen them, and it had been a grand sight. But they had not thought of this plucking. Never mind: a day, and the crew would be back on salt pork.

Cookie took a small bird from the spit and gave it to them, just to spur them on. They spent some time eating it, enjoying every morsel.

'I suppose one has to kill birds to live,' said John thoughtfully.

'Aye,' announced Cookie. 'Just that. The birds, they had happy lives and quick deaths, and now they help us to live. When we be hungry, we cannot be sentimental like. Come on, start again.'

CHAPTER XVI

THE SIRIUS IS WRECKED

FOUR more days, and the boys woke to find another island lying low and flat on the horizon.

'It's Norfolk,' cried John, 'I know it is, Cookie. The dark parts are the trees-pine-trees enough for all the navies in the world, you said.'

'Aye, indeed, and a small mountain at one end. D'ye see it? Mount Pitt we did call it, after the Prime Minister.' He came and gazed out over their shoulders. 'Guess what ye' d find there?'

'Birds--the birds you've told us about so often!'

'Aye, Mount Pitt birds! Petrels somewhat like those ye did see on Lord Howe's Island. Come here in millions they do about this time o' the year.'

John and Martin hung out of the port and watched the island come closer, until it was there before them--no longer low and flat, but wild, precipitous, and strange.

'Washed by a skirt o' white spume a-flouncing and a-flurrying at the foot o' the reddish cliffs,' was the way Cookie described it. 'I told ye it was like that.'

'But how shall we land?' John asked in dismay.

'Ye'll see, lad. Ye'll see. Maybe ye'll ha' to go ashore and jump on a rock. Aye, and mighty quick ye'll ha' to be.'

'Oh, Cookie!'

'Aye, but if the wind does not blow from the south, ye'll land in Sydney Bay, and that won't be so exciting. When we a-come here first, we did sail round and round a-looking for a place to land. Such a wild shore I never did see. Six days we searched.'

'And then?'

'Mr King, he did find a way through the reef into this Sydney Bay in the south, and made the settlement there. 'Tis sheltered by two islands; Phillip's Isle and Nepean's Isle, he called them after the Gov'nor and Mr Nepean. When the southerly does not blow, it be all right for landing.'

'Where is it? This Sydney Bay?' they asked impatiently.

'Ye'll see soon. We be a-going round now to find out if the landing be safe. Look, there be the islands, one like a sugar loaf peak and t' other a flat coral cay. And there be the settlement with the folks mighty excited, a-running here and there, a-thinking maybe we be the ships from England.'

They were certainly hurrying from all directions across the flat land edging the beach, where their huts nestled against a background of rugged hills on which the great pine-trees ranged higher and higher.

'Ha!' Cookie sighed gloomily. ''Tis as I thought. Signal's not up on the lower flagstaff, so we can't go in.'

One look, and even the boys knew that there would be no landing in Sydney Bay that day, for the south-west winds were driving the seas shoreward to smash on the reef and surge on into the beach.

'Then, where will we go, Cookie?'

'To Cascade, maybe, in the north-east. Got two streams o' water a-cascading down, one on each side. That be where the rock juts out into the water for folks to land on. Aye, and mighty quick ye'll ha' to be if ye go ashore at Cascade, mind ye.'

'Do you think we will?' they asked.

'Aye, maybe. I did think I'd like to show ye the birds on Mount Pitt.'

'Oh, Cookie, that would be fine!'

They watched impatiently until the signals went up for the ships to proceed to Cascade.

'Hurrah!' cried John. The notion of landing on a rock pleased him.

'Come on, get back to your work,' Cookie scolded him. 'Ye won't be able to go ashore unless ye help wi' dinner. And set not your mind 'pon it yet, for the winds here, they'll a-blow up and send us out t'sea maybe.'

But Cookie could not stop them taking a peep through the port, as the first boat with a load of convicts approached the shore.

The rock was plain to see—a black mound on the eastern side of the bay, abutting into the water but not quite adjoining the stony shingle of the beach. Behind lay a valley flanked by high pyramidal cliffs, brilliantly red against the dark green vegetation.

'There it is! There it is!' cried John, pointing, and then Cookie grabbed him by the backside of the pants and told him to run off with some rum to Mr Ball.

'And you, too, Martin. Take this to Mr Blackburn.'

Neither boy realised that it was Cookie's way of getting them on deck, so that they could see more clearly what was happening.

The boat was well in to the shore now. It was being backed stern-foremost towards the rock on the smooth water in between the swells. A man was standing up ready to jump. And—he had made it! Yes, he was there, leaping from rock to shingle, and the boat was being backed out almost instantaneously lest it be dashed against the rocks. A smooth patch had come again, and the boat was being rowed in a second time; another man was jumping ashore. Mighty quick he had to be, too, as Cookie had said, for if he slipped he would be cut on the rocks, or sucked into the outgoing swell and carried out into the sea and drowned.

'Ah, here you are!' Lieutenant Ball said to John, when the boy offered the rum. 'And itching to get in that boat, I suppose, to perform that jumping feat. But not today, lad; there are too many others to go ashore. Remember, you really shouldn't be here,' and he smiled broadly.

So there was nothing to do but to watch, in between bouts of work and half-hearted scolding from Cookie.

After dinner the marines from the *Sirius* began to land, and later a boat full of women convicts and their children were rowed past the *Supply* on their way to the rock.

Cookie watched with the boys from the port, a worried frown between his brows.

'If they don't get a-scared, it'll be all right,' he said quietly. 'As long as a sea don't catch 'em,' and he spoke what he saw, for a wave at that moment broke and half filled the boat. 'The poor things! D'ye see them? Won't stay still. A-jumping up in the boat and a-standing! Nervous like. They'll be swamped! Swamped!'

'Oh my!' John exclaimed, expecting to see half of them drowned, then watched almost with awe, as the sailors, by their patience and skill, rowed the boat backwards and forwards at the right moment to land everyone safely on the rock.

'There won't be many more to go,' Cookie said, as they watched Major Ross rowed ashore. 'Tide's getting too high.'

It was in fact already too high, for Major Ross returned to the *Sirius* and did not land until the next morning, when again the unloading was continued, the boats ferrying across the rest of the marines and the male convicts, much of the baggage, and even some of the pigs and geese and turkeys that had been brought from Sydney Cove.

John watched the marines form into lines and march off up a steep hill on their way to the settlement at Sydney Bay, and the convicts straggling in the same direction.

'Oh, Cookie,' he said, 'and we didn't get ashore today either!'

'Never mind, there's always tomorrow,' Cookie told him gaily. 'We ha' nearly done what we be set to do. Landed nigh three hundred o' marines and convicts, ye know. I guess Cap'n Hunter be glad. But there be a few more women and the stores yet. Tomorrow we'll go ashore, ye and Martin and me, and stay all night p'raps, to climb that Mount Pitt and see the birds.'

But again the weather was against them. As soon as the women were landed, the wind shifted to the east, and a gale blew the ships right out to sea.

'Oh dear! Oh dear!' moaned John. 'We'll never get there.'

'Yes, we will,' Cookie assured him. 'There still be the stores. Can't go back to Sydney Cove wi'out a-leaving 'em. Folk can't live wi'out food, and Cap'n Hunter'll be anxious like to send the food after the folk, else they might starve. He must get it ashore.'

Indeed he was so anxious about them, that he began to send some over to the *Supply*, because he believed that the *Supply* had a better chance of getting into Sydney Bay than the *Sirius*.

It was then, as the boats made trips backwards and forwards between the *Sirius* and *Supply*, that the unexpected happened.

'What d'ye think?' Cookie announced. 'Cap'n Hunter, he ha' just heard about ye, and he says ye ha' to go aboard the *Sirius*. Maybe he'll mast ye.'

Both boys were silent. To be placed up there on the mast in the wind and the rain for hours was not very pleasant.

'But, Cookie, it wasn't our fault,' John began to protest. You forgot.'

'Aye, and so I did,' Cookie agreed with a smile, for he was only teasing. 'Why, the truth be, cook on the *Sirius* be gone sick, and Cap'n Hunter says I'm to go across and take his place, and ye are to come wi' me. I got to look after ye, now that I forgot,' and he gave them a wink.

It was the kind of adventure that they accepted joyfully to climb down the ladder into the boat heaving alongside on the swell of the seas, to row across sitting amid the casks of pork and biscuit, and to climb again precariously up the side of the *Sirius*.

Sirius! John returned to her proudly. His ship! The ship in which he and Mamma and Papa and Sue had set out from Portsmouth long ago to come to the new land of New South Wales. No other ship could ever be quite as much his ship as the *Sirius*!

Captain Hunter stood on the quarter-deck. 'Ah,' he said, when he saw them, 'I heard there were some laddies on the *Supply* that shouldna' be there, an' sae they're young fellows called John an' Martin, eh?' Then he continued in a sterner tone, 'Cook, see that we return these laddies tae their mithers safe an' soond, an' see that they dinna' leave the galley wi' oot your orders.'

'Surely he does not mean that,' John said as they went below.

'Aye, indeed,' Cookie reminded him. 'Means every word. No more running about in this ship for ye. Cap'n Hunter won't stand for loafers. Ye'll see.'

'Perhaps the captain won't let us go ashore,' John said mournfully as he thought matters over. 'Then we won't see the birds.'

'Maybe not,' Cookie replied. 'Maybe not.'

The next day John and Martin went about their duties with less vigour. The ships were now off Sydney Bay, and on one of their many glimpses through the port, they saw the *Supply* sail into the roads.

'Oh, Cookie, we've missed our chance!' they both moaned. '*Supply*'s gone in, and if we had been on her, we would have gone ashore.'

'Now, come on, no more running to that port. *Supply* won't be long there, ye mark my words. Winds'll blow her out again.'

And so they did, and for another day the ships beat about the island waiting for the flag to go up to tell them that the landing was safe.

It was up the next morning. 'Hurrah!' cried John, as the *Sirius* moved cautiously into Sydney Bay, and hove to, close to the *Supply*. 'We're here at last.'

'And there's a lovely beach, Cookie,' Martin called, as he scanned the shore. 'I can see it—just in front of the huts.'

'Ah! And not a rock to climb on, eh! Sandy beach will not be exciting enough for ye. Cap'n, he'll not let ye ashore until some o' the stores be landed. Ye'll ha' to bide the time patiently.'

Cookie came to the port to watch with them. Already the ship's long boats were loading stores, and rowing backwards and forwards through the reef to the beach.

One second, one glance, and Cookie caught his breath and stared as tensely as they had ever seen him do.

'My God!' he murmured in an undertone.

'What, Cookie? What's the matter?'

'*Supply*, lads! Look, she's a-drifting to leeward on the rocks. D'ye not see them? Off the western point we call Point Ross?'

They were conspicuous enough, washed by a white swirl that broke and sucked around them.

'Oh, yes! Oh, Cookie! Why haven't they seen them?'

'They have. 'Tis the tide that has swept the ship too far inshore and too far to the west. She'll try to weather the rocks.'

'And she won't,' said Martin abruptly.

'Nay, lad, but she'll tack, see.... Aye, and get clear of 'em... Lieutenant

Ball, he knows this bay... He's turned, he be a-coming towards us, he be a-waving his hat. A-telling us that we be in danger now. Aye, 'tis the *Sirius* that be a-drifting to leeward.... Us that'll be on those rocks soon, mind ye. Listen to him a-yelling to Cap'n Hunter to get out o' the bay!'

'Oh, Cookie, not us! Not us!'

'A ye, and this'll be the time to try ye. Hear ye not the orders being shouted above, sailors a-scurrying, and the long boats a-rowing like mad to get out o' the way? We be in danger all right.'

'What will the captain do? What *will* he do?' John asked nervously.

'Do? Put on more sail o' course, and try to weather those rocks, or ye and I'll be a-floating in the water or a-dashing on the shore afore twelve bells ring.'

John glanced at Cookie to see if he were teasing and decided that he was not. So it *was* serious! What happened in the next few minutes would be vital to everyone. The *Sirius* was drifting on the rocks. He stood at the port with Martin and Cookie and watched her draw close to them. Somehow she must be saved. But how? How? It seemed almost impossible.

'Will we do it? Will we do it?' he asked hoarsely.

'P'raps. Be quiet. Ye'll see in a minute.' Suddenly Cookie put his hand out of the port. 'The wind,' he cried, ''tis changed. Two points to the south. I feel it! I feel it! Oh, 'tis a misfortune, a misfortune!'

'What, Cookie?'

'The change in the wind, ye little ninny. Now the good Lord save us! *Sirius*, she'll not weather those rocks, see.'

'Then what will we do? Oh, what will we do?' John could not bear to think of that lovely ship brought to destruction. His ship, the *Sirius*! And all of those in her—Martin, Cookie, himself, would they be drowned?' Oh, what will the captain do? What *will* he do now?'

'Put her into stays o' course, try to tack, like Lieutenant Ball. All be not lost yet.'

Anxiously they waited. This was indeed the moment. If she failed to tack, what then, what then?

They knew immediately from the shudder of the ship and the

flapping of the sails that she had missed, and that the wind had baffled her.

'Oh my!' murmured John, realising how close to disaster they were.

'Aye, 'twas a misfortune that change o' wind. There be only one thing left to do now, and that be to wear her round. But it'll be a close thing, though, wi' those rocks a-near.'

It would be a close thing. Both boys realised that only too well. If the *Sirius* failed to respond, the rocks would cut deep into her timbers and the seas would flow in, ripping her apart and breaking her up in the course of hours.

John looked to the shore and wondered if he could swim that far. He remembered the day when he had been overturned in the canoe with Nanbaree. Then the water had been calm, now the surf was strong, and it would buffet him and take him where it willed.

But the ship was responding to the efforts of her men. She was being brought round on the starboard tack. She was going to clear the rocks. She had, she had!

'Thank God!' he heard Cookie say.

'We're saved, we're saved,' John yelled, as he and Martin jumped for joy.

'Nay, lads, keep your delight till later. 'Tis not over yet.'

'Why, Cookie, why?'

He pointed to the settlement and the beach. 'Ship, she did wear, but she be now closer inshore, and the reef, d'ye see it?'

Yes, the reef where the surf broke parallel to the shore! They had seen it when they came into the bay. There it was before them—a new danger, for the *Sirius* was drifting towards it.

And there was another. The wind had changed again, and was direct from the south and dead on shore.

'Curse the wind,' cried Cookie. 'With a head sea we'll never get out o' this bay.'

For moments they stood waiting... waiting... as the ship fell to leeward...

'Ha!' exclaimed Cookie. 'Did ye feel her bump! She's shoaled, she's shoaled. We be in shallow water.'

The boys dared not think what that meant. Soon she would be on the reef...

'Come,' said Cookie simply, ushering them up the ladder, ''tis time we went,' and they realised that danger was indeed imminent.

On deck they found the ship being thrown into stays again.

'She'll do it,' murmured Cookie. 'Yes, she might. She's coming round, but oh dear, head into the wind!'

'Then what will we do? Oh, what will we do?' John cried again.

'Throw out the anchor, boy, let go the topsails and the halliards, and pray to God that the ship doesn't drift on the reef. That be all we can do now.'

Men were waiting by the anchor, and up in the shrouds. In a matter of minutes the anchor was out, the sails were flapping in the wind.

'Ah, but 'tis a task beyond them,' Cookie sighed, 'wi' the winds and the tides as they be.' He gathered the boys to him, and looked towards the sea. The swell, the swell will get her —it will throw her on the reef Oh, God, the ship, the ship! Her stern be tailing on the reef...'

And even as he spoke the violent rocking of the hull and the grating of the rocks on her keel told John that the worst had happened, and with a sickening feeling he knew that the *Sirius* was lost.

CHAPTER XVII

MARTIN MUST BE SAVED!

'WE'RE wrecked, Cookie,' said John calmly, as if he were sur-prised that he was still on a firm deck and not wallowing in the water. 'Just like Robinson Crusoe.'

'Aye, lad, so we be, and now we'll all ha' to go ashore.'

'Yes, Cookie,' said Martin lightly, 'and we'll really see those birds.'

Strange how they could joke just then, with the ship set upon the reef, and danger all about them, but it was so. Once the worst had happened, neither John nor Martin was any longer afraid.

'Aye, the birds! But this ship,' Cookie murmured, for he was very distressed, ''tis a great pity! *Sirius*, named after the dog-star, the ship that did bring us white folks to New South Wales. And wrecked now here, in Sydney Bay, in Norfolk Island. 'Tis a tragedy. Poor Gov'nor, I be afeard o' what he will say.'

They heard the carpenter report to Captain Hunter that the ship had bulged and that there were seven feet of water in the hold, heard the master call up that the water was coming in fast.

'That be bad, bad,' Cookie told them. ''Twill be the masts next to be cut,' and he drew them to safety in the companion-way.

'But why? Oh, why?' John cried. This would be the death of his ship, the *Sirius*. What good would she be without masts?

'To lighten her, boy,' Cookie explained, 'before she is full of water, so that the sea will throw her farther inshore, and then you and me and Cap'n Hunter, we all can be saved.'

So there still was danger of their losing their lives, even though they stood upright on the ship's deck, and the ship seemed firm upon the reef.

'Aye, the seas, they'll batter her when the tides do rise, and the winds blow more fiercely from the south,' Cookie said.

'Then shouldn't we jump over now and try to swim ashore?' John demanded impetuously.

'O' course not. That be for the cap'n to say, not ye.' They heard the masts split and creak and crash, and rushing up on deck again, saw them cast away, and the *Sirius* but a hulk being thrown by the swell farther and farther on to the reef.

Poor *Sirius*! John looked sadly about and remembered her as he knew her in her pride. Only last night, only an hour ago, she had been a thing of beauty and movement, almost alive, and now, within a few minutes, she had become a dead thing—a heap of useless timber.

Then he saw Captain Hunter, and noticed how distressed the captain was—tired, worried, overwrought, and he turned to Cookie and said, as the thought came to him, 'Cookie, the captain won't get into trouble, will he, because he lost his ship?'

'Tut, tut, what made ye think o' that? Course not. 'Twas the tides, lad, and the change o' wind, and maybe 'cos we didn't know enough about this bay—all these wrecked this ship. Cap'n, he couldn't help it. Anxious like he be to get the stores ashore, but when he be in trouble, didn't he try everything that be right? Get that notion out o' your head this very minute.' He took them both by the arm. 'Ye two, I want ye to come to the galley again wi' me. Seamen, they'll be needing a bite o' biscuit and some grog, and ye can help by giving it to 'em.'

'But the ship might sink,' John protested.

'Sink! Not *Sirius*! She be fast on the reef, didn't I a-tell ye, until the seas begin to break over her. Now come, we must do a-something to help. Ye be a boy in the King's Navy, ye know.'

Lieutenant Ball had rowed across from the *Supply*, and was asking if he could help, but Captain Hunter ordered him back to his ship.

'We are lost,' he called from the deck. 'Ye canna' help us. Save your own ship by sailing out o' the bay as quickly as ye can.'

The seamen already had begun to lift and heave boxes, trunks, and baggage over the side to send them floating to the shore. Others were bringing provisions out of the hold and securing them on the gun-deck.

'So that they can be thrown overboard too, if they cannot be taken in the boats,' Cookie explained.

Two long boats had nosed their way to the side of the hulk and were being quickly loaded with the bread and flour that was near at hand, but the surf was rising, and they might not be able to come again.

With everyone so busy, John and Martin went more willingly below to help. For an hour or more they ran backwards and forwards with rum and biscuits to the working sailors, and on one trip John took some cold pork and bread to Captain Hunter on the quarter-deck.

'He needs it, poor man,' Cookie said.

'Weel, weel, ye ha' e adventure this time, laddie.' The captain grinned when he saw John. 'Keeping up your spirits, I hope.'

'Aye, sir,' and John stood erect and looked him straight in the eye.

'What be they doing now?' Cookie asked as they ran back.

'Floating a cask tied to a line to the shore,' Martin announced.

'Ah! Be sending a message to Mr King, p'raps, Aye, and a-getting a rope there. Ye'll be going ashore on a grating, lads.'

'A grating?' they repeated. 'You mean a hatch cover, don't you?'

'Aye, used like a raft, maybe.'

'A raft!' they repeated again. 'Poled ashore like Robinson Crusoe. How could it be in that sea, Cookie?'

'Well, not exactly. It'll be pulled ashore by a rope, I guess.'

Now they were eager to take more rum and biscuits, so that they could watch proceedings from the deck.

'The cask is nearly to the shore, Cookie,' John reported on one of their rounds.

'Yes, and the rope tied to the cask has a longer, bigger rope tied to it,' Martin announced.

'Aye, I told you so. That be the hawser. Folk on shore will make it fast high in a pine-tree, and t' other end will be hove taut on board this ship. And on the hawser they will place the heart o' a stay. Ye know—a piece o' wood the shape o' a heart wi' a hole in it—and to this they'll sling the grating like a pair o' scales. Ye'll see.'

'And we'll sit on the grating like a raft?' Martin asked.

'Maybe, and o' course the heart, it has two lines on either side o' it—one to haul it on shore and one to haul it on board. Sailors call it a traveller, 'cos it can travel up and down the rope. And that's why ye'll get there.'

It all sounded very complicated, but each time they went on deck they found it coming out just as Cookie had described.

On shore the folk were watching and waiting. They were only too willing and eager to help. As soon as the cask was within reach, someone swam out and retrieved it. Then ready hands heaved and heaved until the hawser with the wooden heart upon it was drawn in, and soon made fast to a mighty pine-tree.

In their next trip to the deck the boys found that the heart had been hauled back, and that the grating was now being slung underneath, just as Cookie had said, 'like a pair of scales'.

'It's ready,' they told him, 'and soon they'll begin.'

The surgeon's mate was the first.

'Ask Mr King if it is safe for us tae stay here all nicht,' Captain Hunter said to him. 'If it's no', we shall have tae gang ashore—or try tae.'

John and Martin hung over the side and watched the grating slide gradually to the surf.

'Like coming down on a swing,' John thought. But when it reached the water, he saw that it was dragged almost immersed through the swirling seas, bumped and buffeted on the rocks, the man upon it at the mercy of the tides and currents. One weak hold, one false move, and he would be in the water fighting for his life.

Though neither spoke, both boys hoped that they would not have to go ashore that way.

'It's rough,' they told Cookie. 'You should have seen the raft being knocked about.'

'Aye, I guess so. Wind, it be blowing harder, and the seas be rising. Take my word for it, we'll all be a-going ashore tonight. Aye, and on that very rating!'

No, surely not! John was afraid, and Martin, too, though in his stolid way, he said nothing. For both of them the wreck was no longer an adventure, but a very grim and dangerous happening in which there was a grave danger of being hurt and even drowned.

'Oh, Cookie!' was all they could say. 'Not in that surf,'

But when they went on deck again, they saw that Mr King was making signs from the shore. His meaning was quite clear. Everyone was to quit the ship by nightfall! Otherwise the seas might break her up, if the tides rose higher and the winds blew harder during the night. He would send a boat across the lagoon to the reef, and so meet the grating halfway.

'Those laddies must be among the first,' they heard the captain say. 'The cook micht gang tae, but we'll send a few ither loads afore them.'

So it had come, and strange to say they did not rush below and tell Cookie. They waited there on deck, watching the first load buffeted ashore, then the second, waiting, waiting for the captain to give the sign, standing silent, grim, cold and afraid in the fading light of the late afternoon.

When Cookie emerged from the companion-way, they knew that this was the moment. 'And now it's Robinson Crusoe again, eh?' he said, as he led them to the stern and prepared to get them on the raft. 'Why, the great Cap'n Cook never went ashore on a raft! Much more exciting it be than jumping on a rock.'

'Aye, indeed,' boomed a Scotch voice beside them. 'Ye were the laddies that wanted tae see the birds. This is the test for ye. Noo we'll ken whether we ha' e made sailors o' ye.'

Both boys turned and smiled at Captain Hunter, and took heart from his cheery good-bye.

'Will you be coming too, sir?' John asked.

'Aye, that I will later on. I must see some o' my men awa' first.'

A sailor at the stern was holding the raft precariously over the swirling seas below.

John began to climb over the bulwarks. He knew that Cookie would not help him, and he did not want any help, for this was the time when he could show Captain Hunter that he had grown up very much in the last two years, and had learnt, as he said, to be a 'real' sailor.

But in his nervousness he sprang on the raft, and for a moment he knew nothing except that he was clinging grimly to Cookie as the raft swayed and swung in mid-air. Every instant he thought the slant would send them both whirling into the pounding waves below, but Cookie was strong, he was able to steady it, but not without telling the boy just exactly what he thought of him.

'Now sit ye down, ye little ninny, and hang on to the ropes like. Aye, and hold tight, and never ye fear. Mr King be sending a boat across the lagoon to meet us, and I'll be wi' ye all the way.'

John sat on the raft and clung grimly to the rope as he waited for Martin to climb down. The southerly wind was biting deep into his very bones, and raising goose pimples on his bare arms and legs.

'Oh, Cookie, let's start!' he pleaded, and his teeth began to chatter. 'It's cold.'

'Aye, indeed, and colder still it'll be in the water. But here we go. Down and away.'

Down they did go, slowly, jerkily, and with a shock John found that he was enjoying the ride. He forgot the void below, forgot the pounding waves, felt only the pleasant sensation of moving through the air, closer, closer to the shelter of the lagoon and safety.

Then he remembered the water. It was there before them, and they were going down to it. The hawser was long, and it sagged in the middle, down, down into the curdling turmoil. With a plop the raft plummeted in, and he felt the cold of the seas as they laved his legs, poured over his body, then drew back, sucking him with them in their ebbing rush. He grasped the ropes more tightly, braced his body to meet the shock of the next wave, but before it came, the raft bumped on to the coral bed beneath, and lay for a moment aslant on the pinnacle of an outcrop until the wave swept in and, raising it again, carried it on and over, but not yet out of danger.

For behind them the seas were corning—bigger, higher, the waves tumbling in madder and madder, unceasingly, relentlessly. The wind was rising shriller, colder. How much farther? How much farther?

He looked behind and saw one that rose like a mountain of water, and all of a sudden he panicked and longed to draw himself up, to hang on to the hawser, anything to escape that foaming mass. Then he thought of Captain Hunter and his last words, 'Noo we'll ken if we ha' e made sailors o' ye.' Real sailors were calm. Cookie had said to sit tight and to hang on grimly, and so he now waited, hanging on... hanging on...

But dimly he became aware that Martin had seen it too. Martin had panicked also, Martin, who hated danger, but always kept his head. He had risen from his corner, up and up, and Cookie was grasping at him, pulling him down.

Then the wave broke upon them, engulfing the raft, swirling about them, buffeting one against the other. But it swept the raft on until it collided violently with another bundle of ragged rocks, and was brought up with a jolt.

John opened his eyes. He was choking with salt water, sick and cold and terribly tired; too tired to see if they were past the reef, too tired to care if they ever reached the shore, until he noticed with a start that Cookie was holding Martin in his arms, and that Martin was inert, senseless, with blood streaming from a deep cut in his forehead.

'Cookie—!' he gasped.

'Aye, knocked his head against the rocks, he did. Come, ye must help me now. Slip across and try to push the raft away from those rocks.'

'No, not that,' John cried to himself. Let go the rope that had saved him, with a sea coming upon them that might dash him against the rocks as one had done Martin. He looked behind, and saw others rolling in. But Martin had to be saved somehow. Could he slip across before the next wave broke? With a sliding movement he heaved himself over the raft and grasped at the ropes at the opposite corner. He was just in time. The wave broke and crashed with a tumbling roar, but not before he had freed the grating, so that the men hauling could bring them to safety.

And now they were going in. The worst was over.

'See, there is the boat waiting in the lagoon inside the reef,' Cookie said.

But the last exertion had been too great. John was on the point of exhaustion. He scarcely saw the boat, scarcely knew what was happening, until he lay on the keel, staring, staring at something, somebody, as if in a dream.

And yet was it a dream? It seemed so natural that he should see Caesar—Caesar with his black face a-grinning, bending backwards and forwards as he pulled on an oar.

So he was back at Sydney Cove. It had only been a nasty dream. He had not been wrecked on Norfolk Island, and had not been dragged on a raft above a ragged reef. Then he saw Martin lying near him, with Cookie leaning over him, staunching the blood from the cut in his temple.

It was all too difficult to understand.

'Caesar,' he murmured, as the negro lifted him from the boat and carried him ashore.

'Yes'm, mas'r, dis is Caesar. I did come on de *Sirius* ter save you. Too busy you wuz wi' dat cook ter see me lan' on de first day.'

And again John lapsed into unconsciousness.

When he came to, he lay in a rough bed on the floor of a hut. Someone was bending over him. It was Captain Hunter, cut and bleeding, his clothes torn and saturated with water.

'You're hurt, sir,' he managed to say.

'Nae more than ye, John. I came tae tell ye that ye acted like a real sailor. We've made one o' ye at last.'

'But Martin, sir?' and he sat up and looked at the boy beside him.

'He's all richt. Aren't ye, Martin?'

'Well, we got ashore, John,' Martin murmured sleepily. 'Yes,' John replied, as he lay down again, 'and now we'll see those birds.'

CHAPTER XVIII

MILLIONS AND TRILLIONS OF BIRDS

AS soon as the boys awoke the next morning and found that they had recovered, they were up and away down to the beach to see what had happened to the *Sirius* during the night. She was still fast on the reef, more or less as they had left her, with men walking about her decks, and others seated on the grating being hauled ashore.

'But didn't they all come over last night?' John asked a marine standing on guard near by.

'No, indeed, and they'll not all be here before this afternoon. Pray God that the wind keeps fair.'

It was then, as they walked along the beach, that the boys noted that the marines were stationed at intervals along its length.

'Perhaps to guard those things that are being washed ashore,' Martin said.

'Yes'm, mas'r.' The voice came from the bushes, and they knew that behind the greenery was the black face and bushy hair of Caesar. 'Reck'n dey'll stop us furn thievin' dey do, but they woan't—der be ways an' means,' and he came out and winked at them.

Could they ever do anything with such a rascal? Mamma had tried and failed, the Governor had been patient, and in despair had evidently sent him to Norfolk Island.

'Why are you here?' they asked.

'Gov'nor did reck'n I'd not run 'way, p'raps. But up dah in dos hills a man could live fer a while, an' not be pester'd by natives. An' dere be de birds.'

'Birds! Have you seen them, Caesar?'

'I have. Been dah ev'ry night since I set foot ashor' furn de *Sirius* days ago. Come in millions dey do, an' a man kin ketch an' ketch, an' wid a fire roast an' roast.'

'Will you take us?'

'You? Well, now, I could, but mebbe folks 'ud say I shouldn'.'

'What folks?'

'Dat cook, mebbe. Aye, an' de cap'n hisself.'

'If we got permission?'

'Dat wud be diff'runt. Fo'r o'clock ternight we do set out fer Mount Pitt. Meet me by de seventh pine on de track leadin' furn de bay.'

He walked away from them, and went rummaging along the sand in search of goods from the wreck, for a marine was approaching to see that he did what he had been ordered to do.

John and Martin watched him, as he waded into the water to rescue a pair of trousers now floating in with the tide. They saw him pick them up and carry them ashore, first wringing them dry, and then folding them carefully over his arm, and guessed that by some sleight of hand he had taken something from them for himself. Depositing them in a bundle of retrieved goods that was being guarded by the marine, he turned towards the boys and winked, and they saw in his hand the glint of silver. A snuff box!

So there were ways and means, and they could not tell on him. Poor Caesar! He would come to a bad end.

Intrigued with what they could find, they began themselves to ferret among the seaweed. It was good fun to retrieve something of value to be placed on the bundle.

But their empty stomachs soon demanded food, and they went in search of Cookie, not expecting to find him, as they did, already busy with his pots and cauldrons out in the open air.

'Aye, ye be just in time. Sailors a-coming ashore'll need hot food, and ye can wait on 'em. There be soup—'

They could smell it—soup, real soup—soup with vegetables in it, and yes, birds! Soup made of fresh meat, and plenty of it. Already they had gathered two mugs and were waiting for them to be filled.

'Oh, Cookie, how did the birds come?'

'Convicts, they brought 'em in this morning. Been out all night. That Caesar fellow—'

'Yes—' and they paused.

'He brought the most, he did. Queer fellow, that he be. I did think he would not raise his finger to help anyone, and yet there he be, at dawn, a-waiting for me to light the fires. Had made half a dozen others bring birds too. And pretty sulky they seemed.'

'He wants to take us with him tonight,' John began.

'Ah, he does, does he? Well, I'll ha' something to say about that,' and he gave them another mug of soup, and another hunk of bread. 'Eat while ye can,' he said. 'Council'll be a-meeting this morning, and we'll probably go on half ration.'

'Why?'

'Well, why ask me? Ye know the stores, they be on the *Sirius*, eh? And Heaven knows whether we'll get 'em ashore. Nigh three hundred marines and convicts, and all the ship's crew o' the *Sirius*, and nothing extra for 'em to eat 'cept the few casks o' meat and flour that came in the *Supply*. What d'ye think we'll eat—ye and me and the rest of 'em in the weeks to come.'

'But we won't stay here, will we, Cookie?' Both spoke together.

'Stay here? Why not? Wi' out a ship we be. *Supply'll* be full a-going back to Sydney Cove, and they won't want folks who should not be there.'

That was true. Why should they go back in the *Supply* when she would be overcrowded? They had not thought of that. The prospect of spending weeks and months on Norfolk Island was not quite to their liking—especially with food short.

'There are the birds,' Martin reminded Cookie.

'Yes, but they do not last all the year round.' Cookie was in one of those moods when he threw cold water on all their suggestions.

Sailors were now coming up from the beach, wet and bruised and exhausted, and the boys served them readily, remembering their own experience the night before.

It was four o'clock in the afternoon when the last came from the wreck, and the *Sirius* lay lonely and deserted, a forlorn thing, yet defiant still, bow turned to the sea, with the surf breaking and washing around the bulwarks.

'Now we can think o' keeping that meeting ye were a-talking about, with this Caesar,' Cookie said, much to their surprise, when they were packing up the dishes.

'You really mean it?'

'Aye, indeed, I do. Must get some birds for soup tomorrow, that I must. Where did ye say ye would meet him?'

'At the seventh pine on the track leading from the bay.' Caesar was there, waiting behind the bole of the tree in case some marine or officer or overseer should see him, and order him to do something that would keep him from the birds and his appointment.

'A-well, a-well!' he exclaimed. 'Didn' expec' you, dat I did not. An' de cook, too. I sure be mighty honour'd.'

'So ye be, ye heathen,' replied Cookie testily. 'I'll see that ye do not lead these boys astray. And I want some birds—plenty o' birds for the pot tomorrow. How long be this walk to Mount Pitt?'

''Bout two hours, yo' honour,' Caesar explained mockingly. 'Uphill 'long de ridges, al' de way.'

They proceeded up the slope into what seemed to them to be an ordered wood, with mighty pine-trees towering closely at intervals, and below, the loveliest glades they had ever seen. But as they went farther, other trees began to appear among the pines, curtained by underwood that grew and twined and crawled in such a fashion that the woods became impenetrable beyond the track.

'Now if ye went beyond that path...' Cookie murmured.

But John and Martin were quite content to follow it. Birds sang and cooed from all sides, and often the boys were tempted to sneak behind a tree to see if they could find a nest, but they did not try. For beyond the path was only frightening gloom, even if they had had an axe to cut through the brush.

Only twice did they pause as they crept along the spine of the hills, once early to look on Arthur's Vale, the flat valley that had been cleared and was now lush with vegetables of all kinds.

'And it won't be long before Caesar is sneaking there at night to steal,' John whispered to Martin.

'Yes, and getting into trouble again. Don't you see him scheming already, as he makes a note of the lay of the land?'

The second time was when Caesar himself bade them stop and he disappeared down a valley into a jungle of growth, then came back with a finger on his lips, and a handful of bananas or plantains.

'Reckon'd you'd be hungry, mas'rs,' he said, as he shared them around. 'Foun' dat tree, I did, fust time I come heah. 'Tis a secret. Be dah, dos plantains will, when I try ter git 'way, eh?' and he winked at the boys.

So they came at sunset to Mount Pitt, a gradual mound of a mountain, not steep and precipitous as those they had seen at Lord Howe's Island.

Soon they were crashing into the loose soil, floundering as they had done at Lord Howe's Island, and they knew that the mount was honeycombed with nests, and that these were what they had come to find.

Caesar was already adept at the art of dragging a bird from its burrow. Thrusting his arm into the hole almost to the shoulder he pulled it out quickly before the bird had time to peck with its crooked bill, or scratch with its sharp claws.

'Dah, a Mount Pitt bird,' he said, and, spreading its wings, he allowed them to examine it.

They looked at the black bill, hooked savagely at the tip; at the head, as far as the eyes and throat, waved brown and dusky white; at the body, a sooty brown, the under parts a deep ash colour. Then Caesar closed the wings, and they saw that the bird was about sixteen inches long, the tail longer than the body by an inch, rounded in shape, and made up of about twelve feathers. Yellow legs merging into black at the feet, webbed like those of a duck, with a vicious-looking spur as the back toe—and they knew all about the Mount Pitt bird.

'Once de convicts dug 'em outer de nests,' Caesar explained, but' dey doan't now. Jes' wait an' you'll see.'

More and more convicts were arriving, and marines, too, and all around the mountain fires were being lit, triangular blobs of light in the gathering gloom.

And the birds were coming in—coming home to their burrows after a day's fishing at sea, at first singly, then so quickly that they seemed to be everywhere, squalling, squawking, squabbling.

'One has fallen on my hand,' John yelled, as he picked it up and gave it to Cookie.

'And another nearly went into the fire,' exclaimed Martin.

'Aye, that be the purpose o' this fire—to attract 'em, not to cook 'em,' Cookie said.

Now they formed a dark cloud that hid the fading light in the sky, flopping, plummeting squat down just where they flew, dead straight like a falling stone.

'Why,' said John,' they've brought on the night already!'

'Aye,' remarked Cookie, 'they certainly be as thick as gnats on a summer night in England.'

But Martin preferred to call them a shower of hail, for they soon were falling everywhere, respecting no one and no place.

'I believe they would land on my head,' he said, as one, just touching his hair, slithered down and sat in his lap.

For hours the birds flew in—uncountable numbers of birds —millions maybe, or so it seemed, certainly hundreds of thousands, all coming home from the sea.

And among them were the convicts and the marines catching, killing, and roasting, for although Cookie had said that the fire was to attract them, who could resist a roasted bird—when salt pork had been one's food for days and months and even years?

The greediest and hungriest was Caesar. Seated before the coals of the dying fire, he pulled out the body of a bird, then tearing the flesh from the bones with his teeth he ate like a wild animal, licking his lips and rolling his eyes to express his enjoyment. Or perhaps it was for their entertainment. They never could tell.

'Good!' He winked at the boys, and began on another bird, at the same time pulling one from the coals and passing it over to them.

John took the bird and, dividing it in two, gave half to Martin. And while he ate and gnawed, he pondered deeply on this experience. Who would have thought that they would be sitting here on this mountain in the night with the birds still flying and plummeting to earth? What would Mamma say? He pictured the circle that would listen to his tale—Sue's wide eyes and Jenny's look of wonder. And Nanbaree. He had not thought of Nanbaree for days. Oh, why wasn't Nanbaree here? Nanbaree, who had to snare birds so stealthily, so cunningly! John imagined Nanbaree's delight if he could only walk a step and pounce on a bird—just like that! For now there were so many birds that one could not walk without kicking one.

Birds, birds, birds, wheeling, screaming, dipping overhead; jostling, clustering, quarrelling on land. He would never forget the sight.

'Not yet,' he pleaded when Cookie suggested that they should return to the settlement.

'Not yet,' Martin echoed.

But Cookie had enough birds. 'Ye ha' seen all ye can see,' he said. 'Now up wi' ye and along.'

They knew it would be of no use to argue. Regretfully they followed as he led the way, with Caesar lumbering behind with a sack full of birds.

Neither boy on this occasion felt any pity for the birds. It seemed quite right that they should kill them and take them back to Sydney Bay, where food was so short and the future so uncertain.

Both boys followed closely behind Cookie, for the woods were dark, and the way ill-lit by the flaring pine splinter that the old man held high above his head to light the way.

'What are those birds called?' they asked him.

He could not tell them. 'A kind o' petrel, that be all I know. I cannot help a-thinking they be sent by Providence to save us.'

'We'll go again tomorrow night,' they promised one another as, exhausted, they lay down to sleep.

And so they did the next night, but on the following day there were other things to hold their attention.

The council had met and decided to cut the rations by half, and also to declare martial law.

'Just as be done in time o' war,' Cookie explained to them. 'That's how serious things be.'

At eight that morning everyone in the settlement met at the lower flagstaff, the marines drawn up in two lines with the Union Jack and their own colours at their head in the centre, the seamen on the right, and the convicts on the left. There martial law was proclaimed, and Major Ross spoke, telling them that the ration had been cut, that all livestock, except poultry, had to be given to the storekeeper for the use of everyone, and urging them to be industrious and obedient. Then all gave three cheers and, beginning with the Lieutenant-Governor, each passed by the Union Jack, taking off his hat in token of a promise to obey the law.

'Ye, too,' Cookie said, pushing the boys before him. 'Make your promise. Ye might be here for months, haven't I told ye?'

When the midday meal was over, he let them go off to the beach, where the stores were being landed from the *Sirius*.

Two convicts had gone over on the hawser to cast overboard the livestock, which had been without water for two days, and now the geese and ducks and pigs were swimming ashore.

Those on the beach were so interested that they did not notice at first that the men on board were strangely quiet and no longer visible.

When evening began to come on, they grew anxious. What had become of the two convicts? Then suddenly a light appeared through a port and sounds of carousing, and the reason was plain. The convicts had found some grog, and by this time had drunk so much that they were quite merry.

'The silly fools,' Captain Hunter murmured, when he and Major Ross were brought to the beach to deal with the situation.

'Yes, indeed,' said Major Ross. 'That light is dangerous. If they upset it, anything might happen.'

'A fire?' thought John, and quickly his mind raced ahead. If the *Sirius* caught fire, that would mean the end of the stores.

Major Ross called for the marines. 'Fire a volley,' he ordered, 'and see if that will move them.' But the men took no notice; if anything their shouts were louder, more derisive. 'Then fire a three-pounder,' he commanded. 'They can't fail to hear that.'

But when the smoke had scattered, the light on the *Sirius* burned brighter than before. It was a light no longer, but a fire! What Major Ross had feared had happened. The *Sirius* was alight!

'They'll destroy themselves and us too,' he growled. 'Will anyone go on board and send them back?' he demanded of the convicts standing around. 'I'll recommend a free pardon to the man who does so.'

There was one, a man the boys did not know, John Arscott by name, and now he boldly stepped forward.

'I'll go,' he said simply. 'I'm a strong swimmer.'

The dusk was gathering, and they could not follow him as he battled through the surf, but after an interval they saw the light grow smaller, and they knew that the ship had been saved.

The culprits came ashore by the hawser, so drunk that they could hardly keep their grip, but Arscott shouted that he would stay on board all night.

'He's brave,' whispered John to Martin, and Martin agreed, for they both knew that at any time the winds might change and send the surf breaking over the *Sirius* to tear her apart.

Fortunately this did not happen, and Arscott came ashore the next morning none the worse for his adventure. Two fires had been started by the drunken convicts, he told Major Ross, but he had stood over the men while they helped to put them out.

The boys were telling Cookie this, when he said suddenly, 'Come on, let's be going.'

'Where?' they demanded.

'To the *Supply*, o' course. Where else?'

'But you said we'd be staying here.'

'Aye, I ha' said many things in my time. D'ye think they could do wi' out me, eh? And your Mamma, what would she say if I went wi'out ye? Now come on, I ha' got that fellow, Caesar, to carry my bag. And some plantains, too, he brought in for the girls.'

Yes, indeed, they could not go back without taking something. Cookie had always brought them presents, and so must they.

'Where are we boarding the ship?' they asked.

'Cascade Bay, o' course. No sign o' her in the roads, ye can see for yourself.'

That meant a walk over the hills.

'Like waves in a gale at sea, they be,' Cookie complained, as they climbed up and down the sides of the valleys. 'Mighty glad I be I am not a-staying here, or my old heart, it would stop a-ticking.'

The boats were backing into the black rock to pick up passengers and cargo when they arrived.

'And now ye'll ha' your wish, eh?' Cookie teased them. 'Wanted to land on that rock, didn't ye, but ye came ashore on a hawser instead. 'Tis strange that ye do most things ye wish. For now ye be going to jump from the rock into the boat. If I know ye, one o' ye will fall into the sea.'

But neither did. Caesar was there to help for the last time.

'You will never be at hand to save us,' they told him as they regretfully said good-bye, remembering how many times he had rescued them from danger. Please, Caesar, don't try to run away, then you'll soon be back at the Cove.'

'Mebbe, mebbe, mas'r,' he promised, winking broadly, but they guessed that only the smallness of the island would stop him in his designs.

As the sailors backed in, he held each boy by the arm in turn, and in this way helped them to jump into the heaving boat without mishap.

'Good-bye,' they called again and again, when Cookie had joined them, and they were being rowed towards the *Supply*. 'Good-bye, good-bye. Come back to the Cove soon.'

But in themselves they wondered if they would ever see Caesar again. He might come back, he might stay on the island all his life. No one could tell.

The following morning Lieutenant King came on board, for the Governor had ordered him back to Sydney Cove, and with him came some of the officers and seamen who had been on the *Sirius*. Crowded with passengers, the little ship set sail for home.

At dusk the island was still within sight. John and Martin went on deck to take a last look at the place where so much had happened. Above, the birds were winging homewards, and as they watched, amidst the dark blob of green a light appeared, and another, and yet another, and they knew that the marines and convicts were out after the birds.

Sleepy at last, they went below to bed.

'We saw the fires, Cookie,' they told him, so Caesar and the rest must be out catching the birds.'

'Aye, those birds. I call 'em Birds of Providence, that I do, for God, He did send 'em to save those folks. 'Tis almost a miracle.'

'But they'll get the stores out of the *Sirius*, won't they?' John asked.

'Aye, I don't doubt, but there be little enough food for all those on the island. If the ships don't come from England, where will they be wi'out those birds, I say?'

The ships! With prow turned for home, they remembered the ships again. Surely the ships would have arrived at the Cove!

'Aye,' Cookie went on, 'and we folks at Sydney Cove'll be in a bad way if those ships, they ha' not come. It'll be snakes and iguanas and what-not for ye, my lads. Wi' the *Sirius* gone, there be only this little ship between ye and starvation.'

'What do you mean by that?' Martin asked, a little puzzled.

'Well, someone ha' to go somewhere to get food if the ships be not there. *Sirius*, she be a-going to China when she got back. Now there be only the *Supply* to bring ye food from foreign parts, and if we leave ye, there'll be no ship in the Cove for months, no ship to come back here to Norfolk Island. And in that time ye'll just have to live on what ye have. D'ye understand?'

For the first time they began to realise how serious the loss of the *Sirius* had been. If the ships had not arrived from England by this, the

Governor would be worried when he heard what had happened to the *Sirius*. The wreck had been a disaster.

'I wish we had some birds,' John murmured wistfully.

'Aye, indeed,' Cookie reminded him, 'Birds of Providence!'

CHAPTER XIX

BACK TO SYDNEY COVE

THE boys watched the slim line of the coast of New South Wales grow in height, their eyes glued to the spot where the South Head Lookout might be, until a flash of colour against the green on the ridge told them that the sentry had already sighted the *Supply*.

'It might be Dan,' John said.

'Yes, and he will wonder why the *Sirius* is not with us.'

'Maybe he'll guess,' Cookie said, when they pointed out the flag. 'Sailors, they know these things before they are told.'

'And the Governor. Will he know?'

'Aye, as soon as he sees we are alone. Ye watch. Down the harbour he'll come, and mighty worried he'll be. Poor man, he ha' troubles enough wi' out this!'

They were on deck when the *Supply* sailed through the Heads.

'People in the Cove will have seen the flag now,' John said, 'and Mamma and your mother will know that a ship is coming in.'

'Yes,' said Martin, 'and when they're certain that it's the *Supply*, they'll begin to cook us a special meal.'

'Unless they are angry with us for going away as we did.'

Both boys were uncertain about the reception they would get from their mothers.

'They will forget when they hear about the wreck,' Martin replied.

Yes, they would forget, but the boys were not at ease...

A boat was being lowered to take Lieutenant Ball up the harbour quickly. He called to the boys to come with him, and they obeyed readily, for that would mean that they would be home earlier than they expected.

They had rounded Bradley's Head, and were about to turn into the western channel, when they saw the Governor's cutter approaching.

So Cookie had been right. Once the flag had been raised, the Governor had not been able to restrain himself and wait for the ships to arrive. He had come down to see what they were.

Before the boats were within hailing distance, he seemed to sense the disaster that had happened. Perhaps it was the despairing motion of Lieutenant Ball's hand that conveyed the sad story.

'Sailors, they know these things before they are told,' Cookie had said, and the boys saw, before Lieutenant Ball uttered a word, that the Governor knew already that the *Sirius* was lost.

'And the Second Fleet, sir?' Lieutenant Ball asked, after he had told his grim news.

'They have not come,' said the Governor quietly, but the boys felt that he must be almost at the point of despair.

Meanwhile on the hill to the east of her house, Mamma was standing with Papa's telescope at her eye scanning the South Head Lookout.

'What can you see, Mamma? What can you see?' Sue asked.

'The flag flying. Yes, and the sentry walking up and down on the South Head. So it's not the ships from England, Debby. The man couldn't be so casual if it were. He'd be excited—as excited as we would be. And all the men at the South Head would be with him watching and pointing. The ships must be the *Supply* and *Sirius* from Norfolk Island.'

'Then John and Martin will be home,' Sue cried. 'And Cookie, too. He'll be sure to bring us some presents.'

'I hope they're bananas,' said Jenny wistfully.

'Perhaps the boys will bring something,' Debby suggested. 'They will want to please after going off like that without telling us.'

'Yes, indeed.' Mamma smiled. 'The young rascals! I suppose it wasn't their fault, for I have a mind that Cookie arranged it. What shall I do, Debby? Speak to him about it?'

'Well, ma'am, he's always been very good to us,' Debby reminded her, 'bringing us food and things whenever he went away.'

All hearts warmed at the thought of Cookie.

'See, Mamma, there's the Governor's boat going down the harbour,' Sue said.

'Yes, and another corning round Bradley's Head,' Mamma remarked, and they all wondered what was happening down there when the two boats met.

Then the *Supply* came into view, beating round the point, and they knew for certain that the ships were not those from England.

'There, I told you so,' said Mamma, 'Come, Debby, we had better go home and prepare a meal for the boys. I'll send Pete over to invite Martin's parents, and perhaps Cookie will join us when the *Supply* anchors. The boys will need a good meal after so much salt pork.'

Mamma and Debby were putting the pots on the fire when Nanbaree ran in with word from Lieutenant Dawes, which he delivered in his own broken English. John and Martin were in the Governor's boat, and were being brought up the harbour. The lieutenant and even he, Nanbaree, had seen them through the big telescope at the observatory. That meant, of course, the boys would soon arrive.

'I stay here,' he ended, with such a pleading look that Mamma was touched by his devotion. 'Mr Dawes, he come, too.'

'Of course, Nanbaree. Go and see if you can find the girls, and all of you run down to the Governor's wharf and bring the boys home as soon as they land.'

Although Mamma appeared calm, she was not a little excited. As for Debby, she suddenly remembered that she had put the pots on without stoking the fire and rushed to remedy her mistake.

'It's never been the same, ma'am, without John and that young Martin a-rushing in and out,' she now told Mamma. 'I'm mighty glad he's coming back.'

'Yes,' Mamma agreed, 'and so am I; but, Debby, don't forget I have to reprimand him for going away like that,' and she tried to look serious.

'You will be so glad to see him again, ma'am, you'll forget it.'

'No, no, Debby. Just you wait and see.'

They came rushing into the little house, five children and a dog, babbling, pushing and jostling, all in good fun, as if a tornado had suddenly struck at the walls.

'They're here, Mamma, they're here,' Sue's shrill voice skirled.

But there was no great demonstration of affection unless it was a soft light that momentarily came to Mamma's eyes. The boys seemed subdued, uncertain of their reception, perhaps weighed down by the seriousness of the news that they brought.

Before Mamma had time to kiss him or to reprimand him, for John expected one or the other, he blurted out the terrible truth.

'The *Sirius* was wrecked, Mamma,' he said quietly.

'Wrecked? Where?'

'On Norfolk Island.'

Her body grew taut with the shock. 'Was anyone drowned? Captain Hunter? Lieutenant Bradley?'

'No, Mamma, all were saved, and they think they'll get all the stores out of the hulk, but you see—'

'Yes, I do see. We are left with only the *Supply*, and the ships from England as far away as ever. The poor Governor! Is he very upset?'

'Very upset. I heard him tell Papa that all officers are to meet at six o'clock.'

'And the first thing will be a reduction in the ration. Now we'll indeed have to tighten our belts.'

She turned suddenly and watched Debby who was busy at the fire-place, trying in her mind to meet immediately the struggle for food that she knew was before them.

Then she did one of those surprising things that John had always admired in Mamma. Faced with a grave situation, she cast it from her thoughts. Walking across the room, she placed her arms across his shoulders, and kissed him as affectionately as she had ever done.

'This is your homecoming, dear,' she said. 'We must not let anything mar that. Today you and Martin will tell us of your adventures. Tomorrow we'll think of what we shall do to fight starvation. See what Debby is cooking for dinner —roast kangaroo, and roast potatoes, and—'

'Yes, and bananas that Johnnie brought,' Sue interrupted, peeling one for herself and Jenny, as Martin's mother arrived with her small son for another joyful reunion.

Then began the story of Caesar and the night on Mount Pitt. By the time Papa and Lieutenant Dawes and Martin's father joined them, the boys were telling about the birds on Lord Howe's Island, and when Cookie popped in, they had come to the wreck and their journey on the grating through the swirling seas to the reef.

'Aye, ma'am, and ye would ha' been proud o' them,' Cookie said, as he joined them all at the table and Debby heaped his plate with food. 'Ne'er turned a hair, they did, and John, he did help me in a precarious situation like, when Martin be hit on the rocks, and lay there not a-stirring on the grating.'

So much there was to tell, so much that would have another time made Mamma grow pale at the thought of their danger, but tonight she sat and listened, and passed few remarks, attending only to the needs of her guests, and smiling proudly at her son as if somehow she felt that he had matured, grown bigger in body and mind and courage.

He was still talking about his adventures when Papa and Lieutenant Dawes went off to the meeting at the Governor's house, still remembering little bits as Martin and his family departed.

'Thank you,' Mamma said to Cookie, who was the last to leave, 'thank you for looking after the boys so well. I am much indebted to you.'

'Gave them the round o' the galley, I did, believe me, ma'am. 'Twas good discipline. But had I known there be danger, I would not ha' taken them.'

So he admitted at last that he had been responsible. John noticed Mamma look at Debby and smile, and heard Debby say, 'I told you that you would forget, ma'am, and so you did. Aren't you glad now?'

'Indeed I am, Debby,' and they smiled at one another again in that cryptic way that John did not understand.

He was telling Nanbaree, who had stayed the night, about the rock at Cascade Bay.

'But we did jump off the rock, Nanbaree,' he was saying. 'That was when we boarded the *Supply*. Caesar was there to see that we jumped into the boat and not into the sea. The next day we sailed for home.'

As he finished the door opened, and Papa entered, his face grave, his brow knit. And immediately John knew that it would be a long time before he would recount those adventures again, for only the future mattered now, and the future meant a struggle for food, a struggle to live.

'Well,' said Mamma, clearly relieved to see him come and to know the worst, 'what has the Governor decided?'

Papa fell heavily into a chair.

'The ration is to be reduced,' he began.

'Yes,' said Mamma, 'I expected that. What is it to be?'

'Two pounds of pork, two and a half pounds of flour, one pound of rice and a pint of pease for seven days.'

'Oh dear! That's hardly enough to keep a person alive. The pork dwindles away to nothing when cooked, and the rice is full of moving creatures. Is the ration to be the same for everyone?'

'Yes, everyone over the age of eighteen months. There is enough flour to last until the middle of November, pork till the end of July, and rice till the first week of November. When the pork gives out, the flour ration will be increased, and when there is no more rice, the Governor will distribute the seed wheat. In this way he hopes that the provisions will last until the *Supply* returns from Batavia. So we will not starve if the ships from England don't come.'

Mamma sighed. 'But we shall just live. And the *Supply* is such a little ship. What if anything happens to her?'

'Nothing will, dear.' Papa was quite confident of it. 'Lieutenant Ball will see to it. When he arrives at Batavia, he is to charter a Dutch ship to bring back the food. The *Supply* is far too small to carry it.'

John and Nanbaree had been silent, Nanbaree not understanding this strange talk, John thinking of the *Supply*, the ship he knew so well, battling through the seas, through calms and storms and uncharted waters to bring relief and so save them from starvation. Cookie would be going away again—to strange places—and for a moment he longed to be going too, he and Martin down in the galley, darting here and there at Cookie's behest.

'And what of the stock?' Mamma asked. 'Are we to keep our pigs and goats and hens, or are they to go to the stores for the benefit of everyone?'

'No, dear, sows must be kept for breeding; hogs are in too poor condition to be of much use, but the Commissary will buy any that he thinks fit enough to kill. Poultry, too, but larger animals such as your goats are to remain the property of those who own them.'

John knew that Mamma was pleased at that. She relied on the goats to give milk and sometimes cream—luxuries few had round the Cove. She would have been distressed to lose them.

'The hogs belong to John and Martin, you know. They are not ours,' she said now.

Immediately John was very interested. This concerned him closely. If the hogs were partly his, then it would be he who would have to decide what to do with them. Eat them and have pork for dinner every day, when the convicts were living all around on meagre rations? Or sell them to the Commissary to get money that would buy nothing in Sydney Cove, so that everyone would share?

Much as he liked pork, he knew that there was only one decision he could make to help the Governor, and he made it. 'You can sell my hogs,' he told Papa, 'and do what you think fit. I'm sure Martin will agree.'

'Good boy,' said Mamma softly. 'I am proud of you.'

Then Papa began again, 'Convicts, of course, are to work from sunrise to one o'clock,' he said, 'and then spend the afternoons tilling their gardens.'

'Which they won't do,' interposed Debby. 'Not them. They'll rob our garden instead. I know them.'

'Not if the suspicious characters are locked up each night, and that is what is going to happen,' Papa pointed out to her.

'Then they'll rob us in broad daylight, sir. Just you wait and see.' Nothing could shake Debby's contempt of the convicts.

'And what about fish?' Mamma asked. 'Couldn't something more be done about that?'

'Yes, my dear. Fishing parties are to go out each night in charge of an officer or a person of authority to bring in what fish can be caught, and this is to be served from the store instead of pork. We have all volunteered.'

'I'll go too, Papa,' John spoke up. 'And Mamma, Nanbaree and I will catch all the fish we can with spears. Won't we, Nanbaree?'

Nanbaree nodded. Gradually he was beginning to realise that this was a talk about food, about the getting of food, and he knew quite a lot about that.

'Nanbaree, he get kangaroo, bird,' he began.

'Yes, indeed,' said Mamma, 'you will be very useful, Nanbaree. Debby will be pleased to cook every snake you kill, every iguana, and every other creeping or crawling creature you can lay your hands on.'

'The gamekeepers, of course, have to go out each day,' Papa went on, 'to get what they can. Each fisherman is to receive a pound of uncleaned fish for his breakfast in addition to his ration, and the gamekeepers more flour and pork. So when you go fishing, John, you'll earn your breakfast and some for Sue, too, maybe.'

'Then I'll go often, Papa, I'll do anything to help.'

And Mamma wondered at this new John, ready to assist so willingly—the same John who once would disappear from sight as soon as he realised some chore was waiting for him.

'How is the Governor?' she asked Papa. 'Very worried?'

'Of course, my dear, but quite hopeful. He is a man in a thousand. Do you know what he has done? Offered all his private supply of flour to the public store—three hundred weight, no less, because he said he could not live better than the convicts, and that if any convict complained he could see that there was want even at Government House.'

All were silent. What could one say about generosity like that and the motives that prompted it? They had respected the Governor before, but now they honoured him above all men in the colony.

'Such a decision will do him immortal honour,' Papa finished, and got up to come to the table, for Debby had prepared some refreshments for him.

'But, Richard,' Mamma now reminded him, 'we have a private store of flour too, fifty pounds of it left, and sugar and salt and a few other luxuries which I produce from time to time. What the Governor has done, we must do—give it to the public store.'

'No, no, my dear, the Governor would not hear of it,' Papa protested. 'You have the children to think of.'

'Yes, yes,' pleaded Debby, knowing Mamma's weakness in such matters. 'Please, ma'am, please do not give it away.'

'But, Debby, how can we live better than the convicts? They have children, too.'

'Yes, I know, ma'am, but they have not worked as hard as you have in their gardens. Those good-for-nothing convicts—' and again Debby closed her lips firmly to hold back the words that would tell exactly what she thought of them. 'Give them vegetables you can't use, but not flour.'

Mamma thought for a moment. 'No,' she said, 'I am going to offer the flour, and we shall see what the Governor says.'

The Governor refused her offer. Papa came back the next day bringing the Governor's compliments and his appreciation, but also a message to say that he preferred not to accept the flour just at present, and would be glad if she would help all deserving cases with gifts of vegetables.

In the difficult weeks that followed, many came to her door, and few went away empty-handed. Debby watched with an eagle eye to see that the convicts did not deceive her with their tales. She also watched the dwindling supply of flour, and guessed that it was going to the convicts with children.

Mamma, like the Governor, could not eat while others went hungry.

CHAPTER XX

JOEY THE SCHEMER, JOEY THE THIEF

SUE'S pride was a bed of potatoes which she and Jenny and Mamma had grown while John was away.

'Come and see the garden,' she said to him the next morning, and dragged him out to admire the bed as he was about to go to school.

'Ye'll have to help me to keep it from the robbers,' Pete said, for he was hovering about. 'They'll come down like a pack o' crows now that the food's short. That little Joey fellow—'

'Has he been round again?'

'Never stopped coming round, a-looking at your Mamma with those dog-like eyes, so that she can't say no, and a-going off with a cabbage or a turnip.'

Pete picked up a bucket and went down the road with John towards the stream.

As he walked along, John could not help noticing the almost empty look of the Cove. But the emptiness had also an air of forlornness that he did not quite understand.

'Things are getting worse and worse all the time,' Pete said, as if trying to explain. 'Not good times at all these, Master John, and worse to come. Folks who have no clothes and no food can't go on a-working.'

John was accustomed to raggedness amongst the convicts, for the thread that had been brought from England had given out months before, and they had been sorely tried to find something to mend the rents in their clothes. But now he passed some whose clothes bore no resemblance to garments, and he wondered what they would do when the cold winds of autumn began to blow from the south.

'Your Mamma, she has given me extra clothes, and shared the food she has above her ration,' Pete went on gratefully. 'If it weren't for her, I'd be like those poor wretches. Marines, also, be in a bad way,' and he thumbed towards the Governor's sentry, who was shouldering his musket and walking up and down on bare feet.

'Not the soldiers, too!' John stared in disbelief.

'Yes, no more spit-and-polish for them, Master John. They be just the same as the rest o' the convicts. Some have shoes and some haven't. Their clothes be torn and mended like ours. And instead o' parading and such like, they be a-grubbing for food the same as everybody else.'

'And Bennelong, what happened to him, Pete?'

'He be still here, and your Papa says he could escape if he liked. Not fettered any more, he be, and follows the Governor round like a puppy. Lazy beggar, he'll take the food we give him as long as it lasts, then get, I guess. But somehow one can't help liking him—'

Pete broke off short, for on the other side of the stream a ragged figure was sauntering along among the bushes, and both knew by his curious gait that it was Joey.

'Up to no good, I bet,' said Pete, while they rested on the railing of the bridge and watched. 'About to steal someone's potatoes, maybe—the robber! Now one thing be certain. I'm a-going to watch that patch o' Mamma's potatoes, and if that Joey comes near, he'll get more than he's looking for. And if ye meet Joey appearing as if he's fattened overnight, Master John, go straight to the guard. His jacket will be sure to be full o' stolen potatoes.'

John continued on his way to school, and soon came upon a potato on the road. So Pete had been right about Joey! John thought grimly of the punishment for Joey or any convict who was caught in the act of stealing. A hundred lashes from the cat o' nine tails was only a small punishment for a crime like that. It could be even five hundred. With food so scarce, to steal from one's neighbours was almost unforgivable. And yet what could men do, when in their laziness they had failed to work in their gardens, and now had to exist on a meagre ration that did not satisfy the pangs of hunger? For them it was necessary to steal in order to live.

Nanbaree and Martin were already at the observatory when John arrived, and, much to his joy, Midshipman Dan.

'I am glad to have you back,' Lieutenant Dawes told John and Martin after he had questioned them in detail about their adventures. 'Nanbaree and I have been lonely without you. But we cannot spare so much time on schooling now that there are so many things to do—digging, and shooting, and fishing. From now on you are to come to me for only three hours each morning. Your afternoons you are to spend with Nanbaree going into the woods to get game and birds, or helping your mothers in their gardens. Sometimes I'll come with you to the woods and try my hand with a gun.'

The new arrangement began that morning, and was the pattern of many days to come.

Nanbaree was eager enough to help in their rambles, but they knew from the beginning that he would play no part in the weeding. Gardens he did not take to kindly, and they soon found that he would sneak away to catch fish in his own fashion or talk lazily to Bennelong.

And because they, too, often grew tired of the garden, they sometimes sneaked after him to sit at the feet of Bennelong and listen to his jabber about the tribes that lived round Sydney Cove, and his own prowess amongst them.

Bennelong looked almost a dandy, dressed as he was in his red kersey jacket.

'But you should see him on Sundays in his nankeen,' Debby told John when they laughed about it. 'Looks just like a white man, and is treated as such, too. Sleeps in the Governor's house, bless you, in the same room as the steward, and dines each day with the Governor. Quite a gentleman, our Bennelong, though he does try to kiss the women,' and she turned up her nose in disdain.

'Yes, indeed,' Mamma smiled and continued,' he's almost as well-mannered as Arabanoo these days, and can eat with his knife and fork, and drink a toast as politely as the Governor himself. Then some weird spirit gets into him, and he breaks out and does the maddest things—dancing, singing, acting, and above all boasting, but it is great entertainment.'

'And you don't think it is wrong to keep him here, Mamma?'

'Not now that he is not shackled.'

He was in such a mood when one day John and Martin teased him about his enemies, the *Cammeraygal*.

'*Cammeraygal*,' he began to mutter between his teeth, in the usual fashion. '*Cammeraygal*—brrr!'

The sound of the name seemed to arouse fierce animosity that sought to express itself in words and actions.

'*E eye at wange-wahwandeliah chiango wandego mangenny wakey angoul barre boa lah barrema*,' he chanted, and springing up began in slow manner to swing his arms and stamp the earth with his feet, smacking his thighs to the rhythm of his song, gradually becoming more and more violent in his movements until his dancing could almost be taken for a fit of frenzy.

So the boys thought, but Nanbaree and even Abaroo, if she were about, quickly joined in by beating sticks or clapping hands as if it were the most natural thing for Bennelong to behave in this way.

As Mamma had said, 'It was great entertainment.' The Governor thought so, too, for he came out of his house to watch.

Then, as if to show his skill to great advantage, or because he thought he would please the *Beanga*, Bennelong went into further ecstasies or frenzies, whichever they were, stamping more violently, his voice rising to a crescendo, as with a mighty leap he suddenly came to earth and, drawing himself up to his full height, bowed, as he had seen the *Beanga* do many times to Mamma.

It was such an ill-fitting climax after such exertion that the boys laughed loudly.

But Bennelong did not seem to mind. Maybe he did not notice, he was so full of pride at his own achievement. Strutting like a turkey-cock, he went off with the Governor, talking more familiarly with him than any of the officers had ever dared.

'Just like a white man,' John said, and although he did not realise it, Bennelong would have regarded that as the highest compliment he could be paid.

Bennelong was always more entertaining than the garden, and appeared perfectly content.

'And so he ought to be,' Debby said, 'sitting over there at the Governor's house, eating his fill each day, while the rest of us go short. Fish they give him, so it is said, as well as his ration, and even grind corn. Eats enough for six, and never lifts a hand to catch a fish or kill a kangaroo.'

It did not seem fair, but it was wise for Bennelong to be coaxed into staying. It would never do to let him go back to his own people and tell them of the difficulties of the white men. So he was fed his fill, and as long as the food lasted he would be satisfied. Whether he ever noticed the scarcity of it, no one knew.

As the month of April advanced, the scarcity was clear on every hand. The pease in the store ran out, and the ration became two and a half pounds of flour, two pounds of rice, and two pounds of pork. The pork was now four years old, and when cooked shrivelled to a couple of morsels per day. Unless a man was able to supplement his ration, he went hungry.

On 17th April, the *Supply* sailed for Batavia with Lieutenant King on board on his way to England to tell the people at home how badly the colony was faring.

'I'll be back,' Cookie told them, when he said good-bye. 'Be sure o' that. I'll be back, 'cos we know that we must come back, and Lieutenant Ball, he'll see that we do. And bring ye food—aye, tons o' it, and presents maybe, silk for Mamma and Sue, and new trousers and shoes for ye. John, and tea and spice and salt and all kinds o' tasty things. Ye never can tell what we might bring.'

The boys watched sadly from the observatory as the *Supply* disappeared around Bradley's Head and was lost to sight.

'How long?' they asked Lieutenant Dawes. 'How long before she gets back?'

'The Governor thinks it will take seven months,' Lieutenant Dawes told them. 'The food we have has been divided up to last that time.'

And as if to add to the larder as quickly as they could, he took them out into the woods that very afternoon, and shot a crow and two parrakeets and sent them to the Governor by the boys.

'Because I am going there for dinner tonight,' he said, 'and I can't eat the Governor's ration. The invitation asked me to bring my own bread, and now I shall be taking my own meal.'

Papa went to the dinner party, too, with his bread spiked on the end of his sword.

'Oh dear!' Mamma sighed to Debby as she watched him go. 'To think it would ever come to this! Taking one's own bread to dinner at Government House!'

'Yes, ma'am, and if you don't get those potatoes out of your garden soon, you'll lose them.' She was peering through the gloom at a shadowy figure bent over the bed at the far end, and sighed with relief as it took shape and she saw that it was Pete.

'But they're not mature enough, Debby. They must stay another week or so.'

'That may be, ma'am, but I think you're taking a chance. Better to have small ones than no potatoes at all. Now that Joey—'

John grinned, as he listened. Dear Debby! It was only because she cared for them all so much, and for Mamma in particular, that she was so vehement in her protection of their interests.

But Debby was right in her fears. The next day, while Pete was out shooting some birds for supper, Joey brought a female convict to Mamma.

'From Rose Hill, ma'am,' he told her. 'She's been robbed o' a week's food, and now has naught to live on for seven days. I thought, perhaps, ma'am, you might give her some flour.'

The poor thing looked miserable enough, standing there in her ragged dress and shivering with the cold. Mamma weakened immediately.

'Of course I shall give her some flour,' she replied, and ushered the woman into the kitchen to get warm.

'But, ma'am,' Debby protested under her breath, 'it might be some trick to get food from you.'

'Yes, I know that, but she looks so thin and hungry, I must do something.' Mamma began to weigh out some of her private supply of flour while Debby made the woman a cup of tea.

It was not until Pete returned that Mamma realised the way she had been duped. He came in hurriedly from the back garden with a brace of birds, thoroughly perturbed.

'But, ma'am,' he said, 'the potatoes.'

'Potatoes!'

'Yes, the bed has been rifled. Come and see.'

Mamma and Debby saw the havoc before they reached the potato bed-plants uprooted and earth thrown aside.

'Joey,' gasped Pete. 'Joey, ma'am. I saw him as I went out, sauntering behind the hedge. But there was more than one robber to take so many.'

'Yes,' said Debby, 'he was in league with someone, and as soon as he saw you go, he brought that wretched creature in. And when we were weighing the food and giving her a cup of tea, he and his mates made a lightning raid.'

The girls, attracted by the commotion, were almost in tears. 'Oh, Mamma,' Sue cried, 'it's not fair! We work and work, and they come and steal our potatoes.'

'No, dear, it's not fair,' Mamma agreed, 'but I'm afraid they don't know any better.'

'Any better?' fumed Debby. ''Twas all concocted by that Joey fellow, the thieving rascal! And that female, ma'am, who said she'd lost her rations hadn't lost them at all. I'm sure of it.'

They were all staring disconsolately at the pillaged beds, when John rushed through the gate and across the garden.

'Mamma, Mamma, the guard has taken Joey to the guard house. Martin and I saw him skulking under the bridge with his jacket full of potatoes, and we gave the word. There were others, too—' He paused to take stock of the situation. 'So they were *our* potatoes!'

'Yes, and now we shall have even less to eat,' said Mamma sadly.

The robbery had been a great blow to her. The fishing parties had met with little success, and the gamekeepers had brought in only three kangaroos during the month. She had been relying on Pete and sometimes Nanbaree for fresh meat. Rats, snakes, porcupines had all gone into the pot and were relished as the tastiest dainties. But vegetables, especially potatoes, had been the background of all their meals.

'Oh dear!' she sighed.

Yet she was horrified the next day when Papa told her of the sentence given to Joey by the court. 'He's to get three hundred lashes,' he said, 'his flour ration is to be stopped, and he is to be chained to two other robbers.'

'But he won't be able to exist without his flour ration!' she protested.

'Well, he didn't worry whether you could live without the potatoes,' Papa replied. 'Never fear. After a week or so, the Governor will remit the part about the flour, but our friend, Joey, will not be at liberty to steal any more potatoes for the time being.'

Papa, like the Governor, was troubled by the number of thefts. All the convicts pleaded hunger for their misdeeds.

'Oh dear!' sighed Mamma, when he began to tell her of them. 'I do wish the ships would come, and then everyone would have enough to eat.'

The next day she and Debby weighed their dwindling private store of flour.

'You won't give away any more, will you, ma'am?' Debby pleaded.

'No, Debby, not unless they are in very great want.' From then on the convicts had to prove their need to her, and that need had to be very great before she would help them.

Mamma had learnt her lesson at last.

CHAPTER XXI
BENNELONG AGAIN

A T the end of May, thoughts turned again to the celebration of
the King's birthday on 4th June.

'We'll build a bonfire again,' the children said.

'And perhaps,' said John slyly, 'Mamma will let us kill one of my pigs.'

'Kill a pig?' she repeated, horrified at the thought.

'Why not?' said Papa. 'We bred them to eat. Why shouldn't we have a feast for the King's birthday? I'm sure I'd like a nice piece of crackling.'

Crackling! John and Sue licked their lips at the thought.

Golden crackling, crisp to the teeth, blubbery on the mouth!

'The littlest one, ma'am,' Debby pleaded. 'It's thin enough, goodness knows, and we have three more. Spaced each month, you know, they should do until the *Supply* returns. You'd like a bit of fresh pork, now wouldn't you, ma'am? I would.'

'And us,' cried the children again.

Mamma knew she would like a bit of fresh pork. The meals of stale pork and mashed vegetables sometimes almost nauseated her, and being a mother she often served herself too little.

'Now, ma'am!' Debby had a habit of standing over her.

'You haven't given yourself enough.'

'But, Debby,' she would reply, 'the children are growing.'

Debby had noticed that Mamma had lost weight.

'A piece of fresh pork would just about be the tastiest thing I could think of,' she now replied, 'but I am afraid to kill that pig. What would happen if the *Supply* were wrecked?'

It was the black thought in everyone's mind.

'The Second Fleet would still come,' Debby reminded her. 'People at home haven't quite forgotten us.'

'Maybe,' Mamma replied sadly, but she did not relent--not until one morning Pete announced importantly, 'The sow's going to have another litter, ma'am.'

'Oh, then we shall kill the smallest and thinnest pig for the King's birthday!' she ordered, as the children jumped for joy, and Debby smiled broadly. 'If the sow has another litter, I can depend on a little fresh meat for how many months?' She had grown tired of counting them. 'Five months now.'

While they gathered the branches for the fire, they talked about the roast pig and who was to eat it.

'You're to have some,' Sue told Jenny.

'And you, also,' John told Martin.

Nanbaree grinned his widest grin and asked, 'Nanbaree, too?'

'Of course,' said John. 'You like pig?' and from the sound of the sucking and chewing noises that Nanbaree made, John was left in no doubt.

King's birthday in the year 1790 was going to be something to remember.

'Mr White? Mr Dawes?' Nanbaree continued.

'No, they'll be at the Governor's. There'll be a parade, and then all the important people will go to Government House. At least I think there'll be a parade,' John said again, remembering the raggedness of the marines and their lack of shoes.

'But we'll have no guns—not big guns from ships,' said Sue sadly, 'only guns from the soldiers.'

And they all looked at one another and repeated, 'No guns,' until John remembered that Lieutenant Dawes now had a battery and would be able to fire a salute.

'What about Bennelong?' Martin asked. 'Are you giving him any?'

That is why the children came to speak of it to Mamma and Debby.

'Bennelong,' Debby exclaimed scornfully. 'Give fresh pork to Bennelong? Him that has been fed with fish and what-not, and has had a full stomach when we've been hungry? No, ma'am, don't give good pork and crackling away to such as Bennelong.'

But Mamma surprised them all by saying, 'Why Debby, I've come to like Bennelong! He's a gentleman now,' and much to Debby's disapproval she added, 'I think I'll ask him to have dinner with us. Perhaps he'll entertain us with one of his weird dancing turns.'

'Hurrah!' the children cried, and were off at the run.

'Bennelong, Bennelong, you're to come and share our pig on the King's birthday.'

'Peeg?' he repeated in his queer way.

'Yes, pig, Bennelong, the animal that runs about and grunts so,' and they made a vast noise between them, imitating the hog, and pointing in the direction of the pig-sty in Mamma's garden.

'Peeg,' he repeated and nodded. 'Peeg-birth-day.'

Now how could they explain what a birthday was? And the King? Bennelong knew nothing of King George III far away in England. But he did know the Governor as a person of authority—the *Beanga*, he called him.

'King, him big *beanga*,' John tried to explain.

'Yes,' said Martin, 'and our *Beanga*, the Governor, has a picture of the King on the wall of his house,' and they dragged Bennelong to the window of the dining-room and pointed inside.

'King, him big *beanga*,' repeated Bennelong, and then made them all feel silly, for he drew himself up to his full height, and with an imaginary glass drank a toast. 'The King,' he said as impressively as the Governor himself.

'Yes, King, him big *beanga*,' John said again. 'You drink toast to him every day.'

But birthday—how could they explain it? They gave up trying. Sufficient that he should know that it was an occasion to honour this important person, the King, and that for that reason there was to be 'peeg' for dinner.

'King, him big *beanga*,' he repeated.

'Yes,' said John again, 'big *beanga* of the white tribe over the water.'

'Ah!' he nodded. 'Peeg for big *beanga*—white men.' And immediately he began to make movements like those of a man with an axe, and squeals that could only be likened to those of a pig. Nanbaree joined in, and then the children realised that they were looking at a play—a play without words—and that Bennelong and Nanbaree were killing the pig, laying it in the ashes, taking it out and eating it from their hands.

'Peeg,' Bennelong was chanting, 'peeg.'

So that was what they were doing—miming a story. As Mamma had said, 'It was great entertainment.'

But Bennelong was not always so amusing.

A few days later the girls found him sitting morosely in the sun, rubbing his stomach and groaning continuously. 'What wrong you?' Sue asked him tenderly.

'Bennelong seeck,' he replied, and went on groaning the louder.

His keeper hurried them off. 'He's only pretending,' he told them. 'Thinks he's not getting enough to eat, that's all.' Sue told this story at the supper table, just before John and Papa prepared to go off all night with the seine.

'Perhaps I could give him the fish I'll get for my breakfast,' John suggested.

'Indeed you won't,' said Papa, and Debby murmured her approval. 'Bennelong can catch his own fish, if he is so hungry.'

He appeared happy enough, when later John and Papa passed through the Governor's garden on the way to the wharf. 'G'd nite,' he said to Papa, and gave him a mock salute. 'Good night, Bennelong,' John replied, and called back, 'We'll go down to the Cove, all of us tomorrow, and you can catch fish with the fish-gig, eh?'

Bennelong rubbed his stomach. 'If Bennelong not seeck,' he said, and then turned rewards the Governor's house.

The night was cold and long, and the catch poor. The boats came in before the dawn, their crews dispirited.

But as soon as they turned into the Cove, they were on the alert. Something had happened. Robbers? There must have been an alarm.

Lanterns were bobbing about among the bushes of the Governor's garden, voices carrying clearly across the water.

'He might be there. He might be here. No, over the fence, or in the shed.'

Quickly the oarsmen made for the wharf.

The boat had scarcely touched before Papa was on his feet and out, and John was following him.

'What's up, what's up?' Papa called.

And a voice replied—the steward's voice—'That rascal, Bennelong—'

'Has escaped, I suppose,' Papa finished.

'Yes, the beggar,' and John stood as the steward explained to Papa. 'He went to bed in my room as usual. Then about two o'clock, he woke me and said he was 'seeck'. He's been 'seeck' so often lately, that I didn't take any notice of him. It was just his way of complaining that he wasn't getting enough to cat. But this time he went on telling me that he was 'seeck', so I let him out, thinking he would come back as soon as he had relieved his sickness. But he didn't, and now we are searching to see if he really did go, or whether he is only having a joke with us.'

But he wasn't having a joke with them. John stumbled upon his clothes thrown in a heap in the middle of a bed of vegetables, and as the sky paled, and light seeped through the darkness, they saw that he had placed a water butt against the fence to help him to jump over it. 'You'd better wake the Governor,' Papa suggested to the steward, and he went reluctantly inside.

The Governor came out sleepy-eyed and weary, for he had never recovered from the nights spent on the damp ground on his explorations, and he was still in poor health.

'Don't worry,' he said in a tired voice. 'It has been an effort to feed him the last few months. Maybe we'll meet in better times in one of the coves and persuade him to return.' The Governor had so much to worry him. 'If only the ships would come,' John heard him murmur as he went inside, 'then half our troubles would be over.'

Debby was pleased when she heard of Bennelong's escape. 'All the more for everyone else,' she said gaily, as she cooked the extra fish for breakfast.

Mamma was quietly pleased for another reason. 'He'll be back with his own people,' she explained. 'That's far better than living with us. But he was certainly entertaining.'

'And now we won't have him for dinner on the King's birthday,' wailed Sue, 'and there'll be no dancing.'

'You and Nanbaree and Jenny and the rest of you can make one up for us,' Mamma replied. 'Surely you've watched him enough to know what to do.'

That was a suggestion. They began the next time they were all together, Nanbaree directing the boys and showing them what to do, while the girls clicked sticks and clapped hands with Abaroo giving the lead.

They were in the midst of it when, one day, Midshipman Dan came from the Lookout with some potatoes for Mamma, and had to watch the strange antics that went by the name of Bennelong's dance.

'Why not let them come down and stay with me for a few days,' he suggested to Mamma. 'There's still a week to the birthday. And yourself, ma'am? I have never known such perfect days as those which come in May in this country —with the sea before me and the harbour behind, and the bounteous sun touching my body with the gentleness of a blessing. There is no lovelier spot than the Lookout.'

But, of course, Mamma refused. 'I couldn't, Dan,' she said. 'I daren't move out of the grounds. Debby, Pete and I all have to be on the alert. But my children can go, and I think Jenny and Martin will also get permission from their mothers.'

'I hope the ships come while we are there,' John said.

'Yes,' added Martin, 'then we'll be able to raise the signal to tell you they're coming into the harbour.'

Dan and Mamma looked at one another wistfully. 'How do you feel about it?' she asked him.

'Well, when one has watched the seas for days and months, hoping, praying, imagining, one cannot help but wonder and wonder and wonder about ships that never come. Have they been wrecked? Have we been forgotten?'

'No, not that, Dan,' Mamma reproved. 'We could not be forgotten. There must be a reason. They must come soon.'

But the children did not get their wish. The ships did not come on the days they visited Dan at the Lookout at the South Head. They roamed the woods, and climbed the boulders, and made Nanbaree hunt for game, and always, each day, they gazed across the broad expanse of the Pacific Ocean, but there was no sign of a sail. A cloud, maybe, that might be a sail, but always it dissipated before their eyes.

'Well, there's still the birthday,' John said, as they sailed home up the harbour.

And they went to work with even greater zest, gathering branches for the bonfire until it loomed above them at an enormous height, and in between times, when they were not at lessons, weeding in the gardens, or roaming the outskirts of the woods in search of game and honey and anything that would make a meal.

The prospect of a feast spurred Nanbaree into action. Because he thought something special was expected of him, he tracked and speared and snared in a way he had never done before. Early and late he arrived at Mamma's door with gifts of grubs, and roots, and animals of various kinds.

What Mamma and Debby rejected, the children cooked and ate in the old kitchen that was now John's very own hut. It seemed as if the King's birthday would be extended over many days.

'Only three more to go,' Sue sighed, as the evening closed in on the last day in May.

'Yes, we'll kill the pig on 3rd June, ready for the 4th,' Debby went on. 'I can almost taste it already, can't you, ma'am?'

'I can, indeed,' said Mamma, and the children screwed up their lips in anticipation of the good things to come.

They had not tasted fresh pork for many, many months.

CHAPTER XXII

THE SHIPS HAVE COME!
THE SHIPS HAVE COME!

BUT again they planned without thought for the weather.
The next morning dawned dull and cold, with a boisterous
southerly massing clouds for a deluge, which flooded the tiny settlement and water-logged it for two long days.

'Oh!' choked Sue, swaying back in disappointment, as she came
to the door on the third day and looked out. 'Mamma, just look at the
rain again!'

Mamma and Debby gathered behind her, as John ran from the old
kitchen to the new house.

'Aren't we lucky it is not tomorrow?' Mamma said, by way of
comforting them. 'Don't worry, dear, it will probably fine up before
the morning.'

Even Sue was old enough now to know that it would take hours
for the wood to dry.

'But we won't be able to have a bonfire, will we?'

'You never know, dear. Come along and have breakfast.'

It was far too wet for school. John went to the door again, when
the meal was over, and gazed at the bleak outlook before him—not a
solitary person stirring from the shelter of his hut, nothing but mud
and slush and dripping greenery under an overcast and leaden sky.

He was almost twelve now, but still he was disappointed. 'Oh, why
did it rain today?' he sighed to himself 'All our work for nothing!'

'No, indeed,' Mamma said, when she heard him muttering, 'you
can keep the bonfire for the Prince of Wales's birthday next month,
or set it alight next week when the wood is dry.'

'Why then, Mamma? When the ships come?' and he smiled wryly.
It was a forlorn hope.

'But, Mamma—' began Sue again from behind.

'Yes, I know, pet, but these things do happen. You just have to accept them. Let us all hope that the sun shines this afternoon, and all day tomorrow, and then you might have a bonfire.'

But neither of them could settle down. Mamma tried to interest them in their work, Sue writing laboriously on her slate, and John chewing the end of his pen and thinking of news to put in a letter to his grandmother in far away England.

'You might as well write it now,' Mamma said, 'then it will be ready when the ships arrive. Come on, dear, don't look so stumped. Write about Nanbaree and Bennelong—oh, there are lots and lots of things to tell.'

John responded for a while, but his heart was not in it, and he kept going to the door or peering through the curtains, sighing, and then going back to work, restlessly twitching in his chair, and at last, as if he could bear the boredom no longer, teasing Sue in a manner that soon brought Mamma to her rescue.

'Just look what he did, Mamma!' Sue cried. 'He rubbed out all I had written.'

'John, how could you?' Yes, he knew he deserved it. He was a pig, but wet weather always made him a pig, shut up as he was in a small space like Mamma's house. He had grown so accustomed to roaming where he liked, to being always out in the fresh air, and it was a nuisance that rain should come now—of all times.

'Oh, why!' he muttered. 'Mamma, can't I go over to Martin's or to the observatory?' he pleaded.

'No, dear,' and he knew that it would be of no use to ask again.

If only Nanbaree would come or somebody! Anything other than being cooped up in the house for another day!'

And as if in answer to his prayer a knock came at the door, and there was Jenny—Jenny with a sack over her head, and with her usual salutation in such weather, 'Mother said I could come 'cos I was bothering her so much.'

From then on Sue and Jenny retired to Sue's bedroom, and what mysterious pastimes they pursued there were none of John's business.

He did not really care, and for want of something better to do he went reluctantly back to the letter. He wrote:

Nanbaree is a black boy who was brought in to Sydney Cove when he was ill with the smallpox. That was eighteen months ago. Now he can read and write and tells us all sorts of things about the natives...

So intent he was in writing that he did not hear the door open, did not even look up, until there beside him he saw Nanbaree grinning as drops of rain ran off his black nose on to his lips, his black body shining wet, his feet slushed with yellow mud that now lay in broad footprints across Mamma's floor.

Well, that was one thing about being a black boy. One could discard one's clothes and go about in all weathers! But what would Debby say? They knew soon enough, for immediately she was wiping up the mess on the floor and muttering a little about folks who could not stay indoors on wild days such as this.

And Mamma, who never could bear the sight of nakedness, was off for a pair of breeches to save him from getting a cold.

'Now you're here, you had better stay, Nanbaree,' she told him. 'Maybe it's a good thing, with John as restless as an eel, and not knowing how to occupy himself.'

'Peeg,' announced Nanbaree, with no regard for Debby's scolding. 'Peeg killed?'

'No, not yet,' John told him. 'Pete's got it in the little yard. We'll hear him when he starts.'

Now the girls emerged, for the word 'peeg' was a magical word, and demanded that they rehearse the dance again. And so they did, until the small house almost shook with thumping and slapping, clicking and clapping, and Mamma and Debby, when they had got over the first novelty, called again and again for quietness and peace. But it was hard to restrain the actors once they had been worked up to their miming.

'Oh dear,' said Mamma, 'are we to put up with this all day? I think I'll have to send you out to your own hut, John. Debby and I can't stand any more.'

It was then that the squealing in the little yard told them that the life of the pig had been sacrificed for the King's birthday.

Nanbaree was off like a wild thing, breeches and all, and John was only held back long enough for Mamma to hand him a cape to save him from some of the deluge.

As for the girls, she locked them in. 'No,' said Mamma, 'It's no place for you. You are little ladies, not savages,' and for all their entreating they had to go quietly back to the bedroom to play with their dolls.

Nanbaree wanted to snatch up some of the offal that Pete extracted from the pig, and take it back there and then and cook it in the fireplace in the old kitchen.

'No, no,' cried John, 'that's for Gyp—Gyp has to have a share in the birthday, too, Nanbaree,' and it was as much as he could do to stop Nanbaree from grabbing what he threw to his dog, ravenously sniffing at the open doorway of the out-house where Pete was working.

They had brought the carcase into Debby's kitchen in triumph with Pete, and laid it out on the table.

'Where shall we keep it?' Debby asked Mamma. 'There's many a hungry mouth about the Cove that would like to get his teeth into it, ma'am.'

'Hang it in the larder, of course, and I shall keep the key,' Mamma replied, and they were all standing there admiring it, when Debby drew herself up and listened.

'What's that?' she said suddenly.

'What's what?' Mamma asked.

'A noise like people shouting, ma'am.'

'How could there be a noise like shouting on a day like this?' Mamma scoffed, taking the key of the larder from her pocket to open the door. 'No one's going to steal that pig unless over my dead body!'

'And mine, too,' Debby assured her, then again stopped short and listened.

There *was* a noise—the noise of pattering up the wet path, of running feet swiftly directed to the door.

It was opened before they got to it, and Martin rushed in —a

Martin as excited as they had ever seen him, Martin tousled and wet and spattered with mud from the waist downwards, his great coat flapping around his knees.

'The ships!' he gasped.

'The ships!' everyone repeated, each one on edge, keyed up in an instant, waiting for the next word.

'The ships! The flag's up at the Lookout. Oh, don't you hear? The ships! They've come at last.'

The ships at last! It was hard to believe. The ships at last, and on such a day!

But now there was no thought of the day, no thought of the rain or the mud or the wind. The ships had come! They must go and see for themselves the flag flying at the South Head—the flag that brought the good news. For the ships meant food, clothes, letters from home!

'Quick, Debby, get our cloaks,' and when the girls rushed out without any protection, 'Now come on back. You must put something over your heads. And the telescope, Debby, don't forget that.'

The boys had already gone with Pete into the rain, joyously spludging into the wet mud and squelching across the grass, leaping like young animals, yelling, shouting against the wind, 'The ships have come! The ships have come!'

And after them struggled Mamma and Debby, protecting their clothes as best they could, with the girls racing on, jumping over puddles, spattering into the yellow slush, on, on, with the rain beating into their faces, and dripping from their eyelids to fall into their open mouths.

They were on the path now that led to the high ground between the Cove and the Government Farm.

People were coming from all directions—convicts so drenched that their ragged clothes lay dank against the outlines of their bodies, marines with cloaks so tattered that they would have been a disgrace to any army; men, women, and children, panting, shouting, striving to be the first to see the flag.

It was there all right, a bedraggled speck blown by the wild winds bravely from the pole.

They had come! Yes, the ships had come!

Each of them had a turn with the telescope to make sure that the naked eye had played no tricks.

'Oh, ma'am!' sobbed Debby, and the tears streamed down her cheeks.

'Yes, Debby, you said you would be with me through it all, and now we can be glad together,' and they stood there in the wet and the cold, staring happily at the flag flapping on the South Head.

Around them the knot of people was growing. Women were falling on one another's necks, kissing their babies, men clasping hand in hand, shouting above the wind, cheering.

'Hurrah! Hurrah! Hurrah for a platter full of food!'

'Hurrah! Hurrah!' the children echoed and enjoyed every cheer.

And as they watched, eyes fixed upon the moving speck against the horizon, the rain eased, and the sky lightened, and although the wind still blew boisterously, there was a hint of relief from the wild weather of the previous days.

'Hurrah! Hurrah!' cried John and Martin, thinking perhaps the bonfire would now serve a double purpose.

They had all been there for more than half an hour, when Mamma remembered that she had not locked the front door.

'The door, Debby,' she exclaimed all of a sudden, 'I didn't lock it. Did you?'

'No, ma'am, now that I think of it, I didn't. I was too busy getting the telescope. And we were all so excited.'

'Oh, Debby!' and suddenly Mamma realised that she was fingering something in her pocket. 'Look!' she cried. 'The key of the larder! I opened the larder, but did not put away the pig. It is on the table, and the front door's not locked.'

'I'll go back,' and Debby was already off, when Mamma called to her.

'No, we'll all go,' she said. 'We must get the children out of their wet clothes and give them some hot food.'

The children went most reluctantly. They would have stood there on the hill watching for hours on end for the sight of the ships turning round Bradley's Head and coming up the harbour.

'But, Mamma, the ships might come into sight,' John began.

'Well, I promise you that you can come back.'

The door was wide open when they reached the house, and for a moment they drew back, expecting to see a robber scuttling away with the pig.

'There's someone there,' John whispered. Yes, someone was moving about inside.

What could they do? What could two women and a bunch of children do against a hungry robber?

They paused, waiting.

Then Nanbaree, pointing to a recent footprint near the doorstep, smilingly said, 'Papa!' and they gingerly went inside to find Papa preparing himself a hot drink.

'You beauties!' he teased them. 'Leaving a whole pig lying on the table, with the door unlocked.'

It had been a silly thing to do, but Mamma took no heed of his reproof. 'The ships at last, Richard!' she said, her eyes shining. 'Do you wonder we forgot?'

He had come back for the boys, so he said.

'Us?' they repeated in disbelief.

'Yes, the Governor says you are to come down the harbour with us to meet the incoming ships.'

What matter now about bonfires or birthdays or even pork for dinner? They were going down to meet the ships—the ships that they had waited for so long, the ships that would bring them food and clothes and news from England.

The ships! They were exulting words.

'Nanbaree, too?' John asked.

'Yes, Nanbaree as well.'

'Nowees, big *nowees*,' John explained to Nanbaree. 'We go down the water to see the big *nowees*.'

But first Mamma insisted that they should have a hot drink and a hunk of bread.

'Come, they can go as they are,' Papa said, for he was impatient of the delay. 'If they changed, they would soon be wet again. It will be pretty wild on the harbour today,' and he had his way, although Mamma demurred.

'Well, Nanbaree must have something,' she insisted, and she brought out an old coat of John's and made him put it on.

It was cold on the water, for, although the rain had ceased, the winds still blew strongly from the south, biting into their bones and slashing like sharp knives across their faces, and lifting the spray until they were drenched again and again.

Yet strange that they were scarcely conscious of the cold, the dampness, the discomfort, only the ships—the ships that would soon round Bradley's Head and be clear to their view. Huddled together, they sat in the bow and watched...

They had rounded Bradley's Head themselves before they saw her—one ship only, just outside the Heads.

'There she is, there she is!' all cried together, seeing her almost at the same time.

'What do you reckon she is?' Papa asked the Governor, who had already raised his telescope to his eye.

'*Lady Juliana*, London,' answered the Governor, reading the name on her prow. 'Either a transport or a storeship.'

Lady Juliana! So that was her name. Happy name! Whatever she was she was welcome, thrice welcome. She was from home, from England far away, a link with their people who had not forgotten them.

'Hurrah, hurrah for the *Lady Juliana*!' the boys cried, and twirled their hands in the air, although they knew that the distance between the long boat and the ship was far too great for them to be heard.

'Hail that fishing boat,' the Governor told the coxen. 'I'll go back to Sydney Cove, now that I know what she is. You all go on, and bring me news as soon as you can.'

It was just as well that he should return. The day was not one for a man so ill as he to be on the harbour.

So they went on, while the Governor returned in one of the

several fishing boats that had set out down the harbour as soon as the flag had been raised.

And now the *Lady Juliana* was working her way through the Heads. They watched her closely.

She would run on the rocks. No, not that, not now. But it was only the excited state of their minds that made the danger real. She was safe, she had always been safe, and now she was drawing closer to them. *Lady Juliana*, London! With the naked eye they could read the name on her stern.

'Pull away, lads,' called Papa, and the other gentlemen joined him. 'She is from Old England. A few more strokes, and we shall be aboard. Hurrah for the *Lady Juliana* and news from *Home*!'

They were alongside her, gazing at her crew leaning from ports and over the side, the long boat rising and falling with the swell. They were grasping at the ropes, and at the right moment were hauling themselves aboard, one by one, on to the swaying deck.

The captain was waiting. '*Lady Juliana*, sir,' he said to Papa, 'eleven months from Plymouth with two hundred and twenty-five female convicts.'

So she wasn't a storeship! She had brought more convicts, and women at that.

But more ships were on the way. John and Martin listened, and Nanbaree stood still, as the news came pouring out. The King had been sick and was recovered. There had been a revolution in France. News! So much there was to tell.

And why had they been forgotten so long? It had all been an accident. The ship that was to bring cattle, plants, food—the *Guardian*—had struck an island of ice off Capetown, and had been a complete wreck. The cattle had been lost, and some lives, and only after great privation and danger had the captain brought the derelict to the Cape.

But what did the long wait matter now that the ships—at least one ship—had come at last.

The *Lady Juliana* anchored in Spring Cove for the night, and the long boat set out for home with the news and letters—letters for the Governor, for Mamma, for everyone.

Then, like a benison of good hope, the sinking sun shone through the clouds as if promising better things to come, both for the next day and the long years ahead.

Joyfully the boys landed.

'You are to take Martin and Nanbaree home with you,' Pete greeted them. 'They are to stay the night. Martin's mother and father are coming over, and Lieutenant Dawes and Cookie—just like the time you came home from Norfolk.'

So they came, the three of them together, through the gate and up the path to Mamma's front door, turning to one another, sniffing the delicious smell that could mean only one thing—roast pork for supper.

'Yes,' she said as they burst in, 'we've cooked some for tonight. Today is more important than the King's birthday, and we must celebrate. You must all be as hungry as hunters.'

Nothing could dampen her spirits, not the story of the *Guardian* and all the expensive goods that it had been bringing for Papa, now lost for ever; not the reminder that the ship that had come carried two hundred and twenty-five more women to feed. For her the important thing was that a ship had come, and that more were to follow. The people at home had not forgotten Sydney Cove.

Only Papa expressed his thoughts grimly. 'Now,' he said, 'if the *Guardian* had come as planned, it would not have been necessary to send the *Sirius* to Norfolk Island, and then she would not have been wrecked.'

But Mamma would not let him dwell on what might have been.

'Come on,' she called gaily to all her guests, as Debby carried the leg of pork on a great meat dish from the kitchen and laid it on the table for Papa to carve, and they all gathered round just for a minute, taking another sniff before they scattered to their places to sit in state at one of the most memorable meals of their lives.

There never was such a meal. Such joy, such hilarity, such talk of this and that, in exclamations, in words, in phrases, the story of the *Lady Juliana* being told disjointedly, as every one ate and ate of that delicious pig. For once Mamma did not mind when they picked up the golden crackling in their fingers, sucking the blubbery skin with expressive clucks of content and cracking the rind between their strong teeth, until there was fat around their mouths and fat on their hands, and their faces shone greasily in the flickering light of the candles.

The excitement, too, when Dan arrived, having come up from the Lookout after dusk to join in the rejoicing; and Lieutenant Dawes, straight from discussions with the Governor; then Cookie—how could any celebration be complete without him?

All their friends were there—those who had shared their joys and disappointments, those who had been part of the pattern of their lives in Sydney Cove.

And then, when all were more silent because they were so satisfied, there were the letters—letters months old, but letters telling them of happenings back home to their dear ones, recreating in their minds scenes that they had left years before, now dimmed by the passage of time and their new life in a new land.

One by one the children began to show signs of sleep. Jenny, who was hustled home by Debby; Sue, who was carried off to bed by Mamma; then Nanbaree, not accustomed to such late hours; and last of all John and Martin, now slumped in weariness after all the tumultuous and exciting emotions and events of the day.

'Come on, up you get! Bedtime,' said Papa. 'It's the King's birthday tomorrow.'

'But no bonfire,' John reminded him sleepily.

'No, you can keep that until later in the week. The Governor is going to have a service of thanksgiving for the recovery of the King from illness. We'll light it then.'

And so it happened. When the branches were lit a few nights later, and disintegrated into a million starry sparks, while everyone's face glowed in the reflection with warmth and happiness, John thought again of the ships—the ships from England, far across the seas.

They came slipping through the Heads for the next two months— the *Justinian*, *Surprise*, *Neptune*, and *Scarborough*.

Then hearts grew light again, for bodies were clothed and no one was hungry, and Mamma and Debby sang at their work, and the robbers ceased to pillage, and Sydney Cove took on new life and hope.

The ships had come at last, and all was well!

'Now,' said the Governor, 'we can go on with our task of building a new country in a new land.